To my granddaughter, Amberly, for inspiring me to write the best and most realistic descriptions possible of the children in the story.

Chapter 1

One more patient to face. One more blood pressure to take. One hand on the stand with the blood pressure cuff and the other on the back of her neck trying to massage the knots from her muscles, she walked toward room 202.

"Good afternoon, Mr. Kensington. It's time to take your blood pressure."

"Selena! My favorite nurse!"

"You say that about all the nurses, so don't try to butter me up. What is it you want this time?" She smiled in spite of herself. Placing the cuff around his arm she touched the button on the machine and copied the numbers from the window.

"You know what I want. Talk the doctor into letting me go home. I can do the same thing at home I'm doing here and I won't be bored stiff doing it. Besides, my business is suffering and that hurts more than the pain I have in my leg. I'll be forever indebted to you, put you in my will, dance at your wedding, whatever you want from me, if you can do this one little thing for me. Please?" Graham Kensington gave her his most convincing arguments.

As he talked she watched him with curiosity. She noticed, as if seeing him for the first time, his clean-cut looks. His serious, light blue, piercing eyes belied his boyish, clean-shaven jaw line. The light brown almost blond hair, styled long on the top and in the back, had been trimmed close around his ears and off his collar. The closely clipped, blond mustache seemed invisible except for the contrast against his tanned face. His nicely shaped nose and bushy eyebrows drew her attention back to his eyes. Realizing he watched her looking at him, she dropped her gaze to his lips. The upper one dwarfed the lower one until he smiled, as he did now. Fascinated with the transformation, she saw both lips even out to the same size.

She took a deep breath to regain her composure, smiled and shook her head. "You know I don't have that kind of authority, but I'll see what I can do. Your vital signs have been stable for two days, and you're getting around fairly well on your crutches. Let me take a look at your bandage to see if the bleeding has stopped. Take a deep breath while I take the tape off. There, that looks real good. If I see the doctor, I'll state your case, but don't hold your breath." She disposed of the bandage from his leg and replaced it with a sterile one.

When she returned to the nurses' station, three bells sounded from the board that indicated patients had pushed their call buttons. She picked up a pencil and scratch pad on her way to the panel, pushed the buttons, wrote down the requests, and hurried from the nurses' station.

"Hurry seems to be the word for the day," she said aloud, as she went from one room to another. "I haven't even had time to write on any of the patients' charts yet."

"Selena, you have a phone call in the nurses' station." The interdepartmental intercom. *What now? Why can't someone take a message? Whoever it is, they'll have to wait.*

Five minutes later, she picked up the phone and forced a pleasantness in her voice that she didn't feel. "This is Selena. How may I help you?"

"What took you so long? My time is as important as yours. Meet me at my place tonight at seven," said a distinctly familiar voice on the other end of the line.

"What if I don't want to? What happened to asking instead of demanding?" She spoke softly so no one would hear her. "Tonight is not convenient for me. You know it's Wednesday evening, and there's a service at the church."

"I don't care. Be at my place at seven. That is, if you don't want things to get worse," he said harshly, hanging up without saying goodbye.

Selena sighed. She had done everything she knew how to do to keep her life from getting to this place. *Where did I go wrong? How can this happen to someone who's tried as hard as I have?* Not being one to feel sorry for herself, she forced herself to smile and went back to caring for her patients.

The interior of the nursing unit contrasted with Selena's inner feelings. The white walls and light gray carpet gave an impression of a clean, quiet atmosphere to patients and visitors alike. Pictures of abstract objects hung on the walls and lines with muted colors had been painted halfway down each wall in an attempt to add color to the decor. The slightly antiseptic odor had become as much a part of the job as the pictures on the wall and as easy to ignore. All lost on her senses, she moved automatically through the requirements of nursing with a dark cloud around her emotions.

The modern medical technology had helped too much. . Now more work was required of fewer people, making an almost impossible workload for each nurse. She didn't complain. The more she put herself into the work, the less time she had to think; to think about things out of her control. Like Howard.

The split-shift nurse arrived and took over answering call bells and giving pain medication as requested. Only then did Selena have time to make notations on the charts. She wrote down pertinent information for the head nurse to give to the next shift of nurses.

As she made the last notation on a chart Doctor Girard walked into the nurses' station looking for his patients' charts. She located the charts for him and glancing at the one for 202 remembered her promise to the patient.

"You have a patient that promised me the moon if I can talk you into discharging him today." Selena chuckled.

"Graham Kensington insists he will do everything you tell him to if you'll let him go home."

"Well, let's see if we can get you the moon today." Doctor Girard's mouth curved slightly at the corners. "I planned on sending him home today anyway, but we won't tell him that."

Selena accompanied the doctor on his rounds. At 202, he winked at her as he entered the room. "Good afternoon, Graham, how are you feeling today?"

"I feel wonderful. You did a great job on my leg. Tell him, Selena. She already looked at it and said it looks good. I can do all this at home. Tell me what you want me to do and I'll do it. I really need to go home today."

While Graham talked, Doctor Girard wrote. He handed two pieces of paper to the patient. "Make an appointment to see your doctor next week to get the stitches out. Here's a prescription for pain medication if you need it. Don't put any weight on that leg until you get the stitches out. In the meantime, I'm going to call a colleague of mine in Dayton and schedule you for therapy. Your leg sustained quite a bit of damage to the muscle from the fracture and the laceration. Try to avoid those icy patches on the cement in the future."

The doctor shook hands with Graham, turned and walked out. With his back to the patient, he grinned at Selena and gave her a thumbs up sign.

Selena looked at Graham, his jaw slack. "Would you like your clothes, Mr. Kensington?" She handed him the bag containing his clothes, closed the door and went to the nurses' station.

"His mouth is still hanging open," Selena said to Doctor Girard as he left the nursing unit.

"Let me know what part of the moon you get," he responded lightly.

Selena went back to 202 to help Graham into the wheelchair and wait for an escort to take him to the front door. Leaning over to unlock the wheels, she suddenly became aware that his eyes never left her face.

"What!" she exclaimed.

"Thanks. I really appreciate this. If you ever need anything let me know. I'm serious. Don't give me that look!"

She rolled her eyes. "Seeing you get well and go home is all the thanks I need."

"Lean over. You're really great. I have something for you." His lips touched her cheek in a light kiss.

"Watch it. I'm married." She flashed her wedding band. *He doesn't need to know anything about my marital status.*

"I'm sure your husband won't mind me giving you a simple token of appreciation." Graham looked at her thoughtfully. "I know it's none of my business, but I'm curious about the sadness around your eyes.

"Here, just in case . . ." He reached in his wallet, pulled out a business card and handed it to her.

Selena turned to refute the statement about her eyes as the escort walked in the door. A short wave and a wink and Graham left, the escort wheeling him down the hall toward the elevator. She stared at the card she still held in her hand.

Kensington Enterprises
Manager – Graham Kensington
Owner – God

What did that mean? It was the strangest business card she'd ever seen. Staring at the phone number, she couldn't place the location of the business.

He certainly has a lot of nerve. Sadness around the eyes, indeed! She walked to the sink and stared at herself in the mirror. What did he mean? She didn't see any sadness.

She stripped the bed and disposed of the linens in the laundry room. When she walked to the nurses' station she said to Patty, the unit clerk, "Look at me. Do you see any sadness around my eyes?"

Patty took her glasses off and stared into Selena's eyes. Turning her head first one way and then the other she said solemnly, "Is that what that is? I thought it was eye shadow."

"Oh, stop. The patient in 202 said I have sadness around my eyes. What does he know about it?"

Taking a deep breath, she looked around for anything that might have been forgotten, picked up her keys, her purse, and her coat and clocked out. "See you all in the morning," she said as she walked off the surgical nursing unit of Columbus General Hospital.

At least I still have a job, she thought, as she opened her car door in the parking garage. She tried to think of at least one thing to be thankful for each day. If she felt really creative, she thought of something different each time. Lately, she'd run out of new ideas.

Her job, her car, and her apartment had been mentioned several times in her mental discourse in the last couple of weeks.

Selena pushed the button to check for messages on her answering machine at her apartment. As she listened she removed the barrette from the back of her head and shook loose her shoulder length hair. Tucking strands that fell around her face behind her ears, she deleted the message and changed from her nursing uniform into jeans and a cotton blouse.

She tried not to think about the message on her answering machine and the phone call she'd received at work. *Howard.* He seemed intent on making her life miserable, one way or the other. Sure that he deliberately insisted on seeing

10

her this evening because he knew the importance the Wednesday evening Bible study at her church held for her, she wished she had the courage to stand up to him and say no.

Looking through her mail, she found the usual assortment of bills, advertisements, and missent pieces. The mailman never seemed to get everyone's mail in the right box in this building. She would place them in the correct boxes when she went out later.

I wonder what Howard wants now? First it was "I want an open marriage" then it was "I want a separation" then it was "Get your own credit cards". What else could he possibly want that I have?

Selena had said, "No!" to the first demand, "Why?" to the second statement and nothing to the third one. What could she say? She'd done as he commanded, cut up her credit cards, closed their bank account, which elicited another phone call from him ("I didn't tell you to do that! You can pay for the overdraft since I knew nothing about it!"), and changed the locks on her doors.

The last change she'd done on her own. She suspected that he'd been in the apartment on at least two occasions when she hadn't been there. When he moved out three months earlier he'd said that he took

everything with him. She had no reason to doubt him at the time.

Afterward, an open closet door in her bedroom and the contents of the desk drawer in disarray led her to believe he'd been there looking for something.

Selena knew she'd become overly cautious when she left all the lights on in the apartment and turned on the two outside lights by her door before she left. Howard had never physically harmed her and she had no reason to believe he would start now. He denied being manipulative and controlling, saying that he just liked to think he kept one step ahead in getting what he wanted, either from her or from life. His attitude left her uneasy.

Why can't things be the way they used to be when we first married? Howard seemed so sincere when he said his wedding vows, until death do us part, and forsaking all others. Marriage is a lifetime commitment, divorce is not an option, and I plan to do whatever it takes to make this work.

Taking a deep breath she prayed as she drove to the house that he rented from his brother on the other side of town. She pulled into the
driveway, turned her car around and parked on the street. The garage door and front door stood open, in spite of the chill in the air, and lights shone in every room.

She rang the doorbell and waited. He opened the outside door and smiled. She hated that smile. His eyes cold, his face hard, he only smiled like that when he wanted something. He stepped aside and motioned with his hand for her to enter.

Selena, on her guard, stopped just inside the door. She felt dwarfed by his six-foot-four inch height.

"Come on in and sit down. This may take awhile." His raspy voice grated on her taut emotions.

"I'd rather stand." She leaned against the doorframe and waited. She tried to appear oblivious to the burnt grease smell and the clothes and papers scattered throughout the room.

Howard shrugged and sat down on the sofa, giving her an insolent grin.

Selena noted that he wore his usually short, dark brown hair much longer than she'd ever seen it, and he had two days growth of beard on his face. He wore a cotton shirt, unbuttoned, that hung out over his jeans. Dirty bare feet stuck out from the ends of his pants legs.

"I've tried to be tolerant of your strange beliefs and behaviors, but I've come to the end of my endurance. I want a divorce. Now, don't start whining and telling me it's against your religion. It may be against yours, but it isn't against mine." He laughed as if he'd just told the world's funniest joke.

"I've already filed the papers and you'll be getting the notice in the mail next week. Don't try to fight me on this or you'll be sorry. You owe me the down-payment on your car and half the investment on the money your dad gave you last year. That should be enough for a nice vacation and some pocket money for awhile."

"Whatever happened to doing a six-month trial separation and then re-evaluating our relationship?"

"That was your idea, not mine. I've done as much evaluation as I can stomach. I'm tired of trying to live by your goody-goody rules. Give me the money and get out of my life."

"I don't have the money, and you know it." She slowly took a deep breath. She wouldn't give him the satisfaction of knowing he could get to her.

"Don't tell me your sob stories. Just get me the money by next week or I'll see you in court."

Selena quickly opened the door behind her and walked out. She heard him yell that he hadn't finished yet, but she kept on going. Pulling away from the curb, she saw his reflection in the rear view mirror. He stood in the middle of the lawn shaking his fist at her.

He had to be bluffing when he said he would take her to court. Didn't he? He often made threats and seldom followed through. This had to be just another scare tactic. Didn't it? She would find out. If he wanted a divorce, there was nothing she could do about it, but he would have to fight her for the money her dad left her when he died last year. That was hers for emergencies, or for a nice nest egg with which to retire.

A thought suddenly came to her. What if Howard had a copy of the portfolio she'd received when she invested the money? He could take the number of the account and call it in to the broker and get as much money as he wanted. She'd placed his name on the document somewhere and with the phone number and the account number he could get access to the account and make any changes he wanted to.

Running into her apartment, she went to the bedroom, took the gray box out of the bottom of the closet and sorted through the contents. Not finding the portfolio, she scattered the envelopes and papers over the floor. Willing herself to be calm, she picked things up, one at a time, and placed them back in the box. Not there.

She thought back to the day last year that she'd received the large envelope in the mail; she remembered taking a folder out of it. *What did it look like? Think! Think!* A turquoise folder with white lettering on it.

Selena gasped and put her hand over her mouth to keep from crying out. Could <u>that</u> have been why Howard entered her apartment when she was gone? He needed to find the folder? She remembered placing the folder in the gray box; or had she? She couldn't remember now. What if he had found it and taken it? But, if he had it, why would he be asking for the money? He could place the call and get it himself.

Maybe the account had been set up so that only she could make changes in the account. *Why didn't I pay more attention to it when I got it? Everything was written in such technical language that I didn't even try to decipher it. It has to be here somewhere. Where else could it be? Why didn't I take Mom's advice and spend a little money to invest with a broker instead of listening to Howard who insisted I do it myself over the phone?*

Selena finally gave up and went to bed. Since he didn't have keys to the new lock on her apartment door, she didn't need to worry that he would find it before she did. *If* it was in her apartment. But, if he had the portfolio maybe he was saying he wanted her to call and get him the money. She tossed and turned all night.

The next day as Selena accompanied one of the doctors on his rounds, she noticed a florist deliveryman approach the nurses' station and wait for someone to sign for a delivery. Thinking nothing of it, since deliveries occurred daily, she finished with the doctor and returned the charts to the chart rack. "Something for you," said Patty, smiling knowingly. "Somebody really likes you, and it isn't Howard."

"What are you talking about?" Selena took the card out of the bouquet of a half dozen long stemmed red roses. Her eyes opened wide as she read, *My will or your wedding. What is your preference? Thanks for everything. Graham.*

Quickly sticking the card in her pocket, she laughed self-consciously. "They're from the patient in 202--Graham Kensington. He wants to say thanks to everyone for taking care of him during the time he spent on our unit." She thought fast for an explanation."Let me see that card." Patty eyed her suspiciously. "I know it had your name on it. Sad around the eyes, huh? Well, well. What was he doing looking at your eyes? And what would Howard think if he knew someone sent you flowers?"

"What is that supposed to mean? By the way, I'm not taking phone calls from Howard here at work. You can tell him that. He has my home number." Patty's eyebrows went up in surprise.

Attempting to put everything out of her mind, Selena hurried down the hall to assist Mr. King with his bath.

After work she began a thorough search of her apartment. *That portfolio folder has to be here somewhere. What makes Howard think any of the money belongs to him? Well, he'll have to think again.*

She'd get a lawyer and fight him in court if she had to. Maybe. She didn't want to sue him to get it back. But she'd need a lawyer to advise her anyway. Well, as of now, she didn't know if he had the money or not. She'd find out next week if he made good on his threats.

Sunday morning Selena dressed in a burgundy skirt with a white flowered matching blouse and drove five miles to the edge of the city to the church that she'd attended since she was a child. She liked the feeling of knowing everyone there, like seeing family every week. Her best friend, Clarinda, also a nurse, married to a doctor, Ken Jackson, attended the church, too.

Selena found a seat in the middle of the sanctuary and read the bulletin to learn of the activities scheduled for the following week. The service leader walked to the front and raised his hands to begin leading the first hymn. Everyone stood up.

The congregation sang the first hymn, *O For a Thousand Tongues*. Selena looked around to locate guests in attendance. She noticed Ken and Clarinda sitting across the aisle and up two benches. Their three children sat between them. Ken shared a hymnal with the man beside him. The back of the man's head looked familiar but she couldn't place where she'd seen him before.

The service completed, Selena made her way to the back to wait for Clarinda. She caught up with her in the foyer and made arrangements to have lunch with her on Friday. As she turned to leave, Clarinda said, "Oh, Selena, I want you to meet Ken's cousin who's here for the weekend."

Selena turned and found herself face to face with a pair of pale blue eyes.

"Well, if it isn't my favorite nurse! Hello, Selena, how are you?"

Selena's face warmed and she laughed self-consciously. She felt him take her hand in a slow, firm grasp. She quickly pulled it away.

"Hello, Graham

"Do you two know each other?" Clarinda asked. "My days spent in the hospital were brightened by her presence. She prevailed upon the doctor to let me go home. I wouldn't have lasted another day in there." His eyes searched her face as if looking for the sadness around her eyes.

Selena felt his hand lift hers and bend the fingers to look at her wedding band. He raised his eyebrows as she pulled her hand away and covered it with her other hand.

She said all the things she'd been taught to say in these situations, "Nice to see you again," and "Hope you're feeling better."

Making a hasty exit to the Sunday school classroom, she took several deep breaths and gained the control she sought by the time the leader took prayer requests. What was it about Graham Kensington that flustered her? Sad eyes, indeed!

Selena met Clarinda at the mall on Friday. They walked to the Bistro, ordered sandwiches, and sat sipping sodas.

"How is Howard these days? You haven't talked about him much lately. Are you working things out for a reconciliation?"

"Howard? He's being Howard. He says he's going to file for divorce. He said I'd get the papers this week, but I haven't seen them yet so I don't know what he's doing." Selena mentioned the conversation between the two of them the last time she saw him at his house.

"What are you going to do if he follows through with all his threats?"

"I guess I'll wait and see if that happens and then go from there. What can I do? I can't make him stay married to me. At least I still have a job. They're talking about reducing

17

the amount of staff at the hospital again. I just hope and pray they don't cut deep enough to get me. I missed the last one six months ago. That time they cut everyone that had worked there four years or less. Rumors are flying around, but so far no one has heard anything definite." Selena sighed.

"Are you all right? You look tired

"I suppose. The thing that has me more concerned than anything else is that I can't find the portfolio folder to change things in the account. Remember the money I inherited from Dad? I invested it for future use. Now Howard is demanding I give him half of it. I don't know if I'm going to do that or not, but I have to find the portfolio to make a phone call to change it before Howard decides to take it all. I guess I better get going. Mom is expecting me this evening. Thanks for listening."

Selena drove to her mother's house for the evening. Telling her about Howard's threats, she omitted the part about misplacing the portfolio. It would only upset her mother and surely it would show up sooner or later. Wouldn't it? She'd lost count of the number of times she'd searched her apartment. Each time she prayed that God would reveal its location. And each time she returned to where she started, empty-handed.

She told herself over and over that she still had something to be thankful for. She still had the top three: job, car, and apartment. Now she added another, no court papers. She didn't know what it meant, but it was something to be thankful for. Maybe Howard would change his mind and decide to reconcile the marriage.

God answered prayer, didn't He? Selena prayed.

Chapter 2

Selena rolled down the window of her car and breathed in the cool air, saturating her senses with the panorama of pastel colors. Spring in central Ohio brought out the blooms on the dogwood trees, the laurels, the red buds, the forsythia, and the flowering plum trees. Tulips, daffodils, and jonquils added splashes of color to the never-ending display. The crocuses and snowdrops had already lost their blooms and now gorged their bulbs with water and nutrients for a showy display for next year.

It had been several months since Selena spent the day with her sister, Jeanine Sampson. She thoroughly enjoyed the hour's drive through the countryside, no matter what the season.

Driving leisurely through one small town after another Selena smiled. With each town came its own set of memories. Her first date with a boy who lived in this one; her friend in junior high school had lived in the last one and died in a traffic accident on graduation day; the next one reminded her of the time her friends talked her into going skinny dipping with them in the local pond. Her face warmed as she thought of that one, hoping her mother had never found out.

Her mind went back to the old farmhouse, her first recollection of a family home. Her parents, Wilson and Madelyn Cordell, worked hard to provide the essentials for their growing family of three girls and two boys. Every Sunday found them in church, learning good morals and love for each other and their neighbors. A giving family, they gave away the vegetable produce they raised and the milk and eggs from the animals to those in need.

Selena smiled as she thought of the fun times that her parents had encouraged. Friends from school and church spent many hours on the farm.

With children in five grades, creative energy abounded in them and their friends, and Wilson and Madelyn encouraged the children to have a good time--once the chores were done! She wished now she had a quarter for every time she'd heard her parents say that.

Selena wouldn't have given up anything about her childhood, except for one thing. Her parents had taught through their example that everyone had a good heart and could be trusted. She now knew that wasn't true, and she'd learned the lesson the hard way.

Growing up with church the center of her life, she'd determined at an early age that she wasn't going to get married until the right man came along. She set her standards high and kept them there all through high school. After graduation Mister Right didn't look to be forthcoming any time soon, so she went to college and graduated with a degree of science in nursing.

She got a job at Columbus General, the largest hospital in the city of Columbus, Ohio and moved into an apartment close to work so she wouldn't have to drive far. She enjoyed the work and knew that God wanted her to be there. But, as her twenty-fifth birthday crept up on her, she began to wonder if there'd ever be a Mister Right for her.

One day shortly after her birthday, Liza Morgan, a woman she worked with, invited her to spend the weekend with her at Chaqua Lake, a summer resort area in northern Ohio. A family in the cabin next to the Morgans' introduced themselves as the Mulvaneys.

Selena sat in front of Liza's cabin in the evening, fanning herself to get some relief from the heat. She smiled as a young man approached her from the Mulvaney's cabin.

Introducing himself as Howard Mulvaney, he sat on the chair opposite her and talked easily of general topics. Before the weekend ended, he asked for her phone number and said he wanted to see her again. After a half dozen dates, she told him she couldn't see him anymore because he had no interest in church or church related activities.

Two weeks later he called and asked if he could go to church with her. That began a dating relationship, which eventually ended in marriage. When he said he worked and attended college to be an engineer, she believed him. When he said he loved her, she believed him. When he said he couldn't live without her, she believed him. When he said God had worked a miracle in his life and he wanted to be a Christian, she believed him.

They married and Selena felt that her life had finally taken on the meaning she'd been looking for. He had to be Mister Right. Then she discovered that he didn't always tell her the truth. He said he had to quit his job so he could study, but he never studied and eventually didn't enroll for the next semester. He said he loved her, but she noticed the long glances and the insolent smiles at other women. He said he couldn't live without her, but made plans for weekends away that didn't include her. He soon stopped going to church with her and eventually sneered at her friends, her life style, and her God.

She continued to pray for him, but it seemed the more she prayed the more he resisted her attempts to restore their relationship to a loving, caring level. Now he'd filed for divorce, and she couldn't understand what he wanted from her in the first place. Clarinda suggested that maybe he needed her stability. Ken surmised that he needed her good looks to make himself feel important. Selena had laughed out loud at that one.

At five-foot-three, with a medium build, she never considered herself to be an outstanding beauty. Her long dark brown hair with bangs over her forehead accented her large brown eyes and small nose. She had a ready smile, but no one had seen much of it recently.

Howard accused her of being naïve when she refused to embrace his new age philosophies and the multifaced ones of the people she worked with. He accused her of being ignorant when he tried to talk to her about things she'd never heard of before. Struggling with all the issues, she'd chosen to remain naïve and ignorant.

Seeing the sign at the city limits, Granada, Selena slowed down and turned onto the first side street where Jeanine lived. This town and this street looked like most of the others in the county. All of them had been settled about one hundred years earlier. Large elm and maple trees along with a smattering of oaks lined the streets, providing shade for the well kept houses and lawns.

The two story houses with gables accommodated the large families that moved into the area looking for rich farmland and friendly neighbors. Large front porches graced each dwelling as days ended with families socializing in the coolness of the evening. Spacious lawns graced the homes where potluck lunches and Sunday afternoon games provided competition and friendly bantering. Each family had supported the stores needed for the town to be self-sufficient.

Most of the stores were closed now but families stayed. Some chose the small town atmosphere in which to raise their children. Others remained in the house where they were born, generations after the first ancestor had died.

Selena parked in front of the house, knocked on the door once, yelled, "Halloo!", and walked in.

Jeanine looked around the corner of the kitchen door. "Come on in and watch your step."

Selena smiled as she stepped around the toys, books, and crayons of the three children. A twinge of envy came and went. Selena dreamed of having children, but had decided to wait until she worked through her problems with Howard. Now it looked again like having children of her own might never happen.

She found her sister in the kitchen feeding the baby, Tom Jr., kissed her on the cheek and sat at the table. "Where are the other children?"

"I put them down for a nap, and this one will be going soon. We should have some peace and quiet--for a little while anyway." Jeanine smiled.

Selena looked up to Jeanine, two years her senior. Their paths went in opposite directions when they graduated from high school. Jeanine married her high school sweetheart as soon as they graduated, but waited to have children until her husband completed college and started his own business. Even with the differences in their lives they remained close and were each other's confidante.

Selena poured out her heart after Jeanine placed the baby in bed for a nap. Jeanine cried with her and promised to help any way she could, especially by praying for her.

The children awoke from their naps and Selena spent a couple hours entertaining them. She said goodbye shortly after dinner. As she drove home, she wished she could shake the melancholy mood that wrapped itself around her. She'd hoped Jeanine would be able to help by encouraging her more. *Oh, well, it's my problem, not hers.*

Another Monday morning. Selena sighed as she clocked in to begin her shift at Columbus General. The weekend had been stressful. Howard called and left several messages that she didn't respond to. The last one sounded threatening, demanding that she pay him the money she owed him at once or else. . . The threat was non-specific, but she felt uneasy. It must mean, though, that he either didn't have her portfolio, or he wasn't able to get the money he wanted.

That's certainly an answer to prayer. It means my money remains intact in the account. However, it made Howard a presence to be reckoned with if he decided to carry out his threat. She breathed a prayer of thanksgiving that she'd thought to change the locks on the door to her apartment. At least he couldn't just walk in without her consent.

Six o'clock that evening her doorbell rang. Her heart pounded as she looked out the window. She opened the door to the uniformed police officer, wondering if someone she knew had been hurt. Acknowledging her name when asked, she took the large envelope from him.

"What's this?"

"Registered papers, ma'am. Please sign here." He handed her a pen and pointed to the line with a large X at the end.

She signed the form, thanked the officer, closed the door and collapsed on the sofa. She stared at the envelope for a long time, not wanting to read the contents. She finally opened it before she went to bed, and read that Howard had filed for dissolution of marriage due to unreconcilable differences. A court date had been set for August twenty-fifth, with the judgement being final September first.

That meant with time he could still change his mind. She breathed a sigh of relief. *There's still time.* She'd have to pray harder. Even though she'd have to cross that off the list of things to be thankful for.

Selena went to work on Friday hopeful that things would change soon. Howard hadn't called her for two days and that provided some relief. She locked her purse in the cabinet in the nurses' station and began to assess the needs of her assigned patients before she went to the conference room to get the report from the night shift.

Patty walked in behind her, sing-songing, "Pay day, pay day, pay day." Selena laughed. Inwardly she looked forward to pay day as much as Patty.

During her morning break, she went to the Financial Services Department to pick up her paycheck. She opened it to corroborate the amount, then noticed another paper in the envelope. *Probably something about the picnic this summer,* she thought and stuck it back in the envelope before placing it in her pocket.

After lunch the head nurse, Katrina Smart, approached Selena and asked if she could speak to her in the conference room for a few minutes. They chatted amiably as they walked to the end of the hall, went in the conference room and closed the door.

"Have you had a chance to read the notice in the envelope with your paycheck?" Katrina asked. Selena shook her head.

"Please read it."

Selena removed the paper from the envelope. Her face blanched as she placed her hand over her mouth. Tears formed when she looked at Katrina. *What am I going to do now?*

The letter, from the Nursing Administration office, told her what a good job she'd done for the hospital and that she had an exemplary record. However, due to a need for budget cuts and a decrease in the number of patients being admitted to the hospital it had become expedient to reduce their nursing staff by one fourth. If she needed recommendations they would be willing to supply them. Her final day of work would be in one week on Friday.

"I'm very unhappy about this," Katrina said. "You're one of my best nurses. There are others I would rather see leave. Unfortunately, they're not looking at work records; they're going strictly by seniority. After the last cut, I had to take nurses from other units. That still left you the lowest in seniority on our unit. I'm really sorry about this; I wish I could do something."

Selena wiped her eyes and held up her head. Smiling crookedly she said, "Thanks for your support, Katrina. This hits me at a time when I really don't need another problem. But, I guess I better get my resume' out, dust it off and start job hunting."

Getting her records ready to begin job hunting proved easy. Interviewing for positions in a market flooded with qualified nurses who had met the same fate as hers, didn't. With Howard still breathing threats, she didn't want to be out driving after dark, which limited her choice of jobs. The nurses who had been in her position six months earlier had filled the positions she would have accepted now.

Ken Jackson told her that a colleague of his with an office in the same building had a job opening for a nurse. Selena asked for a recommendation from the hospital administration and from Ken. Three weeks after she left the hospital she filled out an application for a job with Doctor Stanford. He looked briefly at the letters of recommendation she handed to him and offered her the job. The pay, lower than she made at the hospital and the hours, fewer with no chance of overtime, initially tempted her to decline the offer.

She went home and prayed for wisdom to make the right decision, looking at her checkbook several times. Could she make it financially if she accepted the job? It wouldn't allow any extras for emergencies. But she hadn't received any better offers. *Maybe I better take it. If I hear of a better job later, I can always change jobs again.*

She called Doctor Stanford's office the next morning, and was told to report for work on Monday morning. Unsure of her decision, she continued to look at the ads in the newspaper all weekend. Dejected, she found nothing.

She reported for work at Doctor Stanford's office Monday morning.

Learning the work routines didn't provide the challenge she'd hoped for. Having cared for Doctor Stanford's patients at the hospital she knew his routine. He was moody in the office, sometimes amiable with the patients and staff, and sometimes distant and short with his answers. She maintained the professionalism she'd learned in college and in her work at the hospital, and did her best to follow his orders explicitly.

Selena walked through the patient waiting area of Doctor Stanford's office, pushing open the door to the examining rooms in the back. As she tore the page off the calendar on the desk she blinked with surprise at the length of time she'd been working there; two and a half months. It seemed like a long time.

She'd been praying. Every day that she arrived at work she prayed she would hear of another job. She still searched the newspapers for openings in large clinics or local hospitals, finding nothing.

She'd worked on her budget the previous evening. There had to be a way to squeeze a few more dollars out of her paycheck. She'd cut back on the amount of groceries she bought, clothes purchases were nil, and she hadn't accepted an invitation to go out for dinner or movies with her friends since she began the new job. Every time she opened her checkbook the truth became more painful--she had more expenses than income. She prayed regularly for a miracle, not really knowing what it would look like if it came. "A better job would be nice," she said aloud one evening.

Howard called regularly, several times a week, leaving messages too numerous to count, and threatened to clean her out when he took her to court. He didn't specify what he meant and she didn't return his calls to find out. She heard him at the door one evening trying to use his key to get in. His attempts thwarted by the change in her locks, he left quietly, then promptly called her when he got home and breathed out more threats if she didn't give him what he wanted--the money.

Tempted to stay in bed on Sunday, she pulled the cover over her head to shut out the light. However, a lifetime of church attendance activated her conscience. She finally got up and drove to church so she wouldn't have to deal with a guilty conscience along with all the unresolved situations in her life.

She sat in the sanctuary listening to the music, feeling a soothing of her spirit. When the music stopped she opened her eyes and looked around as usual to find visitors to speak to after the service. To her right, she saw Ken and Clarinda and their family with a guest. Looking to her left, she saw her mother with a friend she often brought to services with her.

Toward the end of the service, a child on the bench in front of the Jackson's distracted her from the pastor's sermon. Noticing the Jackson's guest looking her direction, she found herself staring into a pair of piercing, pale blue eyes. Her eyes widened and her mouth opened slightly as she recognized Graham Kensington. She saw the smile before she had a chance to turn and pretend she hadn't seen him.

The service ended, she tried to escape out the door before the Jacksons and their guest had a chance to talk to her. Their aisle of people emptied rapidly, hers slowly. They stood in the foyer when she walked out. Graham's smile indicated that he waited to speak to her.

"So we meet again. How are you, Selena?" Graham smiled as he held out his hand.

Her heart pounded; she fought for control. Offering him her hand, she retracted it as soon as politely possible.

She pasted a smile on her face and responded pleasantly. "I'm fine, thank you, Graham. I see you're rid of your crutches. That must be a good feeling, back on your own two feet again."

"You bet it is. And I can thank you for taking good care of me in the hospital." He reached for her left hand and bent her fingers, glancing at her ring finger. His eyes immediately returned to her face, giving her a knowing look.

She pulled her hand away quickly, feeling her face get warm. Turning she walked as fast as she could to her car and drove home, not staying for Sunday school. She couldn't remember later if she'd even said goodbye.

She left her wedding band at home when she went to work. She had to wash her hands so often she'd finally given up taking it off and putting it back on again. Most Sundays she wore it to church so people would think the marriage was intact, even if Howard didn't attend services. Why had she forgotten it on this day? Of all days for Graham Kensington to show up at church with the Jacksons. No one else cared if she wore the ring or not. Why did he make such a big deal out of it? And why did she care what he thought? She didn't even know anything about him. Well, it didn't matter. She had enough problems in her life without worrying about what he thought.

Selena cringed as she looked at her checkbook and realized the landlord expected a check tomorrow. She'd never been late with the payment, but the landlord would have to wait this time. Placing the call to him, she explained her situation and promised to pay on Friday.

She sat down on the sofa and prayed. *Lord, I need a miracle. Something needs to change here. I don't know what to do or where to go. Please help me make the right decisions.*

She found the morning newspaper under her mail and opened it to the apartments for rent section. She took particular interest in the location of units with rates lower than what she currently paid.

The next day she drove around, looking at neighborhoods, and found none where she would feel safe.

29

One neighborhood seemed acceptable, but when she called the number listed, she learned that the apartment consisted of one room in a house owned by a single man. She slashed an X through that ad.

Sunday, Selena placed her wedding ring on her finger and drove to church. She wasn't about to take a chance on seeing Graham Kensington and have him give her that knowing look again. What did he know anyway? He had to be guessing. Seeing the Jacksons already seated, and not with a guest, she sat on the end of the bench with them.

After the service, Clarinda invited her to have lunch at a restaurant with her family. When she declined, Clarinda took her aside and pressured her into telling her the truth--she didn't have the money. Insisting she eat with them anyway as their guest, Selena finally agreed.

"Is the first of the month a bad time for you financially?" Clarinda asked, as they sipped on their sodas at the end of the meal.

"Anytime is a bad time financially. I like the work I'm doing, but I'm not making enough money to support myself on the part-time hours and the decrease in pay from working at the hospital. I've turned my bank account upside down and backwards. I'm going to have to make some drastic changes soon."

"What are you going to do?"

"I'm looking for another place to move, but what I want in a nice neighborhood has the same rent I'm paying now. I feel like I'm up against a wall and there's no way around it. To top it all off, Howard's divorce suit goes to court the end of this month, and I have no idea if the judge will give him half of my investment."

"Did you ever find the portfolio?" Clarinda asked.

Selena shook her head, explaining that she'd looked everywhere to no avail.

Clarinda looked at Ken. "Do you know of anyone else in your building that's looking for a nurse?"

He shook his head. "I thought the job with Doctor Stanford would help. I'll keep my ears open. If I hear of one of the other doctors needing part-time help, I'll let you know."

Chapter 3

Graham eased his car into rush hour traffic as he headed west on Interstate 70. His business was completed, and he had a prospective client to call during the week. He praised God for the referrals since those kept his business prospering.

Easily maneuvering his two-year-old luxury car in and out of the Sunday afternoon traffic, his mind went back to the morning service. The minister had a way of putting things in perspective and bringing the point of his sermon into real life experiences. He thought briefly about the message. He'd written the scripture references on the back of the bulletin to look up later.

Graham smiled as he thought about the look on Selena's face when she saw him. She seemed surprised and. . . he couldn't place the other emotion. Why did he get the feeling that she'd tried to avoid him when she walked into the foyer after the service? She seemed friendly enough. And then the question arose regarding the missing wedding ring. And the husband she said she had that never went to church with her. What did that mean? The sadness remained around her eyes. The smile she gave him today didn't seem as genuine as the ones she gave him when he was in the hospital.

Her face had floated in and out of his thoughts since the day he met her. Just when he thought he'd stuffed it out of sight it would appear out of nowhere. It had been a long time since he'd been so intrigued by a woman, and he couldn't figure out what there was about her that caught his attention.

By her own admission she was married, and that put her off limits as far as he was concerned. The missing wedding ring left questions, but that was certainly no definite indication that she wasn't married.

Why couldn't he get her out of his mind? He thought about her eyes. Yes, the sadness remained, but he also noticed a serenity that suggested she had a deep-down-inside kind of strength. He thought about her smile and the way her lips parted slightly and showed her straight, white teeth when amused or surprised.

Graham decided to think about something else. The long drive home tired him enough without the thoughts that left him feeling out of control.

The two-hour drive was pleasant in good weather and it gave him time to reflect on the priorities and goals he regularly set for himself. He inserted a tape in the tape player to regain the peace and serenity that somehow got lost in the process of operating his own business and parenting his children.

His mind returned to the present by the ringing of his cellular phone. "Hello, Graham Kensington speaking."

"Graham! Where are you, son?"

"Hi, Dad. I'm somewhere between Columbus and Springfield on I-70 heading for home. What are you doing today? I thought you went to Uncle Glen's for the weekend."

"I came home this morning. They had something planned for this afternoon. How's everyone at your place?"

"Everyone is fine as far as I know. I didn't get any calls from home this time so I guess that's good news. When do you think you'll be by this week

"I'm thinking about stopping by Saturday morning and taking them to Kings' Island Amusement Park. They haven't forgotten have they?" "No, they haven't forgotten."

"Tell them I said hello."

"I'll tell them. Talk to you later."

He punched the button on his phone, glad his dad had spent the weekend with his brother. The past year had been rough since Graham's mother died of cancer. He thought back to happier childhood days.

Christened Graham Oliver Kensington II after his grandfather, he'd been the only child of his parents, Sylvan and Stella. His father had served as president of the largest bank in the state and his mother taught economics at the university. She'd been one of only a handful of women who held a professorship on the state level at a university.

As he grew up in his upper class environment, he heard a multitude of times, "You're smart, Graham. Don't waste your intelligence." He had been eager to please his loving and generous parents. Taking his affluence in stride, he had not been cognizant of the fact that not every one had that privilege. He had friends at school from every neighborhood in the city. He didn't know at the time that some of his friends only showed interest in what he shared with them. He'd learned the generosity of his parents and their way of showing respect to everyone regardless of their economic status.

Church attendance had been a weekly ritual in the life of the family. At the age of nine he heard a sermon that encouraged him to have a personal relationship with God. He didn't know what all that meant, but he had been going to church long enough to know that God created everything and therefore controlled all things, so it would probably be a good idea to have Him for a friend.

Graham never had any questions about whether he would go to college. The question of where he would go entailed many hours of discussion. Encouraged to be part of the selection process, he eventually chose a college satisfactory to them all.

His parents encouraged him from an early age to make decisions for himself. Having to take the consequences for those decisions had ingrained in him the difference between making good choices and bad ones. Choosing a college became a natural part of that early instruction.

The honk of a horn brought his mind back to the present. He shifted his position to ease the ache in his leg. Not wishing to continue with the direction his mind had taken he turned the radio up and concentrated on the music. He began to relax as he let the words sink into his spirit.

His attempts at trying to forget that this was an anniversary date had succeeded so far today. However, as he rounded the corner of the road that followed the river he wondered why he'd decided to go this way. He rarely followed this route as the memories reminded him of things he had settled several years earlier.

He pulled his car to the side of the road, stopped, and got out. He stretched his leg slowly as he felt the twinge from the injury. Walking slowly over to the tree forever scarred that night five years ago, his eyes followed the trunk up until he saw the mark several feet over his head. He picked his steps carefully to avoid the brambles and damp rocks.

His eyes sought the spot in the middle of the stream that had become a memorial to a life ended in its prime. It could have been prevented, if only. . .

He took a deep ragged breath and rubbed his eyes with his fingers. Every time he came here, it seemed her face floated in the water, laughing. The words she said to him once wafted softly on the breeze, "You need to loosen up. Life is a lot of fun. Laugh. Party. Be happy."

Kate. He could still see her blue laughing eyes, her soft blond hair, and porcelain-doll-like features. Just like the first time he saw her; they'd attended a youth event sponsored by the youth pastor at the church he attended while at college.

He'd talked his three college buddies, James Stanwyck, Scott Morefield, and Sid Allen into going with him. As soon as they arrived they spotted Kate, a guest of one of the other girls.

"Does anyone happen to know who *that* is?" James spoke for them all.

"No, but I aim to find out." Scott stood up and walked toward the table. His three friends laughed. They could depend on Scott to find out anything that they wanted to know about anyone or anything. He planned to go to law school and his smooth talking could get answers that eluded others.

When Scott returned to the table he smiled. "That, my dear friends, is Kate Worley and she is currently unattached."

Graham remembered shaking his head. How Scott found all that out in less than a minute he would never know. He had tagged along with Scott on other occasions to observe his methods, possibly using them himself someday, but he never determined how Scott took the scanty information given to him and arrived at his conclusions. It was difficult to discredit him since he was right ninety-five percent of the time.

At the end of Graham's senior year, an event changed his life. One night as he studied for final exams, facts were going in circles in his brain like leaves in a whirlwind. Scott knocked on his door and with much persuasion talked him into going downtown to the Pizza Plaza where the students hung out on Saturday night. When they walked in the door, Graham spied Kate sitting with a guy and another couple.

Sid and James walked in glancing about the room as they sat down. Practical jokes had become common among the four friends. Graham took part in them but rarely instigated them.

Spying Kate with her date, James grinned as he said, "Hey, Kensington. This is your chance to end college life with a bang. You've been out with Kate before. See if you can get her away from that geek she's with."

Now, a movement in the brush beside him caught his attention and he turned to see a raccoon scurrying in the other direction. Breathing a sigh of relief, he turned and walked back to his car. He didn't want to go over the events that had happened at the Pizza Plaza that night. He didn't want to be reminded of the dare he had taken from Scott; a dare that had hurt a lot of people and left lingering questions in his mind about relationships.

He walked back to his car and turned in the direction of home, driving safely but longing to be there. Rolling Acres, the road that led to his home, then the sign bearing the name, Serendipity Estate, came into view. He slowed the car and turned onto the winding, tree-lined pavement that led to the buildings.

The entire house came into view. Without melancholy he remembered the excitement all of them felt when they moved here. He continually reminded himself that God had been good to him, even in the midst of some very troubling times, and in spite of the mistakes he'd made.

As he parked his car two children ran from the house. He braced as they flung themselves at him. He grabbed them in a tight hug. Their squeals of delight lifted his spirits. Handing them his jacket and briefcase he walked between them to the house, hand in hand.

Looking at his children, Trevor and Trina, he realized he had failed to mention to the Jacksons that he needed to add another person to his staff. For the past month he'd been looking for the right person to fulfill the responsibilities he had in mind. He had used an agency to hire the housekeeper and chauffeur/maintenance personnel. A close personal friend had recommended the woman he hired to do the cooking. This new position was one he chose to fill on his own.

Graham talked to several of his friends about his desire to hire another person. Two applicants had been interviewed but he decided against bringing them into his home. He wanted someone with outstanding qualifications, since she or he would be spending a lot of time with his children.

Two weeks later, Graham took the airplane to Columbus, rented a car and drove east to Zanesville. He took care of his business on Saturday, and drove back to Columbus to spend Saturday evening and Sunday with the Jacksons. He and Ken had grown up in the same neighborhood and prided themselves on being first cousins, something no one else in the old neighborhood could boast about.

After the Jackson children went to bed, Graham shared with Ken and Clarinda his plan to hire another person. "I've talked to a lot of people but so far I've hit a dead end. School starts again in a couple weeks and I really need someone by that time."

"What qualifications are you looking for?" Clarinda asked.

"I want a mature individual who is good with children, has high moral and ethical standards, is open and honest, spends money wisely, and has a personal relationship with God that is demonstrated daily and openly."

Ken laughed. "It sounds like you want an angel sent straight from the throne of God."

Graham grinned. "I know it sounds like the standards are really high, but when it comes to my children only the best will do. It may be tough finding someone, but God has assured me that there is someone like that out there. I'm willing to do what I have to do until I find her--or him."

The next morning Graham and the Jacksons arrived at church several minutes early. Graham looked closely at those already there, looking for Selena. He didn't see her. Hopefully she would arrive soon so he could speak to her. Puzzled by her attempts to avoid him the last time, he planned to overlook the missing ring and be pleasant. *I should ask her if I've offended her in some way. I can't imagine what it would be about.*

During one of the hymns, he looked around and saw her sitting in the back. She appeared to be alone again. He turned around a couple more times, but she concentrated on the hymnbook.

The service over, he walked to the back quickly, hoping to catch her before she left. He didn't see her in the foyer. Glancing out the window, he saw her drive away. Disappointed, he admitted again that he shouldn't be this interested in a married woman.

Sitting at the table after lunch, Clarinda suddenly said, "You know, Graham, I've been thinking about what you said last night. I know someone who has all the qualifications you mentioned, but I don't know if she'd want to move that far from Columbus. Of course, given her circumstances right now, she might jump at the chance. Do you remember the woman who took care of you in the hospital? Selena Mulvaney?"

Graham stared at her, waiting for her to go on. He suddenly remembered she'd asked him a question. "Of course I remember her. What kind of circumstances is she in?"

"Her husband filed for divorce, she lost her good paying job at the hospital, and she's unable to support herself on the part-time job that she felt she had to accept. I'll give you her phone number if you want to call her."

Placing the slip of paper with Selena's phone number on it in his
suit coat pocket, he thanked them for the information and looked at his watch. It was time to go.

So, in spite of her objections to his observations, he'd been right. That explained the missing wedding ring. He couldn't imagine what kind of person would divorce Selena. She seemed cheerful, pleasant, organized, and giving of her time the three days he'd spent on the surgical unit. He'd been around people enough to know that she was genuine in her love of her work and that she easily related to all kinds of people. *But, will she work for me? I guess I'll find out.*

Chapter 4

Graham picked up the slip of paper from his desk with Selena's phone number written on it and dialed the number. The answering machine came on after the first ring. Almost at the end of his message, she picked up the phone.

"Hello, Selena. I understand you're looking for another job. Sorry to hear you got laid off at the hospital. Were they down-sizing again?"

"Yes. It's been really difficult finding another job with all the layoffs that have happened, not only at Columbus General, but at other hospitals in the city also." She paused, waiting for him to state his purpose for calling.

"I wondered if you would consider working for me. I need someone to help with the children and take on some housekeeping responsibilities."

He waited several seconds for her to answer. Thinking she'd hung up, he said, "Selena? Are you still there?"

"What do you want me to say? I may be in tight circumstances right now, but I certainly think I can do better than baby sitting and cleaning someone's house. Good luck in finding someone." She hung up, not waiting for a response.

"Wait, Selena. It's not like that." He heard the click on the other end. Now what? She probably wouldn't talk to him if he called her back. He sat at his desk for a long time, tapping his fingers and staring out the window. He'd have to try to talk to her personally the next time he had business in the Columbus area. Opening his notebook, he made a note on his calendar.

Selena hung up the phone, seething. How dare he offer her a job like that? If that's all the better he can do, he can forget it. *If I can't manage my finances on what I'm doing now, how will I be able to manage on less?*

43

She'd continued to look for a better job, but had been disappointed at every turn. Looking for another apartment had given her the same outcome. The court hearing was scheduled for next week, and it didn't look as if Howard was any closer to considering reconciliation than when he first filed for divorce.

She had prayed harder than she could ever remember doing about anything in her life. Nothing had changed, except her disappointment changed to discouragement and then to depression. She felt as if her life spiraled out of control leaving her feeling powerless.

When the phone rang and Graham identified himself, Selena had been surprised and curious. Her pulse quickened when he said he wanted to offer her a job. Maybe this was the answer to her prayers. But when he explained what he wanted she took offense. Was that all he thought her qualified for? Surely his memory hadn't failed him. He'd seen what she could do at the hospital.

I guess I'll have to broaden my horizons and buy some out-of-town newspapers. Maybe Cleveland or Cincinnati has nursing jobs to offer, she thought as she turned out the light in the kitchen.

She took her Bible off the nightstand in her bedroom and began reading in Isaiah at the forty-first chapter. She read the first thirteen verses, then stopped suddenly, returned to verse eight and read verses eight through thirteen again. The promise in verse thirteen burned into her mind. "I am the LORD, your God, who takes hold of your right hand and says to you, do not fear; I will help you." Closing the book, she turned the light out and slept soundly for the first time in weeks.

The day of the court hearing came and went and Selena heard nothing from Howard or the courts. Remembering how long it took them to get the papers to her notifying her of the suit against her, she wasn't surprised a week later that she still hadn't been contacted. It had been two weeks since the last time she heard from Howard and that concerned her more than the slow delivery. She had begun to look over her shoulder everywhere she went. Church seemed to be the only safe place. Did not hearing from him mean he got what he wanted when he went to court? What had he asked for?

Suddenly remembering the document she received in April, she retrieved the envelope from the bottom of the desk drawer. She read it carefully. There was an item about the down payment on her car but no mention of the inheritance money. Did that mean he already had it and didn't need the court to get it for him?

Selena sighed. Howard attended church with her long enough to know that divorce was not an option in settling problems. Why couldn't he understand that if they worked together as God wanted them to that they could make a marriage work? *I would even forgive him for all the threats he's made.*

The last words he'd said to her at his house that evening in March rang in her mind, "I'm tired of your strange beliefs." Tears of frustration slid down her cheeks as she realized that in spite of all her hard work she had failed in keeping the marriage together, her dream of home and family in pieces.

One evening she returned from work and found a message on her answering machine from Clarinda. Returning the call, she said, "Hi, Clarinda. What's going on with you? "

"Did you get a call from Graham Kensington?"

"Oh, he called all right. You wouldn't believe what he wanted me to do." Selena recounted the conversation to her friend.

"You're right. I don't believe it. He talked to us about it and it sounded a whole lot different than that. If I had known that was all he wanted I would never have given him your phone number. I'm really sorry, Selena. Have you found anything else?"

"No. Nothing for day hours. I'm afraid to take evening and night hours. I don't want Howard following me around after dark."

"Well, we'll keep praying about it. Something has to happen soon. Do you have the final papers for the divorce yet?"

"No. I haven't heard a thing. I can't imagine what the delay is all about."

"Well, we'll pray about that too."

Sunday, Selena walked into the sanctuary after the first hymn. The usher helped her find an empty seat on a bench in the middle section on the right. As she placed her purse and Bible on the bench, the person beside her handed her an open hymnal. Turning to indicate her thanks she looked into the pale blue eyes she had come to know so well. *How could I have walked to this bench and not noticed who sat on the end? That shows where my mind has been lately. Now what am I going to do? I could get up and leave. That would be too obvious. I'll think about it closer to the end of the service.*

She stood for the last hymn, picked up her purse and her Bible and was ready to escape as everyone closed their eyes for the benediction. She felt a hand on her elbow. She wasn't surprised. She'd felt him watching her during the service, but had refused to encourage him by looking back.

She turned to him as he moved closer and whispered in her ear, "Don't leave. I need to talk to you. There's been a serious misunderstanding." She felt his hand remain on her elbow, making it nearly impossible for her to leave without causing a scene. She tried to step away from him, but his hand was firm. The physical contact unnerved her.

Out of the corner of her eye she saw him studying her as he asked, "Where can we go to talk?"

"I don't see that we have anything to talk about." She removed his hand from her arm and turned to walk away.

"Whoa, come back here." Graham reached out and gently held onto her arm. "Just exactly what is it you think I'm asking you to do?"

"You told me on the phone you want someone to help you with your children, which by the way you didn't say their ages, and you want a housekeeper. If I can't support myself on the part-time wages of a nurse, how am I going to manage on the salary of domestic help? Don't
get me wrong. I'm not beneath doing that kind of work. I'm just not in a position right now to consider working for less money."

Graham folded his arms and smiled. "I understand now why you said what you did on the phone. I didn't mean to insult you. However, if you had let me finish before you hung up on me, I would have explained what I really want someone to do. There's a lot of responsibility involved. Yes, there's childcare, but I want someone who's not only able to get the children ready for school, and to take them to after school activities, but is also able to help shape their lives by being an example to them in the way they should behave and think. I said I needed a housekeeper for lack of a better word to call it. I already have someone who does all the cleaning. I need someone who is able to do the staff scheduling, manage the finances, and generally keep things running smoothly. You would be answerable only to me, and the rest of the staff would be answerable to you

Selena stared at him, speechless. He needed someone to manage his staff, the finances, and the general household?

"What kind of place do you live in?"

Graham laughed. She had let her guard down for one second with the question and he found it refreshing. Her face softened as she expressed her surprise and curiosity at his explanation. He saw her blush as he laughed and he sought to put her at ease. "It's a pretty big place. Would you like to see it and meet the children before you decide?"

"When would be a good time for me to stop by?"

"I wouldn't expect you to drive over. Tell you what-- I'll buy you a plane ticket and meet you at the airport. You can look the place over, spend a few minutes with the children, ask any questions you may

have, then I'll take you back to the airport. You'll be home in time for dinner. Or you can let me take you to dinner, then I'll take you to the airport, still getting you home in the same day."

Her eyes widened, and her mouth opened slightly as she tried to make sense of what he said. "What do you mean the airport? Where do you live?"

"The address is Fredricksburg. I'm not surprised if you've never heard of it. I didn't either until I moved there. I'd pick you up at the Dayton airport, which is about ten miles from the estate. When would be a good time for you?"

She heard the words but had trouble comprehending what he said. She felt as if his eyes held her under a spell, unable to look away.

She willed herself to look away, watching most of the congregation go down the steps to their cars. She finally recovered her voice. "Any Saturday would be a good time for me. I want you to know up front that I still have a lot of questions about what you're asking me to do. Just because I accept your invitation to see your place doesn't mean I'll take the job

"That's fair. I'll call this week and reserve you a plane ticket for this coming Saturday. What about dinner?"

"I don't think so this time."

"All right. I'll call you the middle of the week and let you know when to be at the airport. You can pick up the ticket before you get on the plane."

They stood in the middle of the empty foyer, silent, vaguely hearing the sounds of the trustee locking the doors.

"Selena?" Graham waited until she looked up. "Thanks for thinking about this and doing this for me." He smiled as he looked into her eyes and noticed the sadness remained.

"I haven't made up my mind yet, so don't get your hopes up," Selena said walking through the church door he opened for her.

The first Saturday in September dawned clear and cool. The bright sun promised to warm things by the end of the day. Selena awoke early trying to decide what to wear. This was, after all, a job interview. Remembering snatches of their conversation on Sunday and again on Wednesday when he called to tell her about the plane ticket, she had the feeling this job interview would be like no other she'd been to. She tried to piece together the information he gave her and make some sense of the explanation. She always ended up where she started, with the same question she'd asked him last Sunday at church, "What kind of place do you live in?" He mentioned something about an estate. What did that mean?

Since she had declined his dinner date, she decided to dress casually in jeans, a T-shirt and a vest. She locked her apartment door, drove to the airport, picked up her ticket and walked to the gate to board the plane.

As she fastened her seat belt, she thought about her conversation with Clarinda the evening before. "You're going to love Graham's place. It's the closest place to heaven on earth I've ever seen. Call me when you get back and let me know what you think. Don't worry about the money he's spending on the plane ticket; he has lots more where that came from."

Selena walked off the plane into the terminal and saw Graham standing in the waiting area watching for her. She approached him and smiled. He turned suddenly and walked away leaving her hurrying to catch up.

Halfway down to the main floor he spoke. "Did you have any problems getting the ticket?" She looked at him curiously. His voice sounded funny.

"No. No problems at all."

Watching her walk into the terminal, he first felt a sense of relief. A nagging voice in the back of his mind all morning told him she wouldn't show up; she would change her mind at the last minute.

Seeing her dressed casually he noticed how nice she looked, as usual. The smile she gave him elicited emotions he hadn't experienced before. Taken off guard and momentarily confused by what he couldn't identify he simply walked toward the escalator.

By the time they reached his car and were out on the road, he'd regained his composure and easily engaged her in conversation. He smiled at the natural way in which she expressed herself and breathed a sigh of relief at her relaxed posture and spontaneous answers.

She noted the turns he made onto several side roads. He maneuvered the curves easily as they followed a road that lay adjacent to a river. The road suddenly widened, and she marveled at the rolling lawns in front of large mansions that ended far from the road. The houses had other buildings set behind them that she couldn't identify from the distance. She admired the beauty of each one aloud.

As they turned into the driveway the sign caught her eye. *Serendipity Estate.* What an odd name for a place. Her eyes studied the large mansion on top of the hill. As Graham drove around to the back and parked the car, she noticed a large building down the hill that looked like a stable. Horses grazed in a large corral next to it. Off to the side stood another building. One of the three doors was open, revealing two cars parked inside.

Selena stared at the acres of rolling lawn and wondered inanely how long it took to mow it all. The back lawn ended at the wooded terrain. She couldn't see where the side of the property ended as it dropped out of sight.

The passenger door opened. She blushed self-consciously as she stepped onto the paved driveway.

She turned slowly and took in the quiet beauty, awe-struck by the expanse of the estate. She heard an occasional car on the road, the sound muted and easily unnoticed. The airplane in the sky rose too high up to be heard; seen only by the trail of white smoke-like condensation. A stream meandered across one corner of the woods and disappeared near the only stretch of fence seen from where she stood.

Graham watched her turn as if on a slow moving carousel and take in the wonders of this place he called home. He remembered experiencing the same feelings that showed on her face the first time he'd looked at the estate. He waited quietly for her to saturate her senses.

"So, where do you live?" Selena asked suddenly.

"Come. I'll show you." He walked ahead of her to a back door of the mansion and inserted a key into the lock. Opening the door, he stood aside for her to enter. They walked through a corridor and entered a large kitchen decorated with country style motif in blue and white.

Off to one side in front of an immense window she saw a nook with a table and six chairs. The homey corner seemed dwarfed by the openness of the surrounding area. The large window behind it allowed the light to pour in, giving the whole area a feeling of warmth.

As they left the kitchen, Selena's eyes opened wide at the formal dining room. It looked like one she'd seen in a magazine once. Large works of art hung on the walls. Looking at the rich burgundy colors of the carpet and drapes, she felt as if she had stepped into a palace fit only for a king. Her shoes sank into the soft carpet.

Lined with buffets and china cabinets full of multiple place settings of china, crystal, and serving pieces, the room had a feeling of elegance. Graham opened the drapes allowing the light to illuminate and reflect off of the finish of the rich wood furniture.

He opened a door. Walking past him, she smiled at the warmth in the room. A sofa graced the walls on each side with recliners and other occasional chairs scattered through out. A game table stood in one corner, while a large TV took up the opposite corner. Indirect lighting fixtures gave needed lighting.

Family photographs and paintings of children at play hung on the walls. In the middle of the room a large open area invited activities limited only by the imagination. Bookshelves lined one end, and toys looked as if they'd been hastily pushed into piles.

"This is my kind of room."

"Mine too," Graham echoed.

Graham pushed a button on a box on the wall and said, "Babs, you can send the children down now."

Selena expected to hear thundering footsteps until she remembered the carpet. She waited, not knowing which direction they would come from. Suddenly the door behind her burst open and two children hurled themselves at Graham. He braced and caught them both, one under each arm, and held them there as they wiggled and squealed.

Laughing, he set them on their feet. "I want you to meet Selena. She's a friend of mine. Say hello."

"Hello, Selena." They spoke in unison, their eyes big with curiosity as they stared at her.

Graham finished the introduction. "Selena, I would like for you to meet my children, Trevor, who is ten and Trina, who is eight. Trevor is in fifth grade and Trina is in third."

"How about if I get some sodas?" Graham made it more of a statement than a question. When no one objected he left the room.

Selena smiled at the children. Trevor had Graham's round face and blue eyes, but the resemblance ended there. His hair was darker and shorter and parted on the side. He smiled reservedly through even lips.

Trina's long blond hair curled naturally on the ends. Her large blue eyes, small nose, and light pink complexion reminded Selena of a porcelain doll.

"So, guys, tell me what you like to do. Ride bikes? Play soccer? How about baseball? Play with dolls? Play the piano?"

As Graham neared the door with the sodas, he heard both children talking animatedly at the same time. Selena's laughter mixed in with their voices. He stopped at the door with the tray, and watched her interact with them as if she'd known them all their lives. He hadn't told her that the acid test was meeting his children and watching to see how she related to them. She'd passed with flying colors. He knew that God wanted him to hire her for the job.

The next thing--how to convince her of that.

Graham sent the children outside to play, saying he wanted to finish the tour with Selena. She waved at the children as they left the room then turned to him, waiting for him to continue.

He caught the look and smiled, raising his hands in the air as he raised his eyebrows. "What's the question? I know you have one."

"I'm still trying to comprehend all of this. You really live here

Graham laughed. "Yes, I really live here. God made this available for us to live in. I don't own it, but I take care of it like it's my own

"How did that happen? It being made available to you, I mean."

"Maybe I'll have a chance to tell you about it someday. Right now, we need to continue our tour or I won't get you back to the airport in time to catch your plane, and it's a long walk home." She heard the light-hearted jest in his tone and saw the twinkle in his eye.

He opened the door off the hallway, and waited for her to walk into a formal living room. Sizing it up, she guessed it to be twice as large as her entire apartment. In keeping with the rest of the rooms, this one also had a large window covered with thick, deep burgundy drapes. Graham pulled the drapes back part way to let in the light.

Selena felt as if she'd stepped into another world, one that entertained ladies with hair swept up in piles of ringlets, and dresses that swayed on top of layers of petticoats. She couldn't imagine living in a place with so much luxury at her fingertips.

They continued down the hall to a wide stairway that curved to the second floor. "If you continue down the hall past the stairway you'll find the staff apartments. Each person has two rooms. One room is a kitchen/living room combination and the other is a bedroom. And of course each has a private bath. Let's go up the stairway and I'll show you our rooms, mine and the children's."

The large upstairs rooms matched the downstairs ones in luxury, yet they seemed more functional. Selena noticed the one door he didn't open. She followed him down the stairway through a long corridor that curved slightly as they went. He opened a door and waited as she walked past him into an office.

Windows from the ceiling to halfway down the wall took up two walls. She gasped in delight at the view of the countryside beyond the borders of the estate. "How do you ever get any work done? I'd be sitting here all day looking out the window."

"Believe me, some days it's tempting. I won't bore you with the laundry room, the pantry, and all the other myriad of rooms in this place. The only other formal room that might be of interest to you is the music room. It's right next door, so has the same view. Let's go back to the family room and talk a little about what I expect from the person I'm wanting to hire."

When they'd chosen a seat Selena said, "All right. Now that I've been here, explain to me again what it is you want."

She listened as he talked about the care of the children, the scheduling, supervising the other staff members, and managing the finances for running the household.

He saw the expressions on her face change as she thought about what he told her. He prayed that God would work in her life to bring her here. He wanted her to talk about what she thought, but didn't want to force her. He waited.

Finally, she spoke. "To be real honest with you, Graham, I'm pretty overwhelmed with all of this. I'm just a country girl who grew up with very little. I'm trying to sort out the environment from the job you want me to do. Could I see where I would be living if I accept the job?"

"Actually, there's a room on the second floor. There aren't any more apartments that are livable." Graham spoke hesitantly.

"Also, you haven't said how much you're going to pay the person who takes the job. That's a big factor in my decision."

"How much do you think you're worth? I'm willing to pay a reasonable salary. My children's well-being is worth a lot to me."

"I'll have to think about it. I'm assuming I wouldn't pay you for the room and the food." He nodded in agreement. "Would I need to bring my car and maintain it myself?"

"We have vehicles here you could drive. You haven't asked about time off. You'd be able to come and go as you please when the children are in school. Weekends off are pretty flexible as long as everyone doesn't decide to go to their cousin's wedding the same day."

"Could I see the room on the second floor?"

Graham hesitated, then agreed. Opening the door at the head of the stairway, he stepped aside so she could enter. Selena stared at him. Why didn't he show her this room when they were here before? He'd passed the room, leaving the door closed, as if it had no importance.

As she stepped into the room she noticed the feminine touches. Crossing the floor, she opened the mauve drapes and found large French doors leading onto a balcony. She unlocked the door and walked out to find the same view of the woods, the stream, the stables, and the rolling lawn that she'd seen when they first arrived. She felt infused by the quietness--it was everywhere--and she reveled in it. Turning back into the room, she examined a large dressing area with a private bath, the décor in mauve and green. The large pieces of furniture looked as if they'd been made for the spacious room. She turned to leave and noticed a door adjacent to the door to the hallway.

"Where does this door go?"

He didn't answer. She turned to look at him. "That's my room," she heard him say. Her mouth dropped open, not sure of the implications. Why did he want her in the room that had an adjoining door to his? Recovering quickly, she walked out.

"Thanks for everything today, Graham. You have a beautiful place and a couple of really neat kids."

"When can I expect an answer?" They stood in the waiting area of the airport.

"I'll let you know by the end of next week." She waved as she boarded the plane.

Chapter 5

On Monday, as Selena prepared for work, the phone rang. Without thinking, she picked up the receiver. *Now I know why I don't do this anymore.*

"Where've you been? If you think that not staying in touch with me is a good idea you'll find that's a decision you'll be sorry you made. I want to see you tonight and you better be here or take the consequences." *Howard.*

"Don't hold your breath until I get there," Selena retorted, hanging up the phone. She had no intention of meeting him anywhere, least of all at his house. *Now that we're divorced, I don't have to comply with any of his demands.*

Phone calls like that one made Graham's offer look very good. However, after thinking and praying about it, Selena had some serious problems with the way he wanted things done. It didn't sound like she would have much time to herself. Of course, she could arrange that if she made out the schedule. But, experience had taught her that making schedules for others had its own set of risks.

And what about all the time he wanted her to spend with the children? Congeniality for a few minutes did not guarantee that they would always be that pleasant to be around. And, she was very uncomfortable with the living arrangements. An adjoining door between his room and hers? Whatever was he thinking? What would people say if they knew she agreed to that kind of an arrangement? It would look like there was something going on between them, which there wouldn't be, and she didn't want anyone to think there would be. Maybe she could talk him into fixing up the apartment on the first floor that he said wasn't livable. That is, if she decided to take the job.

That night her phone rang after she went to bed. Howard--still breathing threats, this time because she didn't show up as he demanded. She lay in bed praying. She'd have to do something soon. Howard would eventually catch up with her and she wasn't sure she knew him well enough any more to predict his behavior.

Wednesday, her regularly scheduled day to go to work later in the morning, she picked up the phone and dialed the number on Graham's business card. She held her breath, hoping to get his answering machine and make this quick and easy. He answered the phone on the first ring. She sighed.

"Good morning, Graham. I wanted to ask you a couple more questions if you have time. First, I would really like to know if there are serious behavior problems with your children. And second, I'm not comfortable with having a room adjoining yours. Is there any way the apartment on the first floor could be fixed up for me?"

"To answer the first question, I haven't had anyone tell me that there's ever been any serious behavior problems with my kids. I'll be the first to admit they're not perfect, but they're a lot better than some people's kids I know. They really are just normal kids. As for the second question, there's too much work that needs to be done in that apartment and it would take too much time to get it ready. The room I showed you is ready for someone to move into right away." Graham felt a small pang of guilt at the half-truth he'd just told. It really wouldn't be difficult to get the apartment ready on the first floor.

"I'm sorry, Graham, I don't think I'll take the job

"Would you mind telling me why not?"   W h a t would it hurt? She'd probably never see him again anyway. "You never gave me a firm figure on the salary. I don't like the living arrangements; I've never compromised my reputation before and I don't plan to start now. And I have no idea what

I would do with all the things I have in my apartment here. It just doesn't seem feasible. The scheduling could be a problem when I want to see my family here in Columbus."

"All right. You have some legitimate points. Let's take them one at a time. I'm willing to offer you forty thousand dollars a year. Make me an offer for more if you want to. As far as the living arrangements, I'm sorry that's all I have to offer right now. You wouldn't be the only single female in this house, if that makes you feel any better, and I haven't attacked any of them yet. As for the scheduling, there haven't been any major problems managing the staff in the five years I've been here."

Selena thought about that and replied, "What others do is none of my concern. What I do is of great concern to me. The salary is satisfactory, but I still choose not to walk knowingly into a situation where my reputation would be compromised. I'm still going to have to say no. I need to get to work. Thanks for thinking of me for the job anyway."

She'd done the right thing. Why didn't it feel right? She went to work feeling like she'd closed a door that God wanted to remain open.

Selena drove to her mother's house after work. Talking to her mom always helped her to put things into perspective. She told her about the trip on Saturday and the job offer. Watching her mother's face, she told her she had refused the job and why.

"Do what you think is best, dear," her mother remarked.

She went home feeling the same as when she went to work that morning, restless and on edge.

Saturday, Selena again searched for the missing portfolio, cleaning the apartment as she looked. She stopped and frowned when the doorbell rang. She didn't expect anyone. As she went to the door she prayed it wasn't Howard. She looked out the window and her heart stopped. *Graham.* She looked at her dusty jeans and bare feet and for one minute toyed with the idea of not opening the door. *Oh, well. What can he expect if he shows up unannounced?*

"Graham! This is a surprise. Come on in if you can stand the dirt. I'm in the process of cleaning." Gathering up the newspaper from the sofa and picking up a couple magazines from the chair, she deposited them in the paper rack. She sat in the rocker across the room and smiled.

"What can I do for you?"

As she straightened things, Graham looked around. The apartment looked larger than he anticipated. She had it tastefully decorated. The furniture, in excellent condition and arranged attractively, caught his eye. He glanced into the kitchen, impressed with the quality of the cabinets and the furniture there. He'd wrongly assumed from Clarinda's comments that Selena's things wouldn't be this nice.

"I'm sorry to drop in on you unannounced, but I really wanted to talk to you, and I was afraid you wouldn't agree to see me. I got your address from Clarinda. Don't blame her. I twisted her arm."

"I gave you my answer. What is there to talk about?"

"What would it take to get you to change your mind? Everything is negotiable as far as I'm concerned. If it's the kids, I'll be the guy with the heavy hand; you won't have to be responsible for the disciplinary action. If it's the salary, let me know what you want. What is it?" His blue eyes pierced into hers.

"None of the above." She watched him raise his eyebrows. "It's the room, the living quarters that you say is all that's available. I can't believe that in a place with a hundred rooms and ninety-eight bathrooms, that there's only one room for me to live in." She tried not to stare as he sat across from her saying nothing. She couldn't imagine the thoughts going through his head, but his slowly changing facial expressions indicated something was going around in circles in his mind. He stared at a spot on the ceiling. *I wonder if he sleeps with his eyes open.* She almost giggled.

Her eyes wandered to his face. She started. How long had he been staring at her?

"What?"

"There's a solution to this if you want to hear it."

"I'll listen, but that doesn't mean I'll change my answer."

"We could get married." He watched her eyes slowly widen and her mouth drop open. "Before you say no, hear me out. Your reputation would be intact, and you would move into the house without any questions from the rest of the staff about the amount of responsibility you would assume and the authority I want to give you to make decisions."

"But, that would mean moving into your room with you...and...and.. being a wife again and...and I'm not ready for that yet. I still don't have the problems straightened out from being married to Howard. Look, no offense, but I have a pretty good idea what marriage is supposed to be and I don't think we could ever attain that. I made a mistake the first time that I don't care to repeat. Marriage is supposed to be a life time commitment. I want to make sure that the next time I marry, if there is a next time, that it's to someone who cares enough about me to make the same promises I do. And keeps them." Her face was expressionless, as if she read an article from a magazine.

Graham wondered what she really thought of him. It sounded like a preposterous idea to her maybe, but it could work for him. "I know it sounds far fetched. If you want some time to develop a relationship between us before we actually have a marital relationship that could be worked out. You

63

could still have the same room next to mine and we could change things in the relationship whenever you're ready. It doesn't sound like your idea of marriage is very different than mine. Ask Ken about my character if you want, whether I keep promises and make commitments and keep them. Do me a favor. Think about it before you give me your final answer. That's all I ask. Just think about it."

As he left, he suddenly leaned down to kiss her on the cheek. Startled by the sudden movement, she turned her head and his lips landed on the corner of her mouth. He left, appearing to be calmer than he felt. Her lips had been soft. The softness touched the pit of his stomach. His heart pounded.

Selena stared at the door with her fingers on the spot where he'd kissed her. It had been so gentle that had she not been able to still feel the warmth from his lips and the light tickle of his mustache on her cheek, she would have been unsure that it really happened.

Graham went to the airport and flew home, trying not to think about what he'd talked to Selena about. He hadn't gone there with the idea of asking her to marry him. That had been a spur of the moment idea.

He went to his office with instructions not to be disturbed. Staring out the window he smiled, remembering Selena's comment about not getting any work done with a view like this. Allowing himself now to think about his conversation with her, he wondered what her answer would be. He'd married Kate with only commitment keeping them together and he could do it again. But would it be fair to Selena if she wanted the same kind of relationship with him that Kate had wanted and he couldn't give it to her? Divorce was not an option, so what if they got married and she wanted more than commitment?

It hadn't been enough for Kate. What if he failed again? Was the deep, personal, love between two people that he heard others talk about really important in a marriage? And, if so, why couldn't he seem to get an understanding of it and experience it for himself?

Selena asked Ken about Graham's character, explaining that she'd been offered the job and needed to check his references. Ken gave her the same information Graham had given her, saying he had impeccable character, he was a man of his word, and he had a strong personal relationship with God.

Howard called her several times in the next couple days. She still hadn't received the divorce papers and wondered about it, but her curiosity waned when she thought about checking with the court. If she didn't ask any questions, maybe there wouldn't be any more problems. And if she didn't stay in Columbus she wouldn't receive any more threatening phone calls from him or wonder if he followed her.

An idea began to form in Selena's mind. There might be a way around all of this if Graham would agree to sign a contract that limited the amount of time they spent together and that would place boundaries around their relationship. She sat down at her kitchen table and began to write.

She finished writing, made the changes needed to make it look like a formal document, then called Graham. She left a message on his answering machine.

Monday evening Graham returned her call. "Hi, Selena. I got your message. First I want to say that if you say no I understand. I've done a lot of thinking and I know I've placed you in an uncomfortable position. So whatever you decide I'll accept. And I'll try to do it gracefully."

"So, have you changed your mind then?" Indicating he hadn't, she continued. "Okay, I want you to look at something I've written. When will you be in the area again?"

"It'll be a couple weeks before I get there on business. Why don't you fax it to me? I can look at it and give you a call. Can you give me a hint of what this is about

"I'd rather you'd read it first, then we can talk about it."

"All right. How soon can I expect it?"

"I'll fax it to you tomorrow."

"I'll call you tomorrow evening then. "

About noon the next day, Graham's fax machine rang and then began printing. He'd gone to the kitchen to get some lunch, so the papers stacked up with the rest of his faxes for the day.

At the end of the day, he remembered his conversation with Selena from the night before. He picked up the stack of papers from the tray and sorted through them, stapling the ones together from the same source. In the middle of the stack, he found a hand written document with a note from Selena saying she would type it if he agreed to sign it. He read through it quickly, then went back to the beginning and read it again. Laying it down, he went to the window and stared sightlessly at the fall landscape.

Turning back to his desk, he picked up the document and read it again, this time trying to be objective in his approach.

The Nuptial Agreement of Graham Kensington and Selena Mulvaney.

It is agreed that: 1) The marriage shall take place for the preservation of Selena Mulvaney's reputation, as the living quarters prevent the privacy needed to maintain separate lives. 2) The responsibilities and duties required in the job description will remain the same as discussed, including the salary of forty thousand dollars a year, that a car will be made available for transportation, reasonable requests for time off will be honored, and any undue disciplinary action needed with the children will be attended to by Graham Kensington. 3) At no time will there be displays of affection, nor requests made by either person to act in a marital role, nor requests made to change the stipulations of this document until the terms agreed upon have expired. 4) The terms of this agreement will be non-negotiable until six months from the date of the signatures at which time they are open to discussion and renegotiation.

Signed_____
Date_____
Signed_____
Date _____

He took it one point at a time. The first one was a statement, partly true, but he could let it go. It wasn't worth arguing about. The second one was a contractual issue, which seemed odd to him. If they married, none of those issues applied. Why did she set a limit on the salary? She would have access to a whole lot more than that. But, of course she wouldn't know that since they'd never talked about his business.

He sat down at the desk and read the third one over and over. His heart constricted. How would they ever make a marriage work if she refused to allow even the slightest show of affection between them? What was she afraid of? Did this have anything to do with her ex-husband and the way he'd treated her? Looking at the fourth point he wondered why the six-month time frame. At least she allowed for renegotiation and six months really wasn't a long time, was it? He sighed. The fourth point wasn't the problem.

Turning to his computer he began to type. He changed first one thing and then another. Then he deleted the whole paragraph and started over. He prayed for help. She would never accept a complete change on point three. But, she might accept another point of view if he appealed to her common sense.

The sun had set and the soft artificial light made shadows in the room when he picked up the phone and dialed Selena's number. "Hi, Selena. I received your fax today and wondered if I might make a comment or two on point three. First of all, if you come here I'd need to tell people we're married, otherwise that would defeat the purpose of the marriage as stated in The Agreement. Therefore, an absolute no showing of affection would cause people to ask questions I don't think you'd want to answer. Are you following me so far?"

Selena listened and her heart sank. "I'm following you. What're you suggesting? We can call the whole thing off if you want to. In fact, let's do that and go back to my original answer. No."

"Wait, wait. Not so fast. Before we throw everything out the window, let's consider something else. How about if we give people what they want to see and that way we won't have to fend off the questions. In other words, displays of affection will be allowed in public, and during times at home when other people are around, which may or may not include the kids. What do you think?"

Selena mulled it over. "All right, define what you mean by public displays of affection."

Graham smiled. She was thinking about it. Maybe this would work. He needed to tread lightly or she could easily go the other way again.

Before they hung up they agreed upon a mutually acceptable definition--holding hands, sitting close to one another, no hugging, and no kissing except occasionally on the cheek.

On the way to the airport on Saturday to pick up Graham, Selena wondered for at least the hundredth time if she'd lost her sanity with all her stresses of the past six months. Agreeing to marry someone she didn't love, and who wasn't the type of person she would normally choose to spend her life with, had given her moments of panic the past week. She hadn't expected him to so readily consent to The Agreement. What did that say about him, other than he needed someone desperately to fill the position that was open on his staff? She admitted to herself that living in luxury for awhile would be interesting, to say the least. And it would get her away from Howard.

Graham walked off the airplane smiling. Selena gave him a tentative smile then turned and walked through the terminal. They drove to the license bureau and waited for the clerk to process the information. The application for the marriage license completed and signed, they went to her apartment to sign The Nuptial Agreement.

Selena began to think of ways she could get out of going through with the marriage, The Agreement, and whatever relationship there was between the two of them, which didn't seem to her to be much. People shouldn't play games with marriage, and how could she commit the rest of her life to someone she didn't know or love? Sure, she needed the job, but the job would be over in ten years or less when the children no longer needed someone to coordinate their schedules. And where would that leave her? Or them? She didn't want to go through the pain and embarrassment of another broken relationship. She'd have to talk to Graham and tell him she couldn't do it. He'd have to find someone else for the job.

Graham looked at her as they sat at her kitchen table. He could see she struggled with something. She hadn't said two words in the time they'd been together and she seemed anxious. She wouldn't look at him and she made a point of not touching him. He laid the document on the table in front of him and sat back in his chair watching her.

"You're not going to sign it?"

"I think we need to talk." Graham spoke quietly. "You haven't said a thing since I got off the plane. If you have questions lay them on me now. I don't want you to think that I've forced you into doing something you don't want to do. What is it, Selena?"

He waited, and still she didn't speak. He took her hand and turned her face to look at him. "What part of this is bothering you?"

"It's the marriage. I know what marriage is supposed to be. We're doing this for the job and I don't think that's the way God wants us to do things. I want to thank you for being willing to sign The Agreement but I wish there was some other way for both of us to get what we want without doing it this way."

Graham studied her face, and felt the pain in his chest at seeing the sadness and pain in her eyes. He wanted to promise her that everything would work out all right, but having been down this road before, he couldn't guarantee her that what they planned would work perfectly, let alone work well.

"Selena, I have my own doubts about some of this. Truthfully, I don't know if it will work. All we can do is try. We always have choices, and we can choose to do something different if this doesn't do what we want it to. I appreciate the six-month time frame. That will give us enough time to find out if we can work together. If we can't, we can talk about something else. I understand what you're saying about marriage. I'm sure I see things differently than you do since you've just come through a divorce. I'm ready to try again, but you're not there yet. That's why I'm willing to sign The Agreement and give you time to heal. We won't be out anything if we can't hold things together since we won't really be married anyway. Right?"

Selena heard the words and the feelings behind them. She still had doubts, but felt a little more confident. Maybe they could make it work. Maybe The Agreement could make it work. And they wouldn't really be married anyway. Not really.

"Let's sign it then and get it over with. I thought, if you don't mind, we could spend a few minutes with my mom before you go home. She wants to meet you, and I didn't know when we'd be back here together again." She bit her lip to stop the tremble.

"We'll have plenty of time. I'm not going back until later this evening. I thought it would be appropriate to have dinner together since we're engaged to be married." He smiled, noting the look of surprise on her face.

Selena's anxiety diminished when she noted the ease in which Graham and her mother related to each other. The spontaneous hug he gave Madelyn when they left brought a smile to her mother's face. She heard him promise to stop and see her mother the next time he traveled through the area.

Graham noticed the similarity between mother and daughter, their smiles, their eyes, and their way of expressing themselves. He felt drawn to Madelyn, and momentarily wished his mother still lived.

Sitting at the restaurant that Graham had chosen, Selena looked around and smiled. Located in a section of the city she rarely frequented, and nicer than one she would have chosen, he seemed comfortable with the prices and the atmosphere so she tried not to show her surprise. She wondered if she would ever fit into his lifestyle where money never seemed to be an issue.

After they ordered dinner, Selena decided to voice her concerns. "Graham, I need to talk to you about when you're expecting me at your place and how I'm going to get all my things there. Also, it looks like I'll need to store my furniture someplace. My last day to work is Thursday of next week, so I thought I'd move on Saturday. I'm thinking about selling my car before I move."

"School started this week and I've been managing all right, but when practices begin in a couple weeks I'll really need your help with the kids. Next weekend will be great. You can have a week to get settled in and learn your way around the area. I'll call a moving company and have them move you. You can store your things at Serendipity Estate. I'll have Jerome find a place for them. If you're selling your car, you can take the plane over and someone will be at the airport to pick you up."

Selena watched him as he talked and wished she had half the confidence he showed in making decisions. He always seemed to know what he wanted and how to get it, and yet his easygoing manner and willingness to work with her put her at ease. Catching him looking at her, her face warmed and she looked away. The arrival of their food saved her the embarrassment of answering the question she could see coming.

When they finished eating, Graham placed his hand lightly over hers. "I bought something for you to make the occasion official." Reaching in his pocket, he pulled out a small jewelry box and held it out to her.

Selena slowly reached out and took it from him. She opened it and stared, her eyes widening and her jaw going slack at the sight of the ring. It had a setting of several smaller diamonds surrounding a large one. She'd never seen anything so beautiful or expensive looking.

"Graham, I can't accept this. It signifies a meaning of something we don't have. I'm sorry, but I can't wear it."

"Will you at least wear the wedding band that goes with it?" He handed her another box.

Selena opened the second box and looked at the wedding band. It had a row of small diamonds across the top. She nodded, unable to speak. In spite of its simplicity, it would be the most expensive piece of jewelry she'd ever owned. Trying it on for size, she placed it back in the box and handed it to him.

"What kind of band would you like?" She thought with dismay that it sounded like she asked him anything except something as personal as his preference in rings.

He pulled another jewelry box out of his pocket. "My band is included in a set with yours. This one is all right unless you prefer to choose another one." He opened the box and showed it to her. His band was wider with a Florentine finish and had one diamond in the center.

"If you like that one, it's fine. Why don't you take it with you and we'll know where it is when we need it. When were you thinking about having the marriage ceremony?"

"I thought we'd have the ceremony on Sunday after church in the pastor's office, if that's all right with you

"Sure."

When Selena drove to the airport, she sensed a dilemma. How do you say goodbye to your fiancé who really isn't one?

Graham saw her uncertainty and tried to put her at ease. "Drop me off at the door and you'll be home sooner. I'll call you when I get some of the arrangements made, and I guess I'll see you next weekend then." He leaned over and gave her a kiss on the cheek.

"That's number one of number three. An occasional kiss on the cheek."

Selena laughed for the first time that day and gave him a push on the shoulder as he opened the car door.

"All right, I'm going!"

She watched him until he disappeared into the terminal then eased her car into the slowly moving traffic.

Chapter 6

The movers arrived on Friday instead of Saturday, throwing Selena into a panic. She cleaned out drawers and closets all week, still trying to locate the missing portfolio. When the doorbell rang she stared at the two men and one woman; they stared back at her.

"I didn't expect you until tomorrow. Nothing is ready to go."

"We have instructions to pack for you," the woman said. "You need only pack what you will need for the next few days. We will deliver to your destination, Fredricksburg, on Wednesday of next week."

How can this happen? I will never find the portfolio now. That means going through all the boxes when I get to Serendipity Estate. She felt like calling Graham and giving him a piece of her mind. The least he could have done was tell her he'd hired people to pack for her.

A thought suddenly came to her. The movers arrived a day early. What did her plane ticket actually say? Looking at it closely she found the date--today's date. That did it! *Does the man have a hearing problem? I specifically told him Saturday.* Fuming, she picked up the phone and dialed his number.

"Hello, Graham Kensington speaking. What can I do for you today?" She cringed at his cheerful voice.

"You can start by listening to me when I talk to you. I told you I would be ready to move on Saturday. I told you I would be ready to take the plane on Saturday. What day do you think this is? When I looked at the calendar it was Friday. Maybe one day doesn't make any difference to you, but it makes a big difference to me. And what makes you think I'm not capable of packing my own things? By the time these people get done I won't have a clue where anything is. I may not be able to stop the movers, but I'm sure not flying out of here today. You can do whatever you want to with the ticket. I'm not coming over there until tomorrow, period."

Graham waited for her to talk herself out. When she stopped, he could hear her crying. "Selena, I'm sorry for the mix up. I thought I told them Saturday. I'll call and have the ticket changed to tomorrow. What time would you like for me to make it? Morning? Afternoon? Evening? Tell me and I'll take care of it for you. If it makes you feel any better, the kids have been asking all week when you're coming. They're pretty excited."

The anger and frustration spent, her face warmed with embarrassment. "Right now not much of anything is going to help. Things have been pretty rough on this end. Sorry I dumped on you, Graham. I appreciate you changing the ticket. Make it in the afternoon. I want to spend tonight with my mom. I'll see you tomorrow then."

Graham hung up the phone and stared at a spot on his desk. Had he done the right thing? She seemed to be too upset about the changes. What else was going on that he didn't know anything about? Clarinda had said Selena was having a rough time, but she hadn't said exactly what kind of problems she had. He would just have to take it a step at a time and try to exercise some patience.

Selena stepped off the airplane wearing a smile pasted on her face. She spotted Graham and moved toward him. He took her carry-on packages from her and guided her to the door. Reminding him that she had luggage, they turned to the baggage claim area, retrieved her pieces, and walked out the door. Maneuvering his car into the traffic, he reached for her hand and squeezed it. "You look tired. Are you all right?"

"I'm not sure about right now, but I'll be fine in a couple days." She removed her hand from his. "Mom says to tell you hi, and not to forget your promise to stop and see her when you're in the area."

"I haven't forgotten. Would you like to stop and get something to eat before we go home? There's a nice little restaurant about a mile from here."

Selena would rather have gone on to Serendipity Estate, gone to her room, closed the door, and not come out until Monday morning. Howard had called her three times during the week, threatening legal action if she didn't comply with his demands. Her emotions taut with watching everywhere she went, wanting to avoid a confrontation with him, she wanted to find a safe place and never come out.

She'd sold her car and planned to send him the money for the down payment. *After that he doesn't have any hold on me.*

She instructed her mother, her brothers and sisters, and Clarinda not to give Howard any information if he called them after she moved. She'd given Clarinda's address as a forwarding address at the post office. *Maybe I can get some peace now.*

She took a deep breath, then started. Graham shook her gently.

"Would you rather not stop and eat?"

She grinned sheepishly. The deep breath had relaxed her and she'd fallen asleep from sheer fatigue. "This is fine. We can stop here. I'm sorry. I guess I'm more tired than I thought."

Graham summoned Jerome to help carry her luggage when they arrived at Serendipity Estate, then led her through the house and up the stairway. He opened the door to her room and stepped aside for her to enter. The room smelled of fresh flowers and everything had a shine to it. She smiled absently at a bouquet of carnations in a vase on the dressing table. She walked to the balcony door and opened the drapes. "Do you mind if I have someone bring my sofa up here? I could put it over by that wall and have it reupholstered to match the rest of the room."

"You can buy a new one if you want, but if you'd rather keep your old one it's not a problem."

Selena noticed the closed door to the adjoining room. She walked over to it and tried the knob. It moved in her hand and opened easily. Closing the door, she turned the lock, and tried it again to make sure it wouldn't open. She turned around to ask Graham about the ceremony to be performed tomorrow, and saw the pain in his eyes change to anger. Without a word, he turned and walked out, leaving her standing in the middle of the floor wondering about the look on his face. She shook her head, confused, and began to unpack the clothes and personal items she'd brought with her.

Selena went to the kitchen the next morning to fix herself some breakfast. The children had already begun eating and ran to her excitedly. Graham got up and moved around to the other side of the table, making room for her to eat with them. Everything had been placed on the table, including the china and tableware for her use.

She smiled as she greeted the children and looked at Graham, trying to gauge his mood after the incident the night before. He grinned at her as if nothing had happened. By the end of the meal, Selena laughed as the children entertained her with their stories.

Graham inwardly breathed a sigh of relief. He knew he'd overreacted to the incident with the door. Her action was no more than he should have expected given the circumstances. *I have to prove I can be trusted. I hope it doesn't take long for her to realize that I plan to respect her wishes and her privacy whether the door is locked or not.*

When they removed things from the table, he asked, "Did you sleep well last night?"

"Yes, I slept well, thanks."

"If you need anything let me know

"I found everything I needed." She gave him the relaxed smile that he remembered seeing the first time he saw her at the hospital.

When they pulled into the church parking lot Selena looked at the building. The country church had an A-frame architecture. When she stepped through the front door the surprise showed on her face at the size of the building on the inside. It had looked much smaller from the street.

Many in the congregation greeted her warmly. A combination of open friendliness and covert curiosity showed on most faces. Everyone knew of Graham's eligibility and that he had access to large sums of money. More than one single woman in the church had tried to get his attention.

They went to Pastor Klein's office following the morning service. The small group included the children, the pastor's wife, and Jason, a friend of Graham's. Closing the office door, Graham took the rings and the license out of his pocket.

Selena felt a pang of guilt as she repeated her vows. Her heart felt heavy and she wished she had thought of some way she could easily get out of it. In ten minutes the vows had been said and the license signed. She vaguely remembered that he kissed her tenderly.

Graham told the children to change their clothes and go to the kitchen for lunch. Selena went to her room and hung up her dress, her wedding dress. She hung it in the back of the closet, determined not to wear it again. She put on a pair of jeans and a knit shirt and went to the kitchen. Automatically eating the sandwich set in front of her, she helped clear the table of the dishes, and went to her room without a word.

Hoping to sleep most of the day, she lay down on the bed. But, sleep wouldn't come. How could she have knowingly lied to God, to Graham, and to herself, when she promised all those things? She got up and went to the window, drawing the drapes back and looking at the view. *Dear God, of all the mistakes I've made in my life, this has to be the worst. Please don't let Graham hate me. Help me to be loving. Forgive me for being selfish and thinking only of myself in this situation. Don't let me compound it by making even bigger mistakes. Graham deserves my respect if nothing else. Show me how to treat everyone here as Jesus would treat them. In His precious name. Amen.*

Looking out of the window of Graham's office the next morning, Selena took in the picturesque view. Her gaze followed the sloping lawn. She saw the tennis court and the swimming pool next to the house that she hadn't noticed the first time. Adjacent to them stood a large terrace with furniture arranged attractively in groupings. Large potted plants and trees dotted the entire area, providing shade during the times of the day when the sun shone the hottest.

Graham had asked her to come to his office to talk about her responsibilities. She glanced at the clock on the wall. Ten minutes late. She didn't mind. It gave her time to collect her thoughts.

The door opened suddenly and Graham apologized profusely for keeping her waiting. "Joyce stopped me on my way up here about the grocery shopping. Hopefully, we can get that transferred to you soon. So, let's talk about priorities first. The first thing I need from you is to familiarize yourself with the children's schedules. I want to be informed of their activities, and will take part whenever I can. If you have any questions, talk to me about it. The second thing I would like for you to do is become involved in the meal planning and grocery shopping. Joyce writes all the menus and does the cooking. I would like you to check the menus and do the shopping. You will need to discuss those things with her on Monday. Any questions

Opening the desk drawer he took out a checkbook and handed it to her. "We will need to go to the bank today or tomorrow and have you fill out a signature card for this account. This is the account to be used to purchase household items and anything else you might need. I will deposit funds into it on a regular basis. You can bring the checkbook to me on the tenth of the month at which time I will reconcile the statement and return the checkbook to you."

She looked under the cover at the record in front. Her eyes widened as she stared at the balance, more than she made in one year. "How long is this balance supposed to last?"

"It will vary from month to month. You will probably have a better idea next month. If you aren't sure about the expenses, ask me. Let's go find the staff and get the introductions out of the way. I told them last week about the wedding and that they'd meet you today."

They found Joyce Kelsey in the kitchen. Putting his arm across Selena's shoulders, Graham introduced her as his wife and outlined the change in responsibilities. She guessed Joyce to be about her own age, but much taller and very slender.

Joyce had pulled her dark red hair back and fastened it at the nape of her neck. A fringe of bangs accented her green eyes. Her thin lips appeared much fuller with the lipstick outside the lip line. She gave Selena a smile as she shook her hand, but Selena noticed a lack of warmth in her eyes.

Taking Selena's hand, Graham led her down the hallway to the back door. When they were outside, she smiled. "You couldn't resist, could you?"

"You're not allowed to object. It's in The Agreement. Anyway, Jerome should be in the stable and we wouldn't want him to think we aren't over-the-edge-in-love newlyweds, now would we?"

Jerome saw them coming and met them by the corral. A large man, middle-aged, with a weather beaten face, she noticed the kindly look of his faded blue eyes. The permanent wrinkles had been etched from a lifetime of smiling and squinting in the sun. His salt and pepper colored, short curly hair barely showed from under his cap. His easy smile and firm handshake put her at ease.

"Pleased to meet you, ma'am. Welcome to Serendipity Estate. I'm at your service. Anything you need, you let me know." His deep mellow voice echoed across the rolling lawn.

Selena admired the horses as Graham talked to Jerome about a problem with one of the cars. How many did he have, anyway?

"Which one of the cars is going to be available to me?" Selena asked as they walked back to the house.

"Jerome is going this afternoon to get a van for you to use. That should give you more room to take the kids where they need to go and to do the shopping. If you want, you can go with him to pick it out."

Selena stopped, and stared at him in amazement. "Are you always this generous? Or are you just trying to impress me? If that's it, you can stop. It doesn't take much to get my attention."

Graham wondered about the last statement, but chose not to comment. Instead he said, "You're my wife. We wouldn't want people saying I don't take care of you, would we?"

She looked at him suspiciously. He was following the rules too well. Was this some kind of game for him?

"Let's go see if we can find Babs. She's usually in the north wing on Monday."

Hearing a vacuum sweeper at the end of the hall, they found her in the music room. "This is Babs Smith. Babs, I'd like you to meet my wife, Selena. She'll be in charge of getting supplies, and of the general administration of the household. Anything you need you can talk to her about." He smiled warmly as he looked at Selena.

Selena returned his smile automatically, and held out her hand to Babs. Babs looked younger in her face than her appearance. She had a mature figure with gray hair, appearing to be in her late fifties. Wearing a bandana around her head, she'd tied an apron around her waist. Her brown eyes sat close together under penciled, arched eyebrows.

"I'm real pleased to meet you ma'am," she said in a smooth, high-toned voice. "I hope you're real happy here at the Estate. We're all happy to have you here."

Selena liked her immediately. In spite of Joyce's apparent doubts about her, she liked them all.

Graham went to his office and Selena went to her room. She finished unpacking her luggage and sat them outside her door to carry down later.

She sorted through her clothes and placed them in dresser drawers. Walking to the dressing table, she sighed. How was she going to decide what to place here and what to place in the drawers in the bathroom? Oh, well. She could always change things later.

She placed items in the drawers on the left and opened the top drawer on the right. As she pulled it all the way out to see how deep it went a pink ribbon in the back caught her eye. She pulled the ribbon toward her and looked at the envelope it surrounded. She turned it over. Kate Worley.

Curious, Selena slipped the ribbon off and took a paper out of the envelope. She sat down as she read the letter.

Dear Kate,

Graham said he didn't tell you what really happened at the Pizza Parlor last month. You have a right to know so you can make an informed decision. I'm sorry to have to be the one to tell you this, but I dared Graham to ask you to marry him. It was supposed to be a joke. Sometimes my sense of humor gets away with me. I'm sorry if I've hurt you. Graham won't be insulted if you call off the wedding.

Your friend,
Scott Morefield

She re-read the letter then folded it and placed it back in the envelope. Should she throw it away? Who was Kate? Maybe the best place for it was back in the drawer, at least until she had time to think about it and decide what to do with it.

Graham had proposed to Kate on a dare and never told her? What did that say about him? Why didn't he tell her? If it was a joke surely Kate would have suspected. What really happened that day? Should she ask Graham?

When she left the room at lunchtime she still had not made a decision as to what to do with the letter, but she came to the conclusion that what had happened between Graham and Kate was none of her business. The date was fourteen years ago, before her time.

The luggage outside her door had disappeared. She checked with Joyce. Jerome had carried them to the garage.

"Was there still something in them you wanted, ma'am?"

"Oh, no. Thanks for asking." She didn't want to admit that no one had ever done anything for her before.

Wednesday afternoon the moving company arrived with her furniture and boxes. Jerome instructed them where to store the items. Selena signed the form, almost forgetting to use Kensington. *The less I have to use the Mulvaney name the less chance there is of Howard finding me.*

One evening she wandered about in her room, restless. Joyce had cleaned up the kitchen after their early dinner. The children went to their rooms to do homework and Graham went to his office for a phone conference call. He hadn't said when he'd be finished. She never asked. They'd spent only one evening together and the children had joined them.

Remembering the swimming pool, she found her swimsuit, put on a wrap and her sandals, took a towel from her bathroom and went out the back door.

She stuck her toe in the water and drew it out quickly. Lowering herself slowly into the pool, she shivered, but it wasn't long before she swam the length of the pool and back again. After several laps, she stepped out of the water, dried herself off and sat for a half-hour in the warm fall breeze, running her fingers through her hair. She took a deep breath, let it out slowly, and let the smell of chlorine from the pool and the pungent odor of decaying leaves saturate her senses. She felt more at peace than she had for a long time. Maybe God wanted her to come here after all. She still had difficulty dealing with the guilt surrounding the circumstances of the marriage.

Unknown to her, Graham had finished his phone conference and caught a movement outside from the corner of his eye. Looking out his window, he saw her test the water, then slide her wrap off and ease herself into the pool. Mesmerized by her slow even strokes as she swam from one end of the pool to the other, he remained at the window watching her with rapt attention.

He swallowed hard. Why couldn't their marriage be like it was supposed to be? How long would it take for her to see how much he cared about her? The emotion he felt when he was near her was new to him and he didn't understand it. What was it about her that made him feel this way? The sadness remained around her eyes, but her smile appeared more often and seemed more genuine than when she came here two weeks ago.

She took her responsibilities seriously and gave him the freedom he needed to continue building his business. She asked very little of him, capable of making good decisions for the children, the household administration, and the staff. He often heard her laughing with the children over some incident or something said, and wished she would laugh as easily with him. Patience, he told himself.

Selena grabbed her jacket as she hurried out the back door. The gray October sky looked like rain. Dark clouds traveled rapidly from one horizon to the other. The sharp smell of dry leaves permeated the air. Summer's green had turned to red, orange, and yellow.

She turned left at the road and drove the van toward the mall. Several sets of keys had been made for the vehicle, but no one drove it as regularly as she did. Twice she caught herself referring to it as 'my van'. Jerome had taken care of a minor problem and it purred like a kitten. She expressed her appreciation to him that there was someone to take care of the maintenance for her. Her car in Columbus had always seemed to need something and she either didn't have the money or couldn't find someone dependable to fix it right. Howard never seemed to have the time or the inclination to take care of anything.

She had a list of several items she needed to purchase for Joyce and Babs. Jerome did most of his own shopping since she usually didn't know what he actually wanted when he needed something. He estimated the cost and she gave him the money from the household account. I still don't know how I'm to pay myself for the job I'm doing, she thought, as she remembered she had given Jerome some money before she left.

Parking close to the store where she chose to do her shopping, she purchased the items on her list then went to the clothing department to look at the new styles for the season. She wanted to purchase a new outfit, but didn't know if that would fall into the category of household items.

When she had arrived at Serendipity Estate she transferred her money from the bank in Columbus to the local bank, then promptly purchased a money order and sent it to Howard in the amount of the down payment on her car. She prayed that would appease him and he'd leave her alone.

That had left only a few dollars in her account, not enough to purchase items for herself. *I guess I'm going to have to talk to Graham about how to transfer money into my account so I know how much I have to spend.* She put it off, not wanting to talk to him any oftener than absolutely necessary about anything.

Selena left the store, trying to remember where she'd parked the van. In the middle of the large parking lot the hair rose on the back of her neck. She saw someone staring at her from two rows over. Her heart stopped. *Howard.* She spotted her van, picked up her pace, threw her packages inside, jumped in and locked the door all in one motion. She backed out of the parking space and glanced in the rear view mirror to see if he followed her.

When she pulled into the traffic, she saw a car follow her out of the mall parking lot. She tried to put some distance between them and finally got ahead when a red light forced him to stop. She eased through the yellow light and kept going. Glad she'd paid attention to the area when she took the children shopping and to lessons, she decided on a way home that would be an indirect route. Hopefully she could lose him in the process. She turned at the first road and then turned several more times. Keeping watch in her mirror she no longer saw him after the last turn.

Her heartbeat returned to normal. Could that have really been Howard at the mall? How did he know she would be there today? Would everyone start to look like him now? There was only one person who looked like Howard. Did he still think she would give him half of her investment? She wanted to cry. There'd been a short reprieve from his threats. *Am I going to have to begin the cycle all over again? I don't know how much more I can take.*

Should she tell Graham? Maybe she shouldn't go anywhere alone. She didn't want to get him involved. Tears wouldn't change anything. She took a deep breath and kept her sight on the rear view mirror as she drove home. She parked the van out of sight of the road and carried her packages into the house.

"There you are, Selena. I need to go to the post office and thought maybe we could stop and get something to eat on the way back. We can pick up the kids after we get done eating." Graham studied her face.

Joyce said earlier that Selena had gone to her room. Graham observed that she spent time in her room when she seemed upset about something. He rarely asked her about it, but decided the time had come to start asking if she wanted to talk about anything. She never went out, spending all her free time in her room, and her phone calls were only to family members in Columbus.

"Is this an invitation or an order?"

"It's an invitation. I rarely give orders."

"Then I accept. I don't like to be given orders."

"I'll remember that." The look in his eyes pierced into hers.

The hostess at the restaurant seated them at a booth that had a U shaped seat. Selena sat on the outside end, expecting Graham to sit across from her. Instead, he sat down next to her causing her to move to the inside. Taking her hand, he said, "Whoa. Don't go so far away." She tried to remove her hand, but he held it tighter.

He smiled, wanting to put her at ease. She gave him a tentative smile. Why did she feel so uncomfortable with him? He'd never been anything less than a gentleman. In fact no one had ever treated her with as much respect. Something about his eyes, something about the way he looked at her. She lowered her eyelids self-consciously.

"Is everything going all right at home?" Graham asked.

"Sure. Why do you ask? Is there something I should be doing? Has anyone complained?"

"No. Of course not. You're doing a great job. The kids really enjoy having you there. I've just noticed that you seem upset sometimes, and I want you to feel that you can come to me if you need anything. You can take some evenings off and go out. You don't have to spend all your spare time in your room."

"I don't go out because I don't have anyone to go out with and I don't know where anything is here. Besides, it would be different if I was single. Since I'm not. . ." She paused, twisting her wedding band on her finger. "I don't want to embarrass you by appearing to be single."

Graham struggled with his emotions. One minute she seemed to be distant and the next she was concerned about his feelings. He took a deep breath. "Would you go out with *me*?"

Selena looked at him, startled, his response unexpected. "I didn't mean that. You don't have to do that."

"I know I don't have to. I want to." He smiled as she nodded her head.

Selena decided this might be a good time to discuss the issues of her money with him. He listened as she voiced her concerns.

"I gave you a credit card the day we went to the bank. You can use that for anything you want, anytime you want. You don't have to wait for an emergency. If you still think you want money in your own account, write checks out of the household account every couple weeks and make deposits to your personal one. I know payment for the work you do was part of The Agreement, but you limit yourself by not taking advantage of the benefits of being married to me." His tone was kind but firm.

She listened but didn't understand what he said. What *were* the benefits of being married to him? The luxurious house she shared with him and the children seemed to be benefit enough for her. Surely he didn't mean unlimited spending. That wasn't in The Agreement.

"One other thing I wanted to talk to you about. I'd like for you to go shopping with me sometime and show me what kind of clothes you'd like for me to wear. I need to buy a couple new outfits and I want them to be something that will look nice. You know, we wouldn't want people thinking you don't take care of me, would we?" She smiled as she repeated the phrase he used frequently.

He was so surprised at her display of humor that he laughed spontaneously. She joined in the laughter and he marveled at her beauty when she relaxed. He promised to go shopping with her, pleased that she cared about his preferences. They picked up Trevor and Trina, who expressed their disappointment that they had not been included for dinner. Selena warmed up the dinner Joyce had cooked, and sat with them to listen to stories of their day.

Graham went to his office to check for messages on his answering machine and returned to spend the evening with his children. He stopped outside the kitchen door and listened to Selena's easy way of relating to them. She laughed with them, corrected them if they needed it, and praised them when they deserved it. He never heard her speak sharply to them.

Graham helped Selena remove the food and dishes from the table. After the dishes had been placed in the dishwasher, he put his hand on her arm, causing her to look at him. "You're doing a great job with the kids. Thanks."

The intensity of the look he gave her and the catch in his voice surprised her. "You're welcome. They're really neat kids."

Selena sat on her bed with her Bible open trying to read from the Psalms where she had stopped the night before. The events of the day kept crowding into her mind. Howard at the mall, if it was Howard. How would she ever know? Graham laughing with her at lunch, then his thanks after the children had eaten. His offer to listen if she needed to talk. What would he think if he knew? Would he be angry with her for bringing her problems to his home? Focus. She went back to her Bible reading.

Picking up the notebook that had her prayer requests listed, she heard a noise like a soft thump. It sounded like it came from the balcony. She turned the light out and walked to the window, pulling the drape back slightly with her hand. The moon shone overhead, giving an eerie light to the balcony. Waiting for several minutes, motionless, she moved her hand to let the drape fall back. She grabbed it again when she saw a black draped figure run to her window, stare at her in the darkness, then turn and run the other way toward Graham's adjoining balcony.

Selena let go of the drape and stifled a scream. Running for the door to the hallway she went to Graham's door and knocked. No answer. Looking around for the light switch in the hall, she kept her eye on her door. *This is crazy. He was*

outside. The door was locked which meant he couldn't get in.
Come on Selena, get a grip.

Selena found the light switch in the darkness at the
same time another hand reached out to turn the light on. She
screamed and turned, giving an unsuspecting Graham an elbow
in his mid-section. He doubled over in surprise and pain. She
recognized him and laughed and cried at the same time.
Putting her hands over her face to hide the fear, she sank to the
floor and shook.

Graham felt his abdomen where her elbow had
connected with him and decided he'd be all right. Looking at
her, he didn't know if she would be. Kneeling down beside her
he questioned her. She shook her head rhythmically from side
to side. He took her hands away from her face, shocked at the
fear he saw there. What could have happened that frightened
her?

"Selena, what happened? Come on. Talk to me.
Please talk to me!"

She took several deep breaths, trying to get control of
herself. Finally, she stopped shaking and asked him, "Were
you out on the balcony a few minutes ago?"

He frowned. "No. Why do you ask?"

He felt a knot of fear in his stomach when she told him
of seeing someone out there. He apologized when she told him
he had scared her out of her wits when he came up behind her
in the hallway. He chuckled, saying, "I'll think twice before I
sneak up behind you in the dark again. You pack a mean
wallop."

She smiled as she wiped the tears from her cheeks.
"This carpet has its disadvantages. You can't hear anyone
walking around. I'm sorry if I hurt you. That was a reflex. I'll
be all right now. Thanks. Thanks...for...for everything."

Selena went in her room and locked the door. She
checked the adjoining door. Locked. She checked the French

doors to the balcony. Locked. She opened the drapes, lay down on the bed and covered herself with a blanket; nothing showed but her eyes.

Graham quietly went downstairs and walked around the outside of the house, stopping below the balcony of their rooms. He checked the soft dirt, the side of the building, and the bushes bordering the house. He found nothing.

He went back upstairs to his room, silently opened the door to the balcony, and checked the railing. He found the evidence. Examining the rope fibers that he'd taken from the railing, he fell on his knees in a posture of prayer. *Dear God, please put Your angels around those I love in this house that no harm will befall them. Please defeat the enemy that Your plan and purpose will go forward. I don't know why anyone would want to hurt Selena. Give her a double portion of your protection and peace.*

Chapter 7

Selena looked at her watch as she pulled into the parking lot at the school. Right on time. The errands for Joyce and Graham had taken longer than she anticipated. And this happened to be the evening that Trevor and Trina had practices for two hours, making for another long day.

Her stress level slowly rose. She didn't mind doing any of the things she found added to her schedule, but some days she had difficulty remaining calm. It seemed that everyone thought she had nothing to do, therefore she had plenty of time to make extra stops. Joyce had a request every day that she knew Selena planned to go out. *How long can I keep this up?*

Additional requests started one day when Selena requested a change in menus. Joyce seemed offended. "I've been serving these meals ever since I started working here and no one has complained before."

"I'm not complaining. You're doing a good job. I certainly wouldn't want to think about cooking along with everything else I do. I would just like to see less red meat and dishes with heavy sauces and more fresh vegetables, lettuce salads, chicken, and fish. That's all I'm saying, Joyce."

"Mr. Kensington likes what I do. He said so himself."

"Mr. Kensington doesn't eat here very often. If you need recipes and new cookbooks, I'll get them for you. I'll help you with the menus if you like. I know change isn't easy, but I'm confident you can prepare the meals I'm asking for."

Joyce now spoke to Selena only when addressed. Selena tried to be fair and kind to her, but felt used by the daily written request for some minor item. She planned to let it ride and see if Joyce calmed down. If she didn't, she would have to confront her. *It's a good thing she doesn't know how much I hate confrontations.*

Selena heard a tap on the window. "Are you Mrs. Kensington?"

"Yes. How may I help you?"

"Hi, I'm Lorena Wilkes, Trevor's teacher. I need to talk to you for a couple minutes. Could you come to my room?"

Selena checked her watch. Hopefully this wouldn't take long. She followed Trevor's teacher to her classroom. "Is everything all right with Trevor, Ms. Wilkes?"

"I wanted to let you know that Trevor and another student were sent to the principal's office today for fighting on the playground. Both accused the other of starting it. We need the parent's permission to administer discipline. There's a paper to sign in the principal's office. You may want to go there and take care of it now."

"That won't be necessary. Trevor's dad and I will take care of it. Thanks for bringing this to my attention."

Selena sighed as she walked back to the van. *That's one problem I don't need today. Now what am I going to do?*

For the next two hours, Selena took Trevor and Trina from one place to another. On the way home they bickered back and forth until Selena stopped the van. "One of you get up here in the front seat now. I'm tired of hearing it."

The children stared at each other. She'd never raised her voice before. What would happen if she got angry? "We won't do it anymore, promise," Trina said.

"Trina, to the front, now!" The child scrambled to the front and quickly buckled herself in. The rest of the ride home was quiet.

The bickering pushed her stress level over the top as she tried to come up with an easy way to tell Graham about Trevor.

They walked into the kitchen expecting their dinner to be on the stove and the table set as usual. No sign of dinner. Selena raised her hands in the air in despair as Graham walked into the kitchen. She took items from the refrigerator to make sandwiches for the three of them. Graham said this morning that he wouldn't be home for dinner.

"What's for dinner?" he asked. "Anything hot?"

Selena whirled around. "Oh, am I the cook now too? Where's Joyce? You want hot? Here's hot." She tore a piece of paper off the bulletin board, wrote down a number and slapped it in his hand.

"What's this?"

"Take out pizza!"

The children watched the exchange with wide eyes. What would happen? People in their house never openly disagreed.

Graham stared at the paper, then at Selena. She had fixed meals for them before without getting this agitated. What else had happened? "Tell me what you want me to do, and I'll help you with this."

She glanced his way, sorry she had snapped at him. Her day had not been his fault. "Sorry." Her voice trembled. "You can cut the meat into slices and place the bread on the plate. Trevor and Trina, go wash your hands for dinner, please. By the way, Graham, where is Joyce? She didn't say anything to me about not being here."

"This is her day off. Did you look at the schedule?"

"I don't even know where the schedule is, let alone look at it."

"It's in the pantry on the back of the door. I think maybe it's time for you to take over the scheduling. Then you would know where everyone is. Is this a good time to talk about that—or not?" "Yes, this is as good a time as any. I can handle it. That is if I don't have too many days like today. I guess I tried to squeeze too many things into the time I allotted myself. One of these days I may learn how to pace myself."

After they had eaten, Selena took a deep breath. "Trina and I will put the food away. Trevor has something he needs to talk to his dad about in the family room."

Graham raised his eyebrows in surprise and Trevor's face blanched.

"Can Selena come too?" Trevor asked his dad.

Before Graham could answer, Selena said, "Not this time, Trevor. I'll talk to you later."

Graham looked from one to the other. Trevor finally got up and walked out of the kitchen with Graham following him.

By the time Selena cleaned and straightened the kitchen, Trina finished her bath and began her homework and Trevor went to his room. Selena went to the family room, hoping to find Graham still there.

"I was going to come looking for you. How did you know what happened with Trevor today?"

"His teacher, Ms. Wilkes, told me when I went to pick up the children after school. She wanted me to go to the principal's office and sign a paper giving the school authorities permission to discipline Trevor. I didn't think you'd want that so I decided to have Trevor tell you, instead of me trying to talk to you about something I knew nothing about. That's why I was so upset when I got home."

"You did the right thing, Selena. Would you like to go for a walk? Maybe some fresh air would help quiet the nerves a little."

Selena smiled. She loved to walk around the Estate, but since the incident on the balcony chose to remain inside after dark. She got her jacket and met him at the back door. Taking her hand, he looked at her and winked.

"Are we in public yet?" She smiled up at him. "I'm beginning to think you might have had an ulterior motive to this little excursion

"You'll never know, because I'll never tell. If you get cold, let me know; we can turn back." He pulled her closer.

Selena admitted later as she stacked her Bible and prayer notebook on the bed that the walk had done her good. Graham had not mentioned her outburst again. He said the incident at school was a guy thing and he'd told Trevor to find another way to settle his disputes. He'd instructed Trevor to write down three ways that would be more acceptable than punching someone, and discuss it with his dad by the end of the week.

She gained new respect for Graham. He'd handled the situation as if he dealt with problems like that every day. She'd stressed about it for two hours. *I guess I have a lot to learn. How does Graham know what I need at times like this? Howard certainly never had a clue.*

She reached in the drawer of the nightstand to get a pen. Startled, she stepped back as an envelope with a pink ribbon around it fell forward in the back of the drawer. Her heart beat faster as she remembered a similar looking envelope in the vanity drawer when she first moved here.

She stood for several minutes, staring. Should she read this one too? Slowly, she reached in and turned it over. Kate Kensington.

Kate Kensington? The last one had been to Kate Worley. Had she been Graham's wife? Her curiosity got the best of her. She took the paper out of the envelope.

Dear Kate,

It's taken me awhile to answer because I didn't know what to say in response to your letter. I gave you a chance to back out of the marriage before it was too late but for whatever reason you decided to go forward with it. I'm sorry things aren't working out the way

99

you wanted them to. I know Graham cares a lot for you and would never consent to a divorce. Maybe if you gave it some more time things will work out for you. You might try talking to Graham about your issues instead of going out to all the parties you mentioned in your letter. I don't know what to say about your statement that Graham is being unreasonable and that you think he is seeing someone behind your back. I'm sure you see a different side to him than I do but I find it very hard to believe that he is being unfaithful to you. If you need someone to talk to I think you should probably see a counselor. I don't want to do anything to jeopardize my friendship with Graham. Don't give up.

Scott

Selena re-read the letter several times. Graham and Kate had marital problems? Kate accused Graham of being unfaithful? Had this been Kate's room? Why didn't she share the room with Graham? Graham unfaithful to his wife? This couldn't be the Graham she knew! But, then how well did she really know him? Had her rash decision to get out of one bad situation only dumped her into a worse one?

She folded the letter and placed it in the back of the vanity with the other one. She got into bed and lay there for a long time, shaking.

She got up the next morning after a sleepless night, applied some make-up, put on a smile and determined not to show the world anything but her best. She would decide what to do when it came time to renegotiate The Agreement.

Friday, Selena had some free time in the middle of the day and went to the garage to open her boxes and methodically look for the investment portfolio. She checked the contents of several boxes, then placed them in the corner. As she opened the sixth one without success, a shadow fell across the doorway. She turned slowly, holding her breath, as Graham walked in.

"Looking for something?"

"Oh, it's just something I misplaced. I thought maybe I would find it when I moved here, but now I don't know where the movers may have put it. This gives me an excuse anyway to mark the boxes with the contents so I don't have to go through every box when I want something. What're you doing out of your office at this time of day?"

"One nice thing about working for myself is I can take a break whenever I want. Anyway, I want to talk to you before I leave this evening. Would this be a good time?"

"Sure." Selena wiped her hands on her jeans. "It's so nice out. Want to sit on the terrace?"

She waited for Graham to speak as he pulled up a chair opposite her. He leaned forward and stared at his thumbs. "I don't feel good about leaving right now, but I need to keep this appointment. If anything happens while I'm gone, you can call me on my cell phone. Jerome has been instructed to stay in close contact with you and assist you with anything you need. Don't hesitate to call him on the intercom or knock on his apartment door if you need him. Will you do that, Selena?"

She nodded. Why this concern all of a sudden? That incident the other night turned out to be nothing. Maybe her eyes played tricks on her. Nothing else had happened since then. She had developed the habit of looking over her shoulder so often, thinking Howard would show up when she least expected it. Maybe she just thought she saw something.

And he didn't know anything about the letters. Had they been left there accidentally when the room was cleaned out?

"If you have any problems with Trevor or Trina, I can take care of it when I get back. If my meeting is over early tomorrow, I'll come home tomorrow night. Otherwise, I'll be back Sunday afternoon. Either way, I'll call you tomorrow and let you know."

"I appreciate you going to all this trouble for me, but you really don't have to. I'll be all right here. If I'm not safe here, where am I safe?" She hoped she sounded surer of herself than she felt. "I don't want any of us to take any chances. I don't want any repeats of the other night." The hard set of his jaw and the twitching muscles in his face gave away more of his state of mind than he intended.

"Graham, the room that I'm in--who was the last person to use the room?"

His look was piercing. "Why do you ask?"

She held his gaze, refusing to back down. "I found some things in the drawers and I just wandered who they belonged to."

"What kind of things?"

"Why are you not answering my questions? Your questions are not answers."

"You're right. The last person to use the room was Kate, my wife and the children's mother. If you find anything Trina might want you can give it to her."

"I know this is personal but could you tell me where she is? I mean why do the children never see her?"

"I thought you knew. She died in an accident five years ago. She often drove alone at night. That particular night she missed the curve, sideswiped a tree, and drove into the river a couple miles down the road from here. At some point the door flew open and she was thrown out. They found her body two miles downstream a week later."

"Oh, Graham, I'm sorry. Do the children remember her? I've never heard them talk about her."

"They both have a picture of her. Without that I don't think there would be too many memories." He stared into space for several minutes then abruptly stood up, flexing his leg before he walked into the house. "I need to finish packing."

Selena remained on the terrace. Graham's reaction to her questions puzzled her, as if he didn't want to talk about it. Did that mean the information in the letters could be true? How could she find out and prevent getting herself into the same situation as Kate had? Granted, she would react differently than Kate but what would she do if she found out Graham had a girlfriend while being married to her?

Trevor and Trina gave Graham hugs after they got home from school, knowing he was leaving. Their dad's absence on the weekends had become part of their life.

Selena stood at the door with the children, surprised when he leaned down and kissed her on the cheek. His lips close to her ear he said softly, "Take care of yourself." The intensity of the look in his eyes took her off guard. That look always left her feeling unsettled. He seemed to want to convey a message. But what was it?

He didn't come home on Saturday. Selena, Trevor and Trina went to church on Sunday morning. She had become so used to having Graham sit next to her during the service that his absence didn't feel right.

The pastor began his sermon by announcing the beginning of a new series on marriage. She dreaded to hear what he might say. Guilt had become her constant companion, reminding her of promises she'd made that she had no intention of keeping.

Pastor Klein read from the book of Ephesians, chapter five, verses twenty-two through thirty-three. Selena followed the reading. When he finished, he went back to the first verse he'd read and began to expound on the meaning of the word submit. Selena re-read the last verse. "However, each one of you also must love his wife as he loves himself, and the wife must respect her husband." She read it again. She didn't remember seeing that verse before.

Could she and Graham live as husband and wife if she didn't have the feelings for him she thought she needed to have? It didn't say she had to love him. It said she had to respect him. She had developed some respect for him. But what about the letters? Should she ask him if he had been unfaithful to Kate? If she asked him would he be truthful with her? How would she know? And what about The Agreement? They had signed it in good faith, both intending to live by it until March. Maybe she should leave well enough alone. Things could be a lot worse. How could she possibly be thinking about changing their relationship with all the unanswered questions that hung between them? The answer seemed farther away when the service was dismissed then when the verse jumped out at her. She marked it in her Bible, determined to do further study at home.

Chapter 8

November hung onto fall rather than allow the cold and bluster of winter to wrap itself around her. Selena thanked God for the balmy weather. She could find very little to keep her occupied in the house and took vigorous daily walks. Not seeing anything of Howard since her morning at the mall, she walked down the driveway and along the side of the road. She'd clocked the mileage with her van last week and walked a mile down and a mile back. Sometimes she took the path into the woods and walked twenty minutes then turned around and walked back.

Even though Trevor's and Trina's after school activities increased, Selena's schedule had become routine. Joyce no longer intimidated her in spite of her continued demands. The scheduling of the staff turned out to be easy, since they had been working with the same days off for five years and wanted everything left the same.

She loved Jerome. His 'at your service, ma'am', always on the tip of his tongue, endeared him to her. But she sought out Babs if she needed something. The housekeeper never got upset at any request, and stopped in the middle of her many tasks to help her. She smiled frequently, and had a little laugh that sounded like a bell tinkling. On the worst of days, a few minutes with Babs took her mind off her problems.

Returning from her walk down the road, Selena went to the corral to talk to the horses. One in particular, Thunder, large and black, had begun to respond to her voice. The apple she always brought for him didn't hurt either. Petting the horse's neck, she hollered hello to Jerome as he came out of the stable.

"Good morning, ma'am. Wonderful day to be outside."

She smiled. He said that every day, no matter what the weather. She heard him say it when it rained, and she suspected he would say it when it snowed.

Walking over to the stable, she stopped Jerome before he went back inside. "Do you know anyone that could give me riding lessons? I would really love to learn to ride. Which one of these horses would you recommend for a beginner?"

He gave her the name of a woman, Susan Ballentine, who owned a boarding stable down the road. Looking over the dozen horses grazing in the corral, Jerome spied a mare they had purchased the week before so they could begin breeding without paying expensive stud fees.

"See that mare over there with a star in the middle of her nose? She's the gentlest horse I've ever seen. I'd have to saddle her up a couple times and take her out just to make sure she doesn't get spooked easily, but I'd wager she'd be the best one for you."

"Thanks, Jerome. Another thing. I'd like to use the tennis court. Since I don't have anyone to hit the balls back to me do you think you could fix up a backboard so that I could hit them against the board?"

"No problem, ma'am. I'll get to it soon."

"I really appreciate that. Thanks so much. I'll call Susan or stop and see her today or tomorrow and let you know when the lessons will begin."

When Selena went for her walk the next morning she noticed Jerome had already placed the backboard against the end of the tennis court. She found the tennis rackets with a box of balls in the garage on a shelf above her boxes. She went into the house to cool down from her walk and found Graham in the kitchen getting a cup of coffee.

"Did you ask Jerome to put up the board on the tennis court?" he asked.

"Yes. Is that a problem?"

"Of course not. I didn't know you played tennis. I can hit the balls back to you if you want me to. I need the exercise anyway."

Selena smiled mischievously. "Think you can beat me? Come on then. Show me how good you are."

He couldn't resist the challenge. "Get the rackets while I change my shoes." He grinned. He'd wait to tell her that he'd played tennis in college on the intercollegiate team. That had been several years ago, but surely he could remember a thing or two about the game.

"Do you know how to keep score?" Selena smiled when he picked up his racket.

"I think I can do that."

"Good, you keep score and I'll hit the balls." The volley back and forth was quick and even. Graham grinned, amazed at her agility. She'd obviously done this before. When the game was over he won by a narrow margin and knew he'd met his match. He limped to the side and sat down, wincing as he flexed his leg.

"I thought you wanted to hit some balls. You didn't tell me you'd played before." His breaths came in gasps from the exercise.

Her face flushed, her eyes bright, she laughed.

"You didn't ask. Does your leg hurt?" She wiped her face with a towel and handed it to him.

It was a natural gesture, but to him it was intimate in its simplicity. His heart constricted as he looked at her and saw again the beauty in her smile, her laughter, and the carefree, relaxed way she related to him at that moment. Her concern for him touched him.

"Oh, a little. It'll be all right in a minute

She frowned. His glib response didn't match the look on his face.

"You never told me how you hurt that leg.

107

His face colored slightly. "It was a stupid trick. You really don't want to hear about it."

"Yes, I do! That was a really nasty injury to be nothing."

"Oh, all right. I left a client's house and slipped and fell on the ice on the front porch. It was an old house and had a boot scraper beside the door. Nobody ever uses it; it had been left there for decorum. Anyway, when I fell my body twisted and my leg came down across the corner of the scraper. Trying to get the muscle healed has been worse than the break."

"Would more therapy help?"

"The therapist said there's nothing more they can do. I just need to exercise it regularly. Easier said than done in my case."

"If there's anything I can do to help, let me know. By the way, I'm going to begin riding lessons next week. Jerome says I can use the new mare you just bought. He's going to saddle her up a couple times to make sure she's safe. I hope you don't mind."

"No, I don't mind. I could give you riding lessons but probably wouldn't have time right now. I love to ride, but haven't taken the time lately to saddle up. Just be careful. I wouldn't want you to get hurt."

Why is he always concerned about me, but doesn't seem to be concerned about himself?

The riding lessons began the next week, and Graham laughed at her as she limped to breakfast more than once. One morning she made a face at him as she slid gently into her chair. He leaned over and kissed her on the cheek, congratulating her on her accomplishments.

"How do you know how accomplished I am?"

"I have a view that makes it difficult to work some days, remember?"

"Yuck! You guys aren't going to start getting mushy like Dad and Sue did, are you?" Trina remarked with a disgusted look on her face.

Selena looked from Trina to Graham whose face turned several colors of red. A slow smile creased her face.

"Who is Sue? I haven't heard about her."

"That was really yucky," Trina repeated. Graham pushed his plate aside and lay his face flat on the table. Selena laughed at his discomfiture.

"Come on. Help me out here."

Selena propped her chin on her hand and stared at him, a gleam in her eyes. "You got yourself into this one, you'll have to get yourself out."

When Trina started to repeat it again, Selena assured her there would be no mushy stuff, and to please eat her breakfast. Selena went to her room to get her coat, and heard Graham behind her. "Thanks for your assistance, Mrs. Kensington." She glanced at him, hearing the stern note in his voice. The twinkle in his eye gave him away.

"You're welcome, sir. I guarantee you that you haven't heard the last of that one yet. It will come back to haunt you."

Was Sue the one Kate thought Graham was seeing? The more Selena thought about it the more confused she became. Who was Scott Morefield? If she could find him, maybe he would give her some straight answers.

Graham watched her leave with the children and wondered. He ran his fingers through his hair as he thought of the surprises that had popped up since Selena came to the Estate.

Selena learned one thing about the little church she attended regularly with Graham and the children. When the music department decided to put on a production, the whole church participated. Therefore, it came as no surprise when Stella Sampson stopped Selena on her way out of church one

Sunday and asked if she'd be willing to participate in the Christmas production. She agreed to sing in the choir only if she didn't have to do any solo parts.

The children also took part in the production, but Graham declined, saying that with his schedule he would not be able to attend practices regularly. Thursday evening seemed to be the best time for practice sessions for the majority of the people involved. Selena decided to make the best of it even though another night would have worked better for her and the children. Thursday night meant a sandwich for dinner at a fast food restaurant with only a few minutes to spare between practice schedules. For herself she didn't mind, but with Graham gone so much on the weekends it often meant that Trevor and Trina wouldn't see him from Thursday morning breakfast until Sunday afternoon.

Selena sighed. She wondered if Graham knew how much his children needed him, if only for a few minutes in the evening. She'd have to remember to talk to him about it.

Arriving at church for the first practice, she smiled at the selections made by the choir director, Shawn Stevens. His age appeared to be in the mid-thirties and he had an infectious smile. His unruly cowlick in the back and his thick glasses reminded her of the story about the absent-minded professor. She soon learned to respect him for his love and direction of music. He seemed to have a natural talent for drawing the notes out of people to create the right sound at the right moment.

Shawn introduced the new members of the choir and welcomed them to the production. Selena tried not to look surprised when he introduced her and everyone turned around and looked at her. She'd seen most of these people in church on Sunday morning and thought they knew her. She smiled, acknowledging the introduction.

One very friendly woman introduced herself as Sue Blakely. "I see you walking in the mornings and wondered if I could walk with you sometime

"Sure. I'd like that."

Two weeks before Thanksgiving Selena took courage in hand and mentioned the holiday to Graham. "What do you usually do for the holidays coming up?"

"We don't have any traditions, if that's what you're asking. What did you have in mind?"

"If you don't want to do this, tell me. I wondered if you would mind if I invited my family here to have Thanksgiving dinner with us. There would be twenty, including the children. They could come for the day; we could eat in the middle of the afternoon. If I phone them with the invitations now we would know by the end of the week how many to expect. What do you think?"

"Sure. Why not? It sounds like you have it all planned out. Had you thought about how you're going to get food prepared for twenty-five plus people?"

Selena opened her mouth and closed it, feeling her face get warm. "Major detail. Actually, no. I hadn't got that far yet. Do you have any suggestions short of me spending three days in the kitchen over a hot stove?"

Graham laughed. "That presents an interesting picture. Really, though, Joyce might be able to help you out. If not, call a caterer. There's one over in North Hampton that other people I know have used and were satisfied with. By the way, when will you be available for that shopping trip? I can get away tomorrow morning if you can."

"Tomorrow morning would be fine after nine-thirty. I have an eight o'clock riding lesson, but that's only for an hour."

"Tomorrow at nine-thirty it is then. First time I ever had a date that early in the day." Graham winked at her as he left for his office.

Oh no. Now what does he have in mind? What did he mean by a date?

The riding lesson went well and Susan praised her repeatedly for how quickly she'd learned the basics, not only of riding, but also of establishing rapport with the horse. Selena named the mare Star for the marking on her nose, and often also called her Baby when she groomed her and guided her to respond to her commands. More often than not, the mare was called Starbaby, running the two names together.

After the workout, Selena urged Star to a slow, gentle gallop around the riding trails. She then brushed her down, filled her feed bin and water trough, and went to the house to shower for the shopping trip with Graham.

As they rode through the countryside, Selena noticed with disappointment that the leaves had fallen off the trees now and the branches stood stark and bare against the overcast sky. *Just like I feel sometimes. When will I ever feel totally at peace again?*

Even as those thoughts went through her mind, she realized she no longer felt uncomfortable with Graham. Often surprised by his reactions to things, especially when he deliberately showed her affection in front of other people, she looked forward to being with him. The show of affection was with mutual consent as part of The Agreement so she couldn't object, but it still surprised her that he took The Agreement that seriously.

She couldn't figure him out. He always seemed to enjoy being with her and his show of affection seemed to come naturally. But each time she found herself responding to him she remembered the letters.

When they arrived at the store, she looked on the bargain racks. She allowed him to steer her to the other side of the room. She looked at several pieces that he took off the rack and handed to her. Two of them she made a face at and hung them back. He laughed at her expressions.

"I hope you're only teasing. Those are hopeless."

"Oh, what am I going to do?" He exaggerated his tone. "You don't like my taste in clothes."

"If I thought you were serious, we'd be in big trouble here." It felt good to play along with him.

She picked out her size from the selections and made two choices. She hadn't intended to spend that much money. Graham looked at her and shook his head. "If you like them buy them all. I see I'm going to have to hide the price tags from you."

"I hadn't planned on spending that much."

"Don't worry about it. Here's my credit card. We wouldn't want anyone thinking I don't take care of you, would we?"

"You're impossible. What am I going to do with you?" Selena laughed, then stopped short when she saw the look in his eyes. It was <u>that</u> look. Whatever did it mean? And what was he thinking?

During the ride home she brought up the problem with the long weekend stretch when he didn't see the children, and he agreed to call home to talk to Trevor and Trina when he was away. They arrived home after lunch, relaxed.

Graham stopped her before she went upstairs to hang up her purchases and kissed her on the cheek. "Thanks for asking me to go with you. I need to do that more often."

"You're too good to me, Graham. Thanks for everything."

Selena opened the door to her room and stopped. A blast of cold air greeted her. Slowly opening the door she glanced about the room. The curtains blew into the room by the balcony door. Her heart pounded. Her eyes darted back and forth. She dropped her packages.

Fear propelled her down the stairs and around the curve of the hallway. She burst into his office without knocking. "Graham, please come." He looked up in surprise.

"What is it?" He followed her, barely able to keep pace with her hurried footsteps.

She stopped him at the door. "When I left this morning, the balcony door was locked. It hasn't been unlocked or opened since the night I saw someone out there. I didn't go in by myself when I felt the cold air and saw the open door."

They walked in together. "Check and see if there is anything missing."

She looked in her jewelry box, her closet, and her desk drawer. Everything appeared to be in place. Opening the safe in the corner of the closet, she checked the contents and found all the items in their usual place.

"Everything seems to be here. Why would someone come into my room and not take anything? It doesn't look like they even looked for anything. I don't understand." Her voice showed the fear she felt. Was she not even safe here? How could Howard have found her? If it was Howard, why didn't he go through her things looking for the portfolio, if that was what he wanted?

Graham's face was set, his jaw muscles taut. Whoever did this would answer to him. He thanked God that Selena wasn't in the room when the incident occurred and remembered his request for her protection.

Taking a towel from the bathroom he pushed the door closed. "Don't touch anything. I'm going to have the police come out and dust for fingerprints. I don't know what is going on here, but I aim to find out."

Should she tell him about Howard? Or would he think it was too far fetched to think her ex-husband would drive two hours just to open a balcony door? Did *she* believe Howard would do that? She turned to say something, but Graham had already left the room.

The police report stated that the only fingerprints on the door handle were hers. When she questioned Stan, the police officer, he said whoever opened it evidently had gloves on. If the person had tried to wipe the prints off they would have wiped hers off too. The look that passed between the two men left her with the impression that they didn't believe her when she said she'd closed and locked the door.

Graham saw the hurt in her eyes. What was she thinking? Fear he could understand. Why the pain?

Chapter 9

It was one week before Thanksgiving and preparations for the holiday began shaping up. Joyce agreed in her rather sullen way to do the food preparation and help with serving during the meal. Babs volunteered to also help with serving and Selena thanked her profusely for offering.

The house smelled of cookies, pies, and cakes from morning until night. Selena whisked them away to the freezer as soon as they cooled. She didn't want anyone thinking they could sample the goodies. She indulged their sweet-tooths regularly, but this time they'd have to wait.

Selena left the house with a half dozen lists and as many places to stop. She asked Graham for his list, although she knew her job description didn't require her to run errands for him. "It's easier to pick up what you need while I'm out than to have you make an extra trip. I make stops for everyone else. Why not you?" Her offer brought forth a declaration of appreciation from him, which in turn brought warmth to her face and a smile to her lips.

She returned home in time to take her packages in the house and go back out to pick up Trevor and Trina at school. It was their late evening to get home, but Joyce would have dinner on the stove for Graham. He kept closer track of their schedule and there had been no further confrontations about his dinner.

When Selena pulled into the parking lot of the school, Ms. Wilkes approached the van. Selena rolled down the window and greeted her pleasantly. "I hope you've had no further incidents recently with Trevor."

"Not exactly, but I do need to talk to Graham, er, Mr. Kensington. Do you know when he'll be available?"

"You'll have to call and check with him. I'm sorry, I don't have his schedule with me." No need to tell her she never knew his schedule.

Returning home near bedtime with Trevor and Trina, Selena saw the light on in the family room. She found Graham stretched out in the recliner watching TV.

"What's the occasion?" Selena asked, smiling. "I didn't think you knew how to turn that thing on."

"Very funny." He returned the smile. "It's something to do to pass the time while my family is out running the streets. How did your practice go?"

"Fine. I'll have the kids come down for a few minutes before they do their homework." *I wonder what he meant by family. Probably just the children. Maybe he remembered what I said about spending time with them.*

Saturday morning the doorbell rang. Selena sat in the family room reading a book. She walked to the front door and greeted Lorena Wilkes.

"Won't you come in? What can I do for you?"

"Graham, er, Mr. Kensington, is expecting me." She brushed past Selena, standing with her back to her.

Selena buzzed Graham through the intercom and escorted Lorena to his office.

As they walked around the hallway she wondered what was so important that she couldn't take care of it. Lorena Wilkes walked into Graham's office without saying thanks. Her demeanor changed suddenly as she greeted Graham warmly.

For several days Selena had contemplated investigating the area on the ground below her balcony. Maybe clues left at the scene on the ground would provide answers to the occurrences on the second floor. The weather hadn't been conducive to walking around outside until today.

The sun shone, warming the air. Restless, she slipped into her jacket and boots and went out the back door. The breeze felt chilly as it lifted her hair, but the sun warmed her face.

As she walked close to the building she heard voices. Slowing down, she looked around and realized she had stopped outside Graham's office. She began to pick up her pace then stopped again when she heard her name mentioned. Holding her breath, she debated about continuing on around the building or eavesdropping on the conversation. Her curiosity won out. Ms. Wilkes had said she wanted to talk to him about Trevor. *So why are they talking about me?*

"Selena is my wife and I have given her the authority to make any decisions that need to be made for my children. You could have taken this up with her and saved yourself the trouble of coming out here."

Selena's eyes opened wide at Graham's words. She heard Ms. Wilkes voice, but could not make out the words. Then Graham's voice again.

"No, I will not go with you. I'm married. I don't know what you thought there ever was between us, but you're mistaken. As far as I am concerned this conversation is over."

Selena hurriedly moved on around the house. So, Ms. Wilkes had designs on Graham. How did they know each other that well that the teacher thought there was something between them? The longer she stayed at Serendipity Estate, the more she began to see that Graham had his pick of women to settle down with. He could have married a woman who would have fit more easily into the social life of those with wealth. Though, she had to admit, he didn't travel in those circles. And it looked like some women had no problem trying to date him regardless of his marital status. Had he been out with Ms. Wilkes while married to Kate?

She stopped and looked around. She'd lost track of how far she'd walked. Turning back she stood under the balcony, trying to think how it would look to someone who wanted to get to the second floor. After studying the surroundings for a few minutes, she decided the only access would be with a ladder, which would leave marks in the soft dirt, or climbing up the side with a strong rope. The railing on top had corner posts six inches taller than the middle posts, which had a flat board across the tops of them. Someone experienced with rope climbing could easily throw a looped rope up over the corner posts. That probably excluded Howard. He'd never shown any inclination of being experienced in anything that took physical exertion.

She looked in the soft dirt, not sure what to look for, and found nothing. In the movies someone always left a button, an earring, or a cuff link at the scene to lead the detectives to the criminal. Selena laughed. Real life never mirrored the movies.

Going back around the corner of the house she heard the tennis balls before she saw the person behind the racket. She walked toward the court to offer to hit the balls back to Graham and stopped. He hit them with such force that his frustration plainly showed.

She waited to see if there would be a let up in the thunk, thunk, thunk, of the fast moving balls. Whatever the problem it must be going to take some time to work out. She winced as she watched him hop on one leg, favoring the injured one. Walking into the house she sighed at the sound of the doorbell.

"Yes, may I help you?" Selena stared at the distinguished looking man.

"You must be Selena. I'm Sylvan Kensington. Pleased to meet you

Selena's eyes opened wide. Graham had talked about his father, but she hadn't met him yet. *I should have known.*

Mirror images of each other, she saw the same pale blue eyes and easy smile.

"Please, come in. This is a welcome surprise. Yes, I'm Selena, and I'm very glad to finally meet you. Are you going to be in the area long? I can have Babs get the guest room ready for you if you like."

"No, no. Don't go to the trouble. I'm just stopping by for a couple hours to see the grandchildren. I've promised friends to be at their place in Kettering by dinnertime. Is Graham around today or is he on the road again?"

"He's outside on the tennis court. I'll have one of the children get him for you." She pushed the intercom announcing the guest and the children burst into the room.

Seeing their grandfather the children jumped into his arms. The laughter and giggling continued until Selena said, "Trev, why don't you go tell your dad he has a guest."

Trevor ran through the house and out the back door. He returned with Graham who shook hands vigorously with his dad and excused himself to clean up. Selena invited Sylvan into the family room and went to the kitchen to make hot drinks.

When she returned, Graham walked down the stairway and took the tray from her. "Are you all right with this? I forgot to tell you that Dad never announces his arrivals. I enjoy his visits and I hope you do, too."

"Sure, I'm all right with it. In my world in Columbus no one ever announced his or her arrival. Did you get your problem worked out?"

He jerked his head and stared at her. "Not exactly. How did you know?

She raised her eyebrows and walked into the family room, smiling.

"Would you like a hot drink, sir?

After the drinks had been served, Sylvan stared openly at Graham. "What were you in such an all fired hurry to get married for that you couldn't wait until I got here to help you celebrate?"

Graham smiled. "Well, you know how it is, Dad. You find a beautiful woman, you have to do it before she gets away." He winked at Selena and deftly steered the conversation in another direction.

Selena lowered her eyes to her cup of tea and didn't participate in the conversation.

Trevor and Trina kept their grandfather's attention. Selena gathered up the cups and took them to the kitchen, placing them in the dishwasher. She decided to go to her room just as Graham showed up at the door.

"Takes a long time to wash a few cups, huh?"

Selena shrugged.

"If I said something to offend you, I didn't mean to. What is it?" He gently turned her face toward his and looked into her eyes.

How could she tell him that she was tired of deceiving people, especially close family members? They'd signed The Agreement with the terms non-negotiable until March. Off hand remarks like the one Graham had just made only made it seem that much more of a sham. He'd meant no offense and she had only herself to blame; The Agreement had been her idea, not his.

She still needed to talk to somebody about the letters. If the information was correct, there would never be anything more between them than there was at the moment. But he seemed sincere in his attentions to her. Of course, he'd probably been the same way with Kate in the beginning.

"It's all right. Let's go back in there so you can spend time with your dad." Allowing him to take her hand they walked in together.

Selena looked forward to Sunday morning. She enjoyed the feeling of being part of a family, instead of always sitting alone in church. Graham never failed to play the part of the loving husband. She wondered how much of it was acting and how much he did because he wanted to. She had become used to his gestures and no longer objected. He stayed within the boundaries of The Agreement, so had a ready answer if she voiced a concern about him overdoing the part.

As usual, when they arrived at church, Graham helped his family out of the car and they walked to the front door together. Trina stopped Selena as they got to the door.

"Selena, my barrette keeps falling down. Could you make it stay up?"

Selena had refastened it several times since placing it in Trina's hair after breakfast. Exasperated, she handed her Bible and her purse to Graham to hold, as she told Trina, "This is the last time. You'll just have to put up with it if you don't like it. You can take it out when we get home."

Graham watched the little scene and wondered if Selena knew what she'd just done. She acted like all the other women in the church, expecting their husbands to hold personal items on a moment's notice while they dealt with issues with the children. And they weren't even her children. But observation showed that Trevor and Trina depended on her and asked her advice and opinion on everything now.

The barrette once again in place, she smiled at him, thanked him for holding her things, then placed her hand in his as they walked to the front door.

Surprised, he squeezed her hand. For the first time she'd initiated the contact. He smiled as he felt the sense of satisfaction and the stirring of his emotions as he walked into the foyer, hand in hand with his wife.

Selena indeed had not thought about what happened. She did notice, though, the soft touch of his fingers on the nape of her neck as he helped her with her coat, a feeling that remained for several minutes afterward. He placed his hand near the small of her back as they walked into the sanctuary looking like the loving family they'd agreed to portray.

Chapter 10

Thanksgiving Day dawned bright and clear. Selena crawled out of her warm bed and pulled on jeans and a long sleeved knit shirt to ward off the chill. Drawing the drapes to the balcony aside, she noticed the cloudless sky. In a few minutes the sun would show its face above the horizon.

Joyce planned to arrive at eight o'clock, but Selena began removing the baked items from the freezer. She checked the turkeys, thawing for two days, and found no ice in the cavity. *Good. They'll be ready for the oven soon.*

She opened the door to the formal dining room and counted the places settings, for the tenth time at least, to make sure that everyone would have a seat at the table. She didn't want to have to make any last minute changes. Everyone had accepted the invitations and she wanted to be prepared. She wanted Graham to look good. After all, it was his house. At least that's what she'd told herself over and over the past two days.

She looked forward to this time with her family. It'd been a long time since they'd all been together.

Trevor and Trina got up at the usual time asking for breakfast. Sending Trevor to get his dad, Selena placed sausage in a skillet to brown and stirred pancake mix. He returned saying his dad would be down in a few minutes. Graham walked into the kitchen as she pushed the switch on the coffee maker to the on position.

"This is a nice surprise." He stood close behind her as she turned the sausage. "Are we getting domesticated

Selena's pulse quickened as she felt his breath on her cheek and caught a faint whiff of his after-shave lotion. She poked him lightly in the ribs with her elbow. "Enjoy this while it lasts. Joyce will have enough to do when she gets here

125

without fixing our breakfast. Here, make yourself useful and turn this sausage while I start the pancakes." She handed him the fork.

"Here, guys, put these dishes on the table," she said to Trevor and Trina.

When Joyce arrived she could only guess from the crumbs and dirty containers what breakfast consisted of. Her face registered surprise as she went to the kitchen.

"Good breakfast. We'll have to do this again sometime." Graham leaned over and kissed Selena on the cheek.

"Oh, no. Not again," Trina said.

Graham looked at her sternly. "That will be enough young lady. A man is allowed to kiss his wife without getting a lot of lip from you."

Trina looked at Graham then at Selena, her eyes wide. "Selena, what is a wife?"

"Well, honey, a wife is a woman who is married. The man she is married to is called her husband."

Trina thought about that for a minute. Suddenly her eyes lit up. "Like a mommy and a daddy?"

Selena stared at her, startled. How did she jump from one to the other? "I guess you might say that. When a man and woman get married and they have children they then become a mommy and a daddy

"Since you and Dad are married then that makes you my mom." Trina nodded her head up and down. "I always wanted a mom, I mean a real mom, not one that went to Heaven. Can you be my mom, Selena?"

Selena glanced at Graham, his expression unreadable. "I don't know, Trina. Your dad and I will have to talk about it. Come on, let's get these dishes in the dishwasher

Selena stacked the plates and found Graham studying her.

"What?"

"You'd make a great mom, Selena." He watched the emotions play across her face. She took a deep ragged breath, picked up the dishes and walked to the kitchen. He wondered. Would he ever be able to break through those walls? What's she hiding from? Why wouldn't she talk to him? Couldn't she see how much he cared for her? *Patience.*

Selena's family started arriving at noon. Tom and Jeanine pulled in first with her mother. She met them at the door and threw her arms around them, tears streaming down her face. Graham, right behind her, reached around the women, shook hands with Tom and introduced himself. She apologized and finished the introductions.

The formal living room doors stood open with the drapes pulled to the side. They invited the guests to be seated there, and Selena went to the kitchen to tell Babs that she could begin serving the appetizers and drinks.

"Sure thing, ma'am. I'll be right there. You just relax."

Soon afterwards the rest of the family arrived: Selena's sister, Peggy and her husband Ben Wells with their two children, her brother Ray Cordell and his wife Luann and their three children, her brother Cameron Cordell and his wife Judy and their four children. Each time the doorbell rang Trevor and Trina came from the family room and took the children with them. Selena breathed a prayer of thanks for the large family room and the many activities there to keep the children occupied.

Her brothers and sisters proved to be a lively bunch. The stories came out, one on top of the other, with joking and congenial camaraderie.

Judy sat beside Selena. In awe of the luxurious surroundings, she commented, "If I'd known it was going to be like this, I'd have dressed up." She looked at her jeans. "Where did you find this guy anyway?" She whispered to Selena.

Selena laughed. "I didn't find him. He found me. He showed up on my nursing unit as one of my patients at the hospital. He asked me to do him a favor, and when I did he said he'd be indebted to me forever." The half dozen people who heard the explanation laughed.

"If it's that funny, let's hear it down at this end of the room," Cameron said. And so the day went.

At two o'clock Selena went to the kitchen. "When do you think we can begin serving dinner?" she asked Joyce.

"Anytime, ma'am."

Selena returned to the living room. Knowing her family watched, she stood behind Graham's chair and placed her hands on his shoulders. Leaning close to his ear she said, "We can begin seating in five minutes. I'll try to get the children washed for dinner." Graham reached up and squeezed her hand.

Nice touch. That should convince everyone how happily married we are, she thought.

Graham took a seat at the head of the table and Selena at the other end. With everyone around the table holding hands, Graham asked the blessing, giving thanks for each family there. Selena silently gave thanks for his generosity in allowing her to have her family together. Her prayer spilled over to all of her brothers and sisters, her mom, and Graham's children.

Joyce and Babs had volunteered Jerome to help them in the kitchen. With good-natured grumbling, he reluctantly agreed, saying, "I don't know anything about kitchens." Joyce assured him he would get lots of instructions and she put him in charge of the dishwasher and lifting heavy cooking pans for them. That left the two women to attend to the demands of the serving.

Selena noticed that Joyce sat all the serving dishes within Graham's reach. His attention directed to Ray on one side and Ben on the other the dishes remained there for several minutes. Selena reminded him several times to pass the food. Finally, she stopped Joyce and told her to please start the serving dishes at her end of the table.

"Yes, ma'am," she said frostily.

Selena prayed there would not be a scene in front of her family. The issues with Joyce still had not been resolved, and Selena didn't know what Joyce would do if she felt disrespected.

Before the request Joyce's demeanor seemed friendly and accommodating to the guest's requests. Afterwards, her attitude turned sullen. Selena directed her requests to Babs who smiled and gave her usual response, "Yes, Ma'am."

After dinner they moved back into the living room, and soon the guests began talking about starting home. Graham and Selena stood at the door and thanked each one for coming. When her mother held her close she whispered, "Is everything all right, Selena? You look sad."

"Of course. Everything is fine. Come over sometime and stay with me for a couple days. You could come on the plane. I'd pick you up at the airport. Think about it. I'd love to have you." She gave her mother another hug.

After everyone left, she stood at the window alone and watched the last car turn onto the road. Overwhelmed by the quiet, the tears trickled down her cheeks. Today seemed more normal than any day for as long as she could remember. Since before she married Howard. Nothing had been normal with Howard.

Ray had pulled her aside right after dinner and told her he talked to Howard last week. Howard had been friendly, too friendly, and eventually got around to his reason for stopping by. He couldn't find Selena; did Ray know where she'd moved? He needed to talk to her. Ray truthfully said he didn't know the address and had never been to her house.

Remembering the conversation, she wondered again if Howard was responsible for the things that happened surrounding the balcony. How could he be if he didn't know where she lived?

Half an hour later Graham missed Selena. He found her sitting on the sofa in the living room in the dark. Easing down beside her he took her hand and kissed her fingers.

"You don't have to do that, you know. There's no one watching."

"I know I don't have to. I want to." He watched her in the semi-darkness.

"Graham, thanks for everything today. I can't tell you how much it meant to me to have my whole family here. It was really special and I couldn't have done it without you." Her voice was soft as she squeezed his hand.

Seeing her soft smile, his heart began to pound. *I better stick to the reason why I came looking for her.*

"The kids want to play games. Want to join us?"

Glad for the distraction she followed him to the family room. A collage of memories of the day left her wondering about her true feelings for Graham. Yes, she respected him more than anyone else she knew, but something more than that surfaced. Fear prevented her from naming it or even facing it. She thought she knew once what it felt like to be in love, then realized she didn't know after all. She didn't want to think about it. She might be wrong again. And if he couldn't be faithful to one woman she didn't want to get emotionally involved with him. Better not to think about it. Besides, The Agreement gave her reason to keep him at arm's length.

The children went to bed and Graham went to his office to check for messages. Selena went to the kitchen for a glass of milk and looked around, amazed that the kitchen looked like no one had been in it all day. She shook her head at the efficiency of the staff. She'd have to be sure to express her appreciation tomorrow.

Picking up her shoes, she climbed the stairway and opened the door to her room. Flipping the light switch, her heart stopped. Fear froze her to the floor. She wanted to scream, but no sound came out. She dropped her shoes. The movement startled her and adrenaline took over.

She ran to Graham's door and pounded as hard as she could. He had to be in there. *Please let him be in there. Where is he?* Her fear-crazed mind forgot he'd gone to his office.

Graham heard the pounding and walked toward the sound. He began to run when he realized it was coming from the second floor. Seeing the open door of Selena's room and her pounding on his door at the same time, he ran to her and gathered her up in his arms to stop the pounding. Her ashen face and her wild eyes frightened him.

"Tell me what happened, Selena. Did you see anyone or anything?" He felt her shudder and looked down to make sure she hadn't fainted. He rubbed her face and she blinked her eyes.

"Oh-h-h-h-h. My room. What did he do to my room? Why would he do that to me? What have I ever done to deserve this?"

Graham sat her against the wall and inched the door wider with the toe of his shoe, his face grim. Who indeed would want to dump everything out of every drawer, pull every piece of clothing off the hangers in her closet, empty her jewelry containers, and scatter it all over the room? Clothes hung from the drapery rods, the chandelier and the bedposts. Her personal belongings covered the floor, the bed, and the furniture. He wanted to check the balcony door, but thought better of it. Instead he pulled the phone out of his pocket and called the police.

Graham picked Selena up and carried her downstairs to the family room, laying her on the sofa. He didn't want her to be upstairs when the police arrived. They'd want to talk to her; he'd insist they do that last. By that time she may have recovered enough to answer their questions.

The police again dusted for fingerprints and looked at the balcony door for forced entry. They found the door closed, but not locked. Nothing to indicate that the lock had been forced open, they looked for other evidence. With so many things strewn around they couldn't determine what belonged to her and what may have belonged to someone else.

Selena told the police what she remembered: she opened the door, turned on the light, and fled for help. The embarrassment at having everyone see the personal things that she'd stored out of sight, now laying in the middle of the floor, increased her pain.

The police left, promising to let them know the results of the fingerprinting. Graham sat beside Selena on the sofa and rubbed her back. He didn't know what to say. His anger at whoever would do this to her and his feeling of fear for not providing a secure place for his family immobilized him. It had happened with so many people in the house and no one had heard or seen anything.

How could something like this happen? The sprawling estate, once a haven, now shattered his illusion of safety. He saw it as it really was. The immense house with its easy access, the rooms too far apart, and the carpet too plush, embraced an evil entity that easily hid its identity. The feeling of powerlessness to protect her and his children washed over him. As the husband and father in this house didn't the Bible direct him to be the protector?

He thought again of the prayer he'd said on Selena's behalf and thanked the Lord for the double protection He had granted. He'd never seen her so frightened--that was bad enough--but she hadn't been hurt physically.

Graham sat down on the floor and talked to her. At first she didn't respond. Then, slowly she answered his questions with an almost imperceptible nod of her head. When he had her full attention he talked about the issues that had to be faced.

"Selena, I told you I don't give commands. I make requests. This is one time I'm going to give you a command. You have to unlock the door. If something happens in the middle of the night and you need help I have to be able to get to you quickly."

She closed her eyes. "What door?"

"Don't do this, Selena. You know what I'm talking about. The adjoining door to our rooms."

She opened her eyes to see his piercing gaze.

"All right. I'll unlock the door."

She sat up, then stood up and began slowly pacing. "Graham, I can't take anymore. I'm sorry I brought all this trouble on you. I should have stayed in Columbus. At least there I knew the source of the problem. Howard had been harassing me for months before I came here. I thought that if I came here it would stop. But it hasn't. And now it's involved you and your family and I can't handle that. If I go back to Columbus, I may still be harassed, but at least all of you here will have some peace and quiet."

Graham took her by the shoulders, forcing her to stop pacing and look at him. "Going back to Columbus won't solve anything. I don't think Howard is behind any of this. I don't know what we're dealing with, but I'm going to find out. Odd things happened before you came, but I had no idea anyone would involve you in any of this.

He cupped her face in his hands and pleaded with her. "Please don't go, honey. We'll figure out what's going on and put a stop to it. I promise you that.

As she looked in his face she thought she'd never seen such anguish or sincerity before. Could he pretend this much if he really didn't care about her? Could he be this concerned about her and love someone else at the same time? Her head pounded. She didn't want to think about it.

"What am I going to do tonight?" Selena asked tearfully. "My room is a mess and I really don't want to deal with it now. I think I'll sleep down here on the sofa.

Graham went upstairs to get her pillow and a blanket. As he stepped around the items on the floor, he saw an envelope with a pink ribbon around it propped against the mirror on her chest of drawers. At first he thought it belonged to Selena. Then he saw the handwriting. Looking at the name on the outside, he picked it up, the muscles on his jaw twitching, stuck it in his shirt pocket, and returned to Selena in the family room. He planned to read it later in the privacy of his bedroom.

He handed her the pillow and tucked the blanket around her. Leaning over, her kissed her on the cheek.

She grabbed his hand. "Could you stay with me for a little while, please?" She hugged the pillow close to her.

As he sat holding her hand, she noticed the envelope sticking out of his pocket. A knot formed in her stomach. A small piece of pink ribbon showed at the corner.

"Where did you get that letter in your pocket?"

His hand went to his pocket as his eyes searched her face. Her eyes opened wide and her jaw went slack.

"I found it in your room when I went to get your pillow. I should ask you where you got it since it's not addressed to you."

"When I first moved here I found them in the drawers as I put my things away. That's why I asked you who occupied the room before me.

"Them? How many are there.

"I found two, but not at the same place. Which one do you have there

134

He took the envelope out of his pocket and slipped the pink ribbon off the side. Taking the paper out, he unfolded it and began to read.

Dear Kate,

I don't know how you can stay with that monster after what he's done to you. I wouldn't allow anyone to force me to stay in that mausoleum of a place you live in. I don't understand why you don't move into town where all the action is and really live. I'm sure Bud would let you stay with him. You know how much he likes you. If Graham came looking for you I sure wouldn't tell him where you were. Make up your mind soon before you go crazy out there in the middle of nowhere.

Always your friend,
Gina

Graham's face turned white then red. He tore the letter in two before Selena could stop him. She grabbed his hands and took the letter as he rolled his fists into balls and laid his head back on the sofa.

Smoothing the paper and piecing it together she began to read. She got to the end of the second sentence when Graham suddenly grabbed it out of her hands and tore it into little pieces.

"Would you please tell me what that's all about?"

"They're lies. All lies. No wonder I couldn't get a handle on the problems between us when she had people filling her mind with stuff like that. But, then it probably wouldn't have changed anything if she had different friends. I can't imagine what she wrote that elicited that kind of response. Where are the other letters? And what did they say?"

Selena put her head in her hands and said nothing. After everything that had happened she felt too emotionally drained to confront the issues. "I don't know where they are. But I've never seen this one before.

"I'm going to find them."

She jumped off the sofa and grabbed his arm. "Please, don't go up there again. Please. It's bad enough that the police had to see...see all my really personal things like that. I'll look for them tomorrow.

"All right. But promise me that you'll give them to me when you find them.

"I promise. Now can I get some rest? Will you stay with me for just a little while longer?"

"Sorry. Of course. Move forward a little and let me slide in behind you." His voice soft, he placed one arm underneath her and the other on top, pulling her close with his knees bent behind hers. He lay his head on the pillow, his face in her lightly scented hair, and tucked the blanket around her shoulders. Holding her, he felt her relax.

He thought she was asleep until he heard her say, "Graham, why did she call you a monster? Were the problems that serious between the two of you?"

"We had some problems but I didn't know she hated it that much here. She never told me she did anyway. I wish I'd known."

"What would you have done had you known? You said God brought you here. Would you have moved away without His guidance?"

"I don't know. I'd have done almost anything to make her happy. I'd have given her anything. But, I couldn't give her the one thing that she craved more than anything else."

"What's that?"

He didn't answer for a long time. She was almost asleep when his voice, gruff, roused her. "She wanted an exciting kind of love, gripping, and the thing that controlled her life. She wanted someone who made her the very center of his being, whose world revolved around her

"That's probably every teenager's dream. Most women eventually realize the dream is just that--a dream." She paused for several minutes.

"Did you really ask Kate to marry you as a dare?" She felt him stiffen and take a deep breath.

"Where'd you hear that?"

"I read it in one of the letters I found in the drawer in my room.

"Yes. It's a long story and I really don't want to get into it tonight. You need to get some rest." He tightened his arms around her and moved the blanket closer around her neck.

"We have all night. It won't take longer than that, will it?"

"I guess not." He began, halting at intervals.

"One of my friends dared me to propose to her. I thought she'd laugh in my face and that would be the end of it. She really surprised me when she accepted. I thought about telling her the truth, but never did. I thought we could be happy. Make it work. We'd been friends for awhile and I was committed to the relationship, but she needed more. When the children were born she seemed happier, but it still wasn't enough."

Selena heard the resignation in his voice and reached for his hand. "I'm sure you did the best you could. You can only do what you know is right. You can't make others do the same."

Her last statement--was it for her or for him?

A long conversation one afternoon with the youth pastor at the church he attended while in college had eased his mind and left him with the same thought Selena had just voiced. *I haven't thought about these things since Kate died five years ago. Why are these letters surfacing now?*

He heard her deep breathing, glad she'd found sleep so easily. He dared not move and dared not give into the emotions that lay just beneath the surface.

Sleep didn't come easily for him. He lay beside her, his arms around her, wondering how to keep his promise to her to find the person who did these things to her. He had to get professional help, but who? *I'll have to start making phone calls tomorrow.*

The last thing that went through his mind before he went to sleep startled him. He'd found a woman that he loved deeply and unconditionally, and he'd do anything to stop this madness. In fact, he could easily make her the center of his life, his world. Not because she demanded it, but because God had placed her there.

As the morning sky lightened, Selena stirred in her sleep. Opening her eyes, at first disoriented, it came back to her. She closed her eyes to go back to sleep, and then remembered. *The Agreement. I'm not supposed to be here like this.* She gently and slowly moved Graham's arm then rolled out onto the floor. She heard him move, waited for his deep breathing again, went upstairs, stepped over the items on the floor, crawled into bed and pulled the blanket over her head.

She slept fitfully until the sun came up, then put everything back in its place and went downstairs. She'd put on a smile and stay. Graham needed her. The children needed her. And renegotiation of The Agreement had to wait until March.

She had a spoonful of cereal halfway to her mouth when Graham walked in for breakfast. She stopped suddenly as the realization hit her. Everything in her room had been put back

in its place. Everything, that is, except the letters. They'd
disappeared.

Chapter 11

One evening in December during dinner Selena asked, "What do you do for Christmas celebration?"

Graham smiled. "Didn't we have this conversation a month ago? Oh, right. That was about Thanksgiving. What do we do, guys?"

The children talked at once. Selena laughed and made a T with her hands. "Time out! One at a time. I can't understand a thing you're saying. Wipe that smirk off your face, Graham. You started this."

The list of favorite holiday activities seemed endless. Graham finally explained that they'd done all those things at one time or another over the past five years, but they hadn't done all of them in the same year. Selena suggested they find one new thing to do this year and each one pick two of their favorites from the years before.

Going to the stable to saddle Star for a morning ride, Selena spotted Jerome in the corral mending one of the fences. "Hey, Jerome!" she hollered out the door.

"Good morning, ma'am. Great day to be outside."

She walked over to him. "I understand there are some Christmas decorations stored somewhere. Sometime before the weekend could you bring them into the house and place them in the family room? Who decorated for Christmas last year?"

"Mr. Kensington hired some ladies from the Christmas Store in Dayton to decorate. They did a nice job. I'll get those decorations for you, ma'am." "Thanks, Jerome." Selena finished saddling Star and led her out past the corral into the open field. "Come on, Starbaby, we're going for a nice ride today."

Mounting, she walked her for several minutes then urged her into a canter. She guided the horse onto the trail, rode to the far end of the property and up the steep incline to a place that overlooked the entire estate. Pulling the collar of her coat up closer around her neck to break the wind that always seemed to be present here, she sat atop Star and admired the place she now called home.

Like a kaleidoscope, the events of the past year tumbled over each other as she recalled how she came to be here. Graham's face rose above every memory. His smile. His laughter. His eyes, gentle, smiling, piercing, warm, searching. The grim look on his face after the frightening incidents. Those looks that still puzzled her. His hands, firm, strong, safe. His generosity, there seemed to be no end to it. His silence when she said or did the wrong thing. His integrity, always doing the right thing for the right reason regardless of the cost to himself.

But overshadowing it all were the words from the letters. The words about him seeing another woman while married to Kate. He didn't take his other responsibilities and commitments lightly. Why that one? Could he be capable of infidelity? His character and integrity in every other area seemed strong. But then who knew what he did or who he saw on his weekends out of town? *They say the wife is always the last one to know.*

What would happen in March when they renegotiated The Agreement? He certainly recognized by now that he deserved more than she could give him. She prayed that God would give her the strength to do the right thing until March, and she'd decide what she needed to do afterwards. Graham's words reverberated in the back of her mind. "We're not really married anyway

Galloping back into the field by the stable, Star slowed to a walk and entered the building.

"I'll get that for you ma'am." Selena heard Jerome in the next stall.

She opened the back door and heard Joyce say, "She just walked in. I'll get her for you." Joyce handed her the receiver.

"Call for you, Ma'am."

"Hello. Hello? Hello? Is anyone there?" She hung up the phone.

"Joyce, did they identify themselves?"

"No, Ma'am. Just asked for you."

"Next time, see if you can get a name, please. I think they hung up before I got there."

She picked up the mail and flipped through the pieces. She took a large mailing envelope with Clarinda's return address in the corner and tore it open. Checking the contents she sighed. Still no packet from the court with her divorce papers. If she could remember the name of Howard's attorney, she'd call him and see why she hadn't received them yet.

She picked up the rest of the mail and walked to Graham's office. His door ajar, she saw him on the phone. Walking toward the end of the hall she planned to look out the window until he finished the conversation. Halfway to the end she noticed a door labeled Closet. *What an odd place for a closet.*

Curious, she opened the door, felt for the light switch and found a large knob. Turning it slowly she watched the light change from very dim to very bright.

Her eyes opened wide at the narrow room with a table and a lamp at one end. On the table lay an open Bible. Above the table, a picture of a woman praying hung on the wall. Two chairs sat inside the door. Why didn't Graham tell her he had a chapel here?

She heard a noise behind her and turned quickly. Graham stood in the doorway. "Am I trespassing?" she asked.

"Of course not."

"I didn't know this was here. I'd have been down here a long time ago had I known."

"Sorry. I forgot to tell you. While we're here, have a seat." He closed the door. "We need to pray about some things. The police called with the results of the fingerprints. They found only yours. Whoever's responsible for this is probably a professional. Also, I have a friend in Columbus following Howard. I'll just say this. I think we can count him out."

"But, if it isn't Howard, then who is it? Who would want to frighten me and why? None of this makes sense to me." Tears welled up in her eyes.

"I don't know. I've been praying, and the more I pray the more I'm convinced it has more to do with me than with you. There are people who would like to see my business fail and I'm beginning to think they will go to any length to make sure it does." His face grim, his eyes downcast, he leaned forward and placed his face in his hands.

"I don't understand what you do that'd interest anyone enough to do something like this."

Graham thought for a moment. "I'll tell you this much. I'm a certified public accountant. My clients are internationally known evangelists and religious leaders. Someday I'll tell you who they are. Right now, I need to have you stand with me, united in prayer. We're going to need the power of God to work for us to get through this."

Selena looked into his eyes as he took her hands and earnestly asked for her prayers. "Of course I'll stand with you, Graham. Exactly what is it that we're standing for or against?"

"This thing could be bigger than you or I. We need to pray that the power of the evil behind this is broken, and that God's purpose will go forward in the world. I'm also praying personally for strength and wisdom to know how to get to the bottom of this and put a stop to it. The hardest thing for me is to see you being attacked. I feel powerless to do anything about it." His voice cracked.

Selena wanted to put her arms around him and tell him everything would be all right. The Agreement stood between them, and the way things looked now everything wouldn't be all right. With the deceit already in the relationship, she didn't want to add more.

She squeezed his hands and said softly, "Let's pray about it." She prayed, asking that the power of God be made known in a personal way in their lives. She ended by thanking God for bringing them together and giving them the privilege to do whatever work he had set before them. She asked for wisdom to discern the truth from the lies.

Graham prayed for wisdom and strength to make the correct decisions and asked God to continue his double portion of protection for her and his family. He prayed for the evil to leave his house and his family, and that the instigator would show his face. He ended by thanking God for Selena and the strength and stability she brought to his family.

Halfway to the family room she remembered the mail that she'd left in the Closet. She retrieved the mail and stopped by Graham's office. He stood with his back to the door, looking out the window. Tapping on the door, she walked in. She watched him turn and smile softly.

"I picked up your mail. That's why I came over here in the first place. Clarinda sent me an envelope of stuff. She said to tell you they send their love and they're looking forward to seeing you next weekend." She laid his mail on the corner of his desk.

She looked at him awkwardly. He still smiled at her, not saying anything. She felt something pass between them while they prayed together. Not wanting to think about what it might have been, she made an excuse about going somewhere and left.

The next day, as she put her coat on to run errands in town for Joyce and Babs, the phone rang. Picking it up she said hello and waited. No answer. She heard someone cough.

"Who is this?" No answer. She hung up the phone.

"Joyce, have you been getting phone calls where no one speaks?"

"No, Ma'am."

Unable to make any sense of it, Selena forgot about it. She focused on the events coming up, presents to buy, and the children's schedules. Along with their usual round of activities, they'd added skating parties, Christmas parties, and Christmas programs.

Some days Selena thought she couldn't go on like this. They expected too much of her. One person shouldn't be required to do all the things they asked her to do. Then someone would express appreciation for something she'd done and she'd give herself a good talking to, to keep on going, to think about the money she placed in her personal account each month. At least until March. By then she would be financially stable enough to take her time to look for a good job if she needed to.

Selena completed her Christmas shopping and thought it might be a nice gesture to ask Graham if he needed help with his. Walking to his office after lunch, she tapped on the door and entered. She seldom talked to him in the middle of the day, but since he planned to be gone for the weekend there wouldn't be much time to discuss anything with him.

"I hope I'm not bothering you." Selena walked to the window to admire the snow-covered landscape.

"You are."

She turned quickly to apologize and saw the grin on his face and the light in his eyes. "You love doing that to me, don't you?" She laughed.

"I just came to admire your view." She kept her face expressionless. She watched him roll his eyes to the ceiling in mock despair then laughed at his response.

"No one wants to talk to me. Everyone just wants to look at my view."

"Seriously, is this a good time to talk, or do I need to make an appointment to talk about family issues?"

Walking over to stand beside her at the window, he said, "This is fine. I need a break."

"I wondered if you need help with your Christmas shopping."

"Are you offering to help me with my shopping? If you are, you're on."

"Also, what do you think of the idea of having an Open House either before Christmas or between Christmas and New Years for our friends, neighbors, and family."

"If you want to have an Open House, do it. It sounds great."

"What do you want to do about decorating the house for Christmas? Jerome said you had someone come in the last couple years to do it for you."

"What do you want to do?"

"I thought at one time I wanted to do it. That is until I saw all the boxes of ornaments, bows, and candles. I'm not sure I'll have time to do it all. One thing I would like to do is decorate the tree in the family room. I didn't see one in the boxes. Does that mean you buy a real one?"

"Jerome usually finds one somewhere. I can have him get one for us again."

"Have you ever shopped for a tree? I used to go with Dad when I was a kid. Those times are my fondest memories. Trevor and Trina would probably have a good time picking one out and it would be nice if you could go along. You know, kind of a family thing.

"You've been good for us, Selena. We've done more family things in the past three months than we did in the past five years. When would you like to go?"

"Saturday of next week would be a good day."

"That'll work. After this weekend I'll be home until the middle of January. How about if we go shopping next Wednesday? Let's make a day of it. Jerome can make sure the kids get where they're supposed to go."

"Wednesday? I think I can work that out. There usually isn't much going on after school then anyway."

"Thanks for making me take a break. I feel better already." His soft smile tempted her to walk into his arms. A thought about The Agreement turned her to the door instead.

He watched her walk toward the Closet when she left his office. He felt a new strength since he'd asked her to pray with him about the situation. He thanked God for the bond that had been formed between them.

He'd been more upset than he let on when she said she wanted to go back to Columbus. How would he ever convince her of his love for her if she lived two hours away? He'd found her and convinced her once that he needed her, but how could he convince her now that he just wanted to be with her? He prayed that she would find something worth staying here for. *The more bonds we form between us the less likely she will leave. Please, Lord, make it so.*

Selena pulled her boots on as the phone rang. Picking it up, she waited. She heard the same sound in the background she always heard when no one said anything. This time a low rumbling laugh that sounded like something in a horror movie came over the line. Her face paled and she quickly hung up the phone.

Turning to go out, she ran into Graham who'd walked up behind her unnoticed. She screamed and jumped back. Her

hands shook as she placed one up to her mouth to keep from screaming again. Joyce ran
from the kitchen and Jerome stuck his head in the back door.

"What's going on?" Graham demanded from behind her.

Selena whirled around. "You scared me sneaking up on me like that."

"Why did you hang up the phone like that? Who was there?"

"There wasn't anyone on the phone."

"Selena, look at me. You were upset when you put the phone down. What's going on?"

"I've been getting phone calls where no one says anything. Sometimes there's a cough or it sounds like someone is clearing a throat. Just now I heard weird laughter."

"Joyce, Mrs. Kensington will not be taking any more phone calls. All calls are to be directed to me. You may take messages and give them to her at which time she can return calls at her convenience. Under no circumstances is she to answer the phone." Graham felt the knots in his stomach as he attempted to control his anger.

He turned on his heel and left the kitchen. Selena ran after him. "Graham, stop. I'm an adult here, remember? The least you could do is discuss it with me before you start barking orders to the staff. I'm not your child, and I refuse to allow you to treat me like one."

She ran out of the house, got in her van and drove down the driveway, too angry to stop when he called after her. She arrived at the school early and did some deep breathing exercises to cool down before classes let out.

She couldn't afford to alienate Graham from herself. They had to stand together to fight this thing or it would destroy them both. She wished now she had turned back when he called to her, if even for a few minutes.

Graham sought her out later in the evening. He paced the floor. "Selena, I'm sorry about what happened earlier. It's not my intention to treat you like a child. You're right; I should have talked to you about it first. I guess it's been too long since I've had to discuss things with anyone, and I forget to take that into consideration. I wish you'd told me about the calls. I could've had them traced and maybe we'd know who's behind it." The muscles over his jaws worked as he clenched his teeth in frustration.

"I'm sorry I spouted off at you, Graham. But, what do you say about a call where no one speaks? I had no idea when they started that they'd continue. I wasn't trying to keep anything from you. I just didn't want you to worry about me."

"It's a little late to be thinking about that, don't you think? As long as I'm married to you I'll worry about you. Especially with everything that's happened. I need you to tell me these things so I can do something about it." He willed himself to remain calm.

"All right. I promise not to spring any more surprises on you. Are we still on for the shopping trip to find a tree tomorrow? I could really use some time away from here."

"Me too. I'm looking forward to it."

She turned away from the look in his eyes; the look that always left her confused and puzzled.

"All right, this is what we're looking for." Graham turned to the children when they pulled into the Christmas tree sales lot. "No big open spaces. About this high, and bushy." Selena laughed as Trevor and Trina went out opposite sides of the car and ran to the area where the trees stood side by side.

"Nice try." She gave him a playful pat on the arm.

Graham took her hand as they walked together. They discussed the pros and cons of each tree.

"We found it!" they heard from the other side of the lot. Laughing, they ducked under branches as they looked for the children.

Selena looked at the tree in dismay. Lop sided, the top had been broken off.

"All right. Tell me what you like about it." Graham tried to be diplomatic. All they would say was, "We love it!" Selena smiled as he gave in and bought the tree. She winked at them as she walked between them, her arms around their shoulders, going back to the car.

Graham summoned Jerome as soon as they got home to help place the tree in the stand so it would stand upright. The tree topper would cover up the broken top. A couple snips with a trimmer evened the sides out nicely.

Trevor and Trina begged to begin decorating the tree. Graham and Selena carried the boxes of decorations into the family room.

"What do we do first?" Graham asked.

"We need to put the lights on first. Why don't you guys decide which ornaments you want to go on the tree and your dad and I will untangle the lights and wrap them around the tree."

They dug into the boxes as if looking for buried treasure. They had a hard time deciding; they wanted to put them all on. Selena looked over at them and laughed. They had named the piles of ornaments, one--definite, one--maybe, and one--never.

She took the light cords out of the boxes and Graham plugged them in to check for burned out bulbs that needed to be replaced. She stared at the tangled mess and sighed. They looked as if they'd been thrown in the box and the lid taped down before they all sprang out.

Selena suggested that Graham hold one end and she'd take the other and start the untangling process. She smiled as she glanced at him and found him watching her in fascination as she straightened the cord, weaving the line in and out. She draped the straightened cord over his shoulder.

The children's voices rang out as they argued over which pile to place the last of the ornaments on. Graham turned and suggested they leave the rest of them in the box. Selena saw the cords slip off his shoulder and grabbed for them at the same moment he turned back toward her.

They stopped as their faces came within an inch of touching. Her arm bent at the elbow, her hand fell across the back of his head, lying softly on his neck. She struggled to keep the cord from landing in a tangled pile at their feet.

He looked deep into her eyes and noticed that the sadness had disappeared. Her eyes wide with surprise, and her mouth slightly open, she stepped back, handing him the cord. He reached for her. When his hands touched her arms, she took another step back. He caught her as she stumbled over an empty box.

"Why don't we finish this later?" She tried to ignore her shaky voice. "I'll see if I can find us something to eat."

She went to the kitchen and sipped on a glass of water until she stopped shaking. Rummaging through the cabinets she found vegetable soup, then placed it on the stove to heat while she fixed sandwiches.

"What's the matter with me?" she asked herself a dozen times. "I work for the man. That's all. That's all The Agreement will allow. Besides, I don't even know if he's the kind of man I want to be involved with. There's still the letters to think about. Get hold of yourself, Selena."

They took a break from the decorating and ate dinner. When Selena went back to the family room, she found Graham had the rest of the cords untangled and ready to place on the tree. They handed them back and forth until the light bulbs outnumbered the pine needles, according to Graham. Trevor and Trina placed the ornaments on the tree, then wound the garland over the branches and placed the icicles on the very tips of each branch. They all declared the finished product the best decorated tree they'd ever seen. After the children went to bed, Selena stacked the empty boxes and took them to the back of the house to be carried out to the garage. She walked back into the family room after the last trip.

"Wait a minute, stop right there," Graham said as she walked through the doorway. He walked to where she stood and placed his hands on the doorframe behind her, an arm on each side of her head. He looked up. "This is an exception to The Agreement, so don't start with me."

She followed his gaze. Mistletoe hung from the doorframe overhead. Her eyes looked into his, her entire body motionless but taut, as he slowly leaned down. She closed her eyes and waited.

When his lips softly touched hers, her heart pounded, and then beat erratically. He backed slowly away, but she didn't notice. She could still feel the soft touch of his mustache against her cheek and the warmth of his lips against hers. She didn't move, leaning against the doorframe with her eyes closed.

Opening her eyes slowly, she saw him looking at her with a soft smile on his face and a light in his eyes. She smiled at him, not knowing what to say.

His eyes seemed glued to her face. The look that had puzzled her the last three months bathed her features. Suddenly it made sense. How had it happened? And when? And why had it taken her so long to realize that Graham Kensington loved her?

If he loved her that much could he possibly love someone else? What would he say if she asked him? If he denied it could she honestly say she believed him?

153

Chapter 12

Selena scanned her calendar for events of the coming week. Two weeks before Christmas, and she felt like she ran from one thing to another, barely able to keep up with everyone's schedules. School break promised a breather or she'd have threatened to hole up somewhere and refused to come out.

Tonight Trevor's class held their Christmas program; Wednesday, Trina's class did their performance; Thursday evening, the last practice for the Christmas program at church on Sunday; Friday both children planned to attend a combined Sunday school class party; Saturday, Graham's party with his associates. *Graham's party!* She almost forgot. The panic began to rise in her throat.

Graham talked to her long and hard one evening, convincing her to go to the party with him. Sure she would feel out of place, unable to fit in with his associates and their wives, she'd begged not to be included. What could she say when he said the one thing that always swayed her to his opinion? "We want to show people how happily married we are and that I'm taking good care of you, don't we?" She reluctantly agreed, then determined not to think about it until the time actually arrived.

"What am I going to wear? I have no idea what people wear to these things. I could ask Graham, but he'd think I don't have a brain in my head. Oh, boy. How do I ever get myself into these messes?" She moaned aloud. "I could go shopping, but I don't even know what to look for. I'll think about it later. This would be a good day for a brisk walk."

Selena dressed in her jeans and flannel shirt, heavy socks, and hiking shoes. Pulling a sweatshirt with a hood over her head, she put on her heavy coat, gloves, and scarf and stepped out into the cold December air. The sun shone bright, but the temperatures remained in the twenties with a brisk wind. Hurrying her pace, she followed the driveway to the road.

She'd walked about a half mile when she met Sue Blakely walking towards her. "Sue! I haven't seen you out for a long time. Want to walk with me?"

Sue turned around and walked with Selena as she finished her mile one way and turned and walked back. They chatted about church activities, families, and upcoming holiday events. As they approached Serendipity Estates, Selena said, "Would you like to go horseback riding with me?"

"Sure. I haven't done that for a long time," Sue said. Jerome threw fresh hay to the horses in the stable. As the women walked in Selena greeted him. "Good morning, Jerome. We're going to take Star and Lightning out for a ride."

"Good morning, Ma'am. Good day to be outside. Good morning, Mrs. Blakely. Good to see you again." He placed a saddle on Lightning. "This one's a little frisky this morning. You'll need to keep a tight rein on him."

They walked the horses to warm them up then set off for the trail. "I noticed you and Jerome knew each other. How did you meet?"

Sue looked at her strangely, then laughed. "I dated Graham for a while before I married Ollie. I thought you knew."

Selena laughed. "No, I didn't know that

They rode on the trail, then to Sue's estate, smaller but equally as nice as Serendipity Estate. Selena led Lightning home as she rode Star, and took them both to the stable.

"Thanks, Jerome."

"At your service, Ma'am."

She smiled. A recently recurring thought came to mind. Did she really want to leave in March? These people treated her like family.

Graham, in the kitchen getting a cup of coffee, looked up when Selena walked in from outside. "Out for a ride I see. Who's your riding buddy?"

"Sue Blakely. Said she used to date you. Interesting how many women have told me that." She laughed. Suddenly she remembered Trina's very vocal statement at breakfast several weeks earlier.

Selena's eyes grew wide with understanding as she stared at him. His face turned red as she exclaimed, "Is that the Sue that Trina mentioned? The mushy kisses? I don't believe it!"

"Would you stop? It wasn't like that at all. It was just a kiss. I didn't even know the kids were around. It was nothing. Honestly, nothing."

Selena smiled, a gleam in her eye. "Nothing, huh? Then why are you protesting so vehemently? And why is your face red? Nothing, huh? I wonder." Graham waved her away and walked out of the kitchen.

"Graham." Selena stopped him. When he turned around she blew him a kiss and laughed. He smiled and kept on going.

The doorbell rang and Babs went to the door. A deliveryman needed a signature.

"Who is it?" Selena called out.

"A delivery, Ma'am. I'll take it to Mr. Kensington."

"I can take it to him."

"I'm sorry, Ma'am. I've been instructed to take all packages to Mr. Kensington."

Selena stopped. So it had come to this. She couldn't answer the phone. She couldn't answer the door. She couldn't receive packages. She couldn't get the mail. She stomped into Graham's office as Babs walked out.

"What're you going to do next, hire a body guard to follow me everywhere I go? I'm beginning to feel like a prisoner in my own home, if this is my home. Sometimes I feel like I'm a visitor that should go home."

Graham, unprepared for the outburst, blinked his eyes several times. "What's this all about? Why didn't you dump this on me five minutes ago?"

"Because five minutes ago I didn't know that I'm not to answer the door or accept packages. I found out yesterday that I'm not to get the mail. That on top of not answering the phone makes me feel pretty unimportant around here." She could hear herself starting to babble. The reasons for the decisions appeared evident. The tensions of the situation had built to where she felt that if one more thing happened she would not be functioning well.

Graham took a deep breath as he got up and walked over to her. He wanted to hold her, but she backed away. Crossing his arms, he noticed the pain in her eyes. "Honey, the reason I've made those decisions is because I don't want you to get hurt. I don't know what we're dealing with yet; I don't know what someone might do."

"You said you'd talk to me about these decisions before you talked to anyone else. Once again I'm the last to know. Thanks a lot. I may as well go back to Columbus. At least I was appreciated there." She tried unsuccessfully to stop the tears and the irrational statements.

Graham walked to the window and stared sightlessly into the bright morning sky. Why did he always hurt the person he cared the most about? He stuffed his hands in his pockets and wondered why life with Selena had to hurt so much. He heard a sound behind him and saw the tears running down her cheeks. She closed the door behind her as she left. He went to the door to call her back. She'd disappeared.

Selena left his office and went to the Closet. Kneeling by one of the chairs, she poured her heart out to God. She stayed there until she received the peace she so desperately searched for every day in this place. She longed for a normal life, not this constant upheaval, wondering what would happen next.

She went to her room, washed her face, changed her clothes, practiced smiling in front of the mirror, then went downstairs to place a call to the caterer regarding some questions about the Open House. Last minute decisions, already in the discussions since the caterer had several bookings for the next three weeks, kept her busy.

The next evening after the children went to bed, Graham looked for Selena and found her in the family room reading a book. She'd been cordial since their discussion the day before, but he could see the pain remained in her eyes. He sat down on the sofa beside her as she placed a marker in her book.

"Selena, I didn't mean to hurt you. And I'm sorry I didn't tell you. I could say again I'm not used to discussing my decisions with anyone, but I don't know how many times you'll accept that as a good excuse. What can I do to make it better for you?"

"Nothing, Graham. I'm just going to have to accept the fact that things are crazy here. You have to understand that as long as I can remember I've made my own decisions. I'm not used to being told what I can and can't do. It's a bittersweet pill. I don't like being treated like a child that has no say in family decisions, but I really appreciate you caring enough about me to want to protect me. All of this seems like overkill to me. I'm trying to accept that this is the way it is. I'm sorry I yelled at you yesterday. You didn't deserve that

He rubbed his thumb lightly on her cheek. "I'd give all I have in this world to make things different for us if I could. I'll try--I promise I'll try--to remember to talk to you if anything else happens. Promise me one thing. Please don't leave us. Hearing you say that hurts more than anything else you could say or do."

He sounded so convincing. She wanted to move into his arms and have him hold her like he did one night, all night, not so long ago. The Agreement. It shouldn't have happened then, and she wouldn't let it happen now.

"I won't leave. I promised I'd stay. I just meant that was the way I felt, not that I actually planned to do it."

"I have something for you." He left and returned promptly. He held out a box, explaining that this package had caused all the commotion the day before.

Taking the lid off, she gasped. She lifted a green velvet dress from the folds of the tissue paper. The bodice, closely fitted with a wide band of satin ribbon around the top that fit snugly under the arms, attached to the skirt below the waist. Spaghetti straps of the satin ribbon went over the shoulders. The skirt, with a slightly flared style, looked to be shorter than her normal length. Laying aside the tissue paper in the box she found a short jacket of matching material that had a satin underlay, and long closely fitting sleeves. Brocade lace started at each shoulder and went halfway down the front opening.

Graham saw the look on her face and knew he'd made a good decision. "I thought you might want a new dress to wear to my party Saturday evening."

"How did you know?" She laughed. "I didn't even know what kind of dress to look for."

Saturday evening, as Selena dressed for the party, she sorted through her jewelry box, trying to find pieces to complement her new dress. Surprised when she put the dress on that it fit perfectly, she remembered the shopping trip and Graham's interest in her outfits.

She moaned when she thought about the jewelry unable to find pieces that she thought looked nice enough with the dress. Hearing a tap on the adjoining door, she said, "Come in."

Graham walked in dressed in a three-piece black suit, with a red and black geometric design in his tie and a matching handkerchief in his pocket.

"Wow!" Selena couldn't hide the admiration. "You look great."

"Thanks. I planned to give this to you for Christmas, but I'd like to have you wear it tonight."

Untying the package, she found two boxes. Opening the smaller one, her eyes widened. Diamond earrings nestled in a bed of cotton, the most beautiful setting she'd ever seen. Two diamond teardrops dangled from a flower design. With tears in her eyes she opened the other package. The light from the chandelier sparkled off the diamonds in a matching necklace.

Selena looked at him and tried to smile. Instead her lip trembled. Grabbing a tissue she dabbed at her eyes to catch the tears before they smeared her makeup.

"How can I ever thank you?"

He spoke softly. "You already have. Here, let me help you with the necklace." He draped it around her neck and fastened it as she held her hair up.

His fingers touched her neck. She felt the feathery touch at the base of her spine. She watched him in the mirror. He lifted his eyes and their gaze held for a long moment in the reflection.

Turning, she thanked him, said she would be ready to go in a few moments, and busied herself with last minute details.

He closed the door, leaned against it and took a deep breath. Did he dare approach her about renegotiation of The Agreement before March? Things had developed faster than he initially thought they would. *How much longer can I keep up the pretense that I like things just the way they are?* Selena, put at ease immediately when they arrived at the party, relaxed and joined in the conversation around her. Graham stayed close to her all evening, either holding her hand or placing his hand on her elbow. The wives of the men he worked with, open and friendly, found common interests to discuss with her. Graham introduced her as his new wife amidst hearty congratulations from all of them.

"Did you enjoy yourself?" He broke the silence as they rode home.

"Yes, very much. Thanks for inviting me."

"Selena! What do I have to say to convince you I *want* you beside me? It wasn't *just* an invitation. I wanted you to meet these people. And I wanted them to meet you, my wife, the most beautiful woman in the world."

"You don't have to do this now."

"This is not a have to, this is a want to."

Selena went to her room and sat on the edge of her bed, thinking about the events of the evening. She had hoped to gain some insight into his business from conversations with his associates. The people had treated her with respect and included her as if she'd always been part of their group. But, no one talked business. It had been strictly a social gathering. She'd been deeply moved by the way each person laced his or her remarks with the work of God in each life. What was this group that Graham worked with? Were they all certified public accountants? No business names had been mentioned. Did everyone there assume she knew? How could so many people work for or with an organization that size and no one talk about it? One would think that in a group of a hundred people someone would've said something. *I guess I'll have to be patient. Graham said he would tell me everything someday.*

Sylvan invited them to spend Christmas Day with him. Trevor and Trina could hardly contain their excitement as the holiday drew near. Their parties and programs over, they looked forward to family Christmas events.

The program at the church had been deemed the best ever. Some of the choir members already talked about how they could do something better next year.

Selena promised Trevor and Trina that after the first big snowfall they could go sledding down the hill behind the corral. Every night before they went to bed the children prayed for snow. Selena grinned, remembering saying the same prayers herself at their age.

The next morning they looked out the window. It had started snowing during the night. Unfortunately, the wind blew the snow in circles and lowered the wind chill temperatures to the single digits. Selena would not allow the children outside in such conditions. *Today would be a good day to go to the garage and finish those boxes I started last fall.*

After breakfast, Selena passed Babs in the hall. "Babs, if anyone needs me I'll be in the garage."

She caught the door before it banged against the house as a gust of wind blew hard against it. Bracing herself she walked to the side door of the garage and stepped inside. She went to the corner where she'd stacked the boxes. *That's strange. They've been moved. Maybe they were too close to Graham's car and he couldn't get in or out.*

Opening a box that had no writing on the outside, she stared in disbelief. The packers had wrapped everything. Now all of the glass and ceramic items lay unwrapped and the paper lay loose in the box. Setting that one aside she opened another one. Personal papers that had been placed in file folders now lay outside the folders. What would anyone have been looking for?

She walked into Graham's office and waited for him to finish typing. She paced back and forth from his desk to the window. Had she not promised him that she would tell him about anything unusual, she wouldn't even be here. She'd avoided being alone with him since his Christmas party. Still shaken by the feelings that had risen to the surface during the kiss they shared under the mistletoe and the time they spent together at his party, she decided not to let it happen again.

Stopping his typing, he listened to her account of the problem with her boxes, put on his coat and followed her to the garage. "I'm going to file a report with the police. How long do you think it will take to determine if anything is missing?"

"Probably all day if I have to go through every box. I'll have to rewrap all the glass items and sort through all the papers."

Graham called and filed the report then stayed and helped wrap the breakable items. When they had examined all the boxes, except the one with the personal files, Jerome carried the boxes with the files into the house and she finished the examination in the family room. As far as she could determine nothing was missing.

"Selena, I'm going to have Jerome carry all your boxes to the vacant room next to his and lock it. I'll call tomorrow and have a locksmith change the lock and give you the only key. Are you comfortable with that?"

Selena smiled. "Yes. Thank you." At least he told her before it happened. He'd kept his promise.

One thing became very clear when she finished sorting her files late that night. The portfolio had been taken, or misplaced, or something. She stared at the wall for a long time. *Now what? How am I going to find out where I've sent the money?*

Christmas with Sylvan Kensington became a warm memory for Selena. They got up early and drove an hour to his house east of Dayton. She hadn't been told that a family tradition of attending a Christmas Day service at his church began several years ago. She apologized for not dressing for the occasion.

Sylvan placed his arm across her shoulders and squeezed her shoulder against him. "You look fine. I'm just glad you came with them. This is indeed a pleasure."

When Sylvan and Graham exchanged knowing looks she wondered what it was all about.

The theme woven throughout the service spoke of peace and Selena listened with an ache deep inside. Would she ever experience the kind of peace the angels spoke about so long ago?

They returned to Sylvan's house where he served cinnamon rolls, fruit, and hot drinks. Trevor and Trina fidgeted and played with their food but did well in curtailing their energy.

Finally, Sylvan laughed and said, "All right, kids. Bring them out." They walked quickly to the other end of the house and made several trips back, stacking gifts in the middle of the family room floor.

Selena looked around. Graham's parents had surrounded themselves with expensive things. Several paintings hung on the walls, either original works by well-known artists, or very good copies. The plush furniture and the carpet reminded her of that which decorated the rooms at Serendipity Estate. The house, smaller then Graham's, had the same touch of elegance.

Trevor and Trina sorted through the gifts, stacking each box beside the person whose name had been written on it. Graham laughed. "I wonder which of those stacks belong to the children."

"Probably this little one over here with my name on it. I bet I marked those boxes wrong."

The children protested good-naturedly as everyone laughed.

Everyone opened packages at once. Selena laughed as she watched paper, bows, and boxes fly in every direction. She heard comments like, "cool", "wow", and "great" above the ripping and the rustle.

Graham looked at Selena and saw the contentment on her face. Looking a little closer he realized the sadness around her eyes which had become her constant companion until the night they decorated the tree had not returned. He grinned, feeling some contentment of his own.

Selena, watching the children, almost forgot about her packages. She unwrapped the largest one, laid aside the tissue paper in the box, and took out a multicolored silk neck scarf.

"Thank you so much. This is beautiful." She smiled at Sylvan.

The second package, about envelope size, looked small and felt flat. Opening it carefully, she read the name of a travel agency on the outside of a small brochure. Puzzled, she turned the front flap back and found a paper on the inside that read, "Redeem as soon as possible to your favorite international destination." Holding it up, she looked at Sylvan. "What's this about?"

Sylvan grinned. "Am I correct to assume that my son has not taken you on a proper honeymoon yet?"

Selena looked at Graham who grinned sheepishly and shrugged his shoulders. "Well, no, he hasn't."

"Then choose two weeks, make X's on every day on his calendar, and drag him off to some exotic port of your choice. All you have to do is contact the travel agency, make the arrangements and go. If <u>you</u> don't do it, it will never get done. Believe me, I know my son." Sylvan ignored voiced objections from Graham as he directed his remarks to Selena. She smiled, enjoying the obvious affection between father and son.

They had their own gift exchange that evening at home. Selena's eyes teared up, overwhelmed with the gifts from the children. Trina gave her a set of perfume and powder, an expensive line at the department store in the mall. Trevor gave her leather gloves and a silk scarf to wear with her coat to church. Graham handed her a box, gift wrapped in the most beautiful paper she'd ever seen. Carefully loosening the tape, she unwrapped the box and removed the lid. A knit sweater of soft yarn, decorated with ribbon and pearls, lay folded in layers of tissue paper. She found matching slacks in the bottom.

Selena tiptoed through the paper to Trina and gave her a long hug and a kiss. Stepping over the boxes she gave Trevor a hug and a kiss, then looked at Graham, not sure what to do. To do nothing would be too obvious a slight in front of the children. To do the same, would be an infraction of The Agreement. She hesitated.

I have to do something. Walking over to his chair, she said hesitantly, "Thanks, Graham. It's beautiful." Leaning down she kissed him quickly on the cheek. *That's in The Agreement, right?* She quickly went back to look at the games they'd given the children.

Graham sighed inwardly. It was a response, but much less than he anticipated.

Selena gave Graham a desk set that he'd admired once when they went shopping together. He almost remarked about the money that she'd spent, then thought better of it. He knew how much it cost, much more than she'd have spent on herself. Would he ever get her past counting every penny?

One of the traditions of their family had been to place the outgrown toys from past years in a box to make room for the new ones. As they did that, Selena gathered up the paper and boxes to be disposed of the next day. Placing her gifts together to be carried to her room, she looked at Graham and said, "What do you want me to do with this certificate from your dad?"

He thought for a moment. "Why don't you put it in your safe in your closet? That seems to be about as secure a place as any right now

"Do you think he'll say anything if we don't use it right away?"

"We'll deal with it if and when he does. Don't worry about it. Why don't you go ahead and choose a time when you'd like to go and I'll see if I can get my schedule together."

What did he mean by that? Did that mean he thought they would still be together after they renegotiated The Agreement in March?

"Graham, what did your dad mean today about just being glad I was there?"

He looked at her thoughtfully and decided he may as well tell her the truth. She would find out eventually anyway. "Kate always made excuses about not going to their place for Christmas. I went alone with the children every year except one while she was living."

Selena looked at him, puzzled. Not be part of a family Christmas? She couldn't imagine why Kate had made that choice.

Later she unlocked the box in the bottom of her closet and placed the gift certificate on top. She fingered it slowly before she closed the lid. Would they ever really take the trip that Sylvan had so generously paid for?

She sat on the side of the bed with her hand on the switch to turn out the lamp. Glancing at the sofa, she caught her breath. The light reflected off a pink ribbon. She slowly walked to the sofa and removed the familiar looking envelope from between the cushions.

The writing on it looked different but the name on it was the same: Kate Kensington. She laid it on the sofa without opening it. Maybe she should give it to Graham and let him do with it what he wanted. Then again there might be information in the letter that she needed to know that he wouldn't tell her if he saw it first. Quickly, before she changed her mind, she slipped the ribbon off and took the paper out of the envelope.

Dear Kate,

I can't believe you'd stay there and let him do that to you. Those bruises you showed me were nasty looking. What will it be the next time? Will he push you down the stairs? Are you just going to stand there and let your husband hit you? You need to call the police and have him arrested for assault and battery. Why you stay and take that I will never know! When you get enough, call me. You always have a place here with me.

Love always,
Bud

Selena sat down on the chair, her legs weak, her mind in a whirl. What would Graham do if she gave him the letter? True or false he'd certainly deny the accusation and there'd probably be another scene like the one when he read the last letter. If he got angry would he turn on her? *Dear Lord, how am I ever going to get the answers? I thought it was safe here with him. How could I have been so wrong?*

The next day the sun shown bright, making a dazzling display on the snow that had fallen during the night. The wind blew itself to some other part of the country, leaving the air cold, but tolerable, with the sun in a cloudless sky. Trevor and

169

Trina again begged to get the sled out. Selena laughed and gave in. In spite of the new toys the school recess would drag on forever if they didn't get out and run off their energy.

Instructing them to put on warm clothing, she looked for Jerome to get the sled from its storage place. The children met her at the door as she pulled it behind her to the house, their coats half buttoned and carrying their hats. Finally bundled up, they took off at a run to the hill behind the corral. "Hey, you forgot something. Don't you want to take the sled with you

As they pulled the sled behind them she stooped down and scooped up a handful of snow to see how well it packed together. Heaving it towards the children, it landed on the sled. They ran faster to dodge the snowballs.

Graham caught a movement outside of his office window. Turning his chair, he saw the three of them heading for the hill with the sled. He grinned. It'd been a long time since he'd played in the snow with the children. He watched Selena throw the snowballs and a thought went through his mind.

Selena heard the back door of the house close and turned around to see who came out. Surprised to see Graham all bundled up in boots, hat, scarf and gloves, she stopped until he caught up with them. "Is everything all right?"

"Sure." He grinned and took her hand. "Why should you guys have all the fun?"

Remembering the letter from the night before, Selena couldn't be sure if the pounding of her heart came from his interest in her at this moment, the way he looked at her, or from the doubts that had begun to surface in her mind about his character. He surely wouldn't do anything in front of the children. *I'll just forget it and have fun today.*

They found the steepest part of the hill and made dozens of flights down. At least they felt like flights to Selena, and

170

from the squeals of the children they thought so, too. Finally tired of climbing back up the hill, Selena pushed them off and built a snow fort large enough for two people to duck behind.

Trina helped her pack the snow and make snowballs. They worked quickly, hoping to begin the attack as soon as Graham and Trevor came back from the ride down the hill.

Stooping down, Selena said softly to Trina, "Now!" and they both threw at the same time. Trina's snowball flew way off target, but Selena's hit Trevor on the leg.

"Hey! Dad, look what they did!" Thus began a fast exchange of snowballs. Graham threw his to destroy the fort, which turned out to be pretty successful. Selena threw hers to hit whatever moving target she could find. Trevor and Trina threw in the general direction of the enemy. When the fort lay in ruins, providing no protection, Selena and Trina stood up laughing and threw one snowball after another. Advancing on Graham and Trevor, Selena laughed. By the time she stood in front of Graham, trying to make new snowballs, she collapsed in the snow. She looked up and saw the look of glee on his face as he walked towards her with a snowball in each hand.

"Oh, no!" She screamed as she tried to run. Their footprints had packed the snow all over the top of the hill, leaving no traction for their boots. Her feet slid out from under her and she went headfirst down the opposite side of the hill from where the sleds had gone.

Graham started after her, his feet ahead of the rest of his body as he slid down the hill beside her. She grabbed a handful of snow on the way down to retaliate whatever he had planned. When her body stopped moving next to the woods where the riding trail started, she sat up and looked around for Graham. Startled, her eyes followed the trail as far as she could see.

Graham slid into her trying to right himself. He heard her say, "Graham, were you out walking this morning?"

"No. This is the first I've been out all day. Why?"

"Whose footprints are those, then? They had to have been made today since it snowed so much last night."

He dropped his snowballs and stared. Who *would* be walking in the woods on a day like this? Had the prints been made before they came out or had someone been watching them? Either way, why? Feeling uneasy, he said, "Selena, please take the children back to the house. I'm going to see where these came from. "Graham, please be careful."
Hearing the fear in her voice, he touched the back of his gloved hand to her cheek and said reassuringly, "Of course

By the time Graham walked back to the house, the children had dry clothes on, drinking hot chocolate. He smiled for Selena's sake. "Must have been someone out for a walk. The footprints went to the stream and came back." He purposely failed to mention that the one set joined with another that had come in from the road that bordered the property. The marks of tires on the side of the road indicated someone had parked a vehicle there.

Making an excuse to change into dry clothes, Graham went to his room and called the police with one more report to add to the files. He suggested if they investigate that they begin with the footprints from the road, so as not to unduly frighten his family.

A flurry of activity ensued the next week as the caterer made one delivery after another of items needed for the Open House on Saturday evening. By Friday Selena wished she'd never thought of the idea. Her head spun with trying to remember all the details. Graham stayed in his office all day, out of the way. The children had trouble containing their excitement because this would be the first time they'd received permission to attend the party.

Joyce took all the phone calls and sounded very informed on the phone, but grumbled all week about not being included in the preparations or the serving. Selena tried to explain to her that without a caterer the task loomed too large. It didn't seem to change her attitude.

Saturday morning, Graham approached Selena who looked stressed. "You don't have to take this on yourself. That's why we hired a caterer, remember? Why don't you go to your room and get out of the way? If anyone has any questions I'll answer them, and I'll get the phone. I'll keep the kids occupied. You need to rest. I don't want you sick by this evening

Selena managed to take a short nap and remain in her room for a couple hours. She felt better when she wandered into the kitchen for lunch. Several people she didn't know arranged trays and decorated the formal living room as well as the dining room table where they planned to serve the refreshments. Everything seemed to be under control. She went to the family room where she spent the rest of the afternoon reading.

Choosing her green dress for this occasion that Graham had given her to wear for his Christmas Party, she also wore the diamonds he'd given her to complement it. When she walked downstairs, minutes before the guests were scheduled to arrive, he stood at the bottom of the stairs and watched her. Her face warmed at his look of appreciation, and the kiss he planted on the back of her hand. He looked into her eyes and whispered, "Lovely." She pushed the feelings of confusion down to an unconscious level. *I don't have time right now to deal with all the questions.*

The invited guests arrived during the designated hours. Graham and Selena made an effort to speak personally to each one. She noticed how relaxed he looked in a setting like this. He made a perfect host. He caught her eye across the room several times during the evening and winked at her. By the time the last guest had departed, she felt exhausted, but deeply satisfied that she'd pleased Graham and had also enjoyed the

time she spent as hostess of Serendipity Estate.   S h e
stretched out on the sofa in the family room for a few minutes
before going upstairs. Graham finished putting the children to
bed and found her there.

"You were wonderful, Selena." He leaned down and
kissed her on the cheek. Unconsciously, she reached up and
placed her hand on his face. Moving his lips down her cheek,
he found her mouth, and lightly kissed her. She responded to
the kiss and smiled as he walked out.

Her eyes popped open. She sat straight up on the sofa.
Her feet hit the floor. She stood up and paced back and forth
across the room. How could this have happened? It wasn't
supposed to happen, was it? She'd come here to do a job, not
fall in love with Graham Kensington.

For it'd suddenly occurred to her that there wasn't
anywhere else on earth she would rather be than right here with
Graham and the children. Sure, things were crazy here, but
hadn't Graham said that if they stood together things would get
better? He'd become the central person in her life and she
didn't want anyone else there. She couldn't imagine life
without him.

But, how could she have these feelings when there were
all those things about him in the letters? Had he really been
unfaithful to his wife? Was he capable of hurting her? If he'd
done all those things to Kate how could Ken say his character
was impeccable? Could he have hidden all those things from
Ken?

Graham walked out of the family room, wanting to take
Selena in his arms, tell her how much he loved her, how much
he enjoyed her warmth, her personality, her strength in the face
of terror, but he couldn't do that until they renegotiated The
Agreement. He lost count of the number of times he wished
he'd never signed the thing. But, then she would never have

come here and he didn't know which would have been worse. Oh, well, it was done now. But, his patience had worn thin.

He started up the stairway, turned around, and walked toward his office. Passing the office door, he unlocked the door to the Closet and fell on his knees in the dark. A long time later he found the peace he sought, and retraced his footsteps to his room.

Chapter 13

An Arctic freeze grabbed hold of the area the first of January and wouldn't let go. Selena shivered as she looked at the thermometer. The mercury hadn't risen above zero for a week and a half. The snow that fell during the holidays turned solid, crunching with every step. Too frigid to stand outside, each morning she drove Trevor and Trina to the end of the driveway to wait on the bus. All of the evening activities had been cancelled. She breathed a prayer of thanksgiving.

She walked to Graham's office to check for her mail, then changed her mind and opened the door to the Closet. She looked forward to their weekly prayer times, even though her new feelings for him left her wondering about the wisdom of spending a lot of time with him, anywhere. He pushed the boundaries of The Agreement to the limit, and she liked it too much. Too much, considering the allegations made in the letters.

She went into the room and turned the light down low, hoping no one would notice. Picking up the Bible she turned to the fifth chapter of Ephesians and started reading at the twenty-second verse. "Wives submit to your husband as to the Lord."

She stopped. The first sentence spelled trouble. Submitting to the Lord had been a slow process but one she did without pain as her understanding grew. She'd submitted to Howard, and he'd abused the authority she'd given him. Verbally she had married again, but had she ever thought out the Biblical concept of marriage?

Once again the guilt surfaced. Not being in right relationship with Graham caused its own set of problems. But, she'd justified that decision for four months. Now, according to this scripture, she'd jeopardized her relationship with God also.

She thought she had everything covered with the thirty-third verse, her relationship with God and Graham, the respect she had for Graham. That had led to the change in her feelings for him.

But, submission? That would mean talking to him now about renegotiating The Agreement. That would also mean telling him the information in the letters. *Am I ready for that? What if he does to me what the letters say he did to Kate? At least Howard didn't hit me!*

She poured her heart out to God. For the first time since arriving at Serendipity Estate she admitted her fears, her insecurities, and her wrong attitudes. The scripture verses 'With God all things are possible', and 'I can do all things through Christ who gives me strength' spun in circles in her mind. Tears of repentance coursed down her cheeks as she opened her heart and spirit to the cleansing, healing Spirit of God.

On her way to the kitchen for lunch, she stopped by Graham's office to pick up her mail. Not getting an answer to the knock on the door, she pushed the door open and went in. He'd stepped out.

Walking to the desk to pick up her mail, she caught sight of a movement outside; someone was walking toward the house from the stable. She watched closely, mystified, trying to recognize the figure. Who would be out at the stable at this time of day? It definitely wasn't Jerome and he was the only one who had business out there. *Get hold of yourself, Selena, you're getting paranoid.*

As she walked to the kitchen she saw Graham approaching. "I stopped and picked up my mail. Hope you didn't mind."

"Of course not. I wanted to tell you I took a phone call from Trevor. He wanted to know if three of his friends could come over for a couple hours after school. I told him I didn't think it would be a problem. I hope I didn't inconvenience you by giving him permission."

"No. No inconvenience at all. He'll still have plenty of time to do his homework. And that will give me a chance to spend some quality time with Trina. I haven't done that for awhile. Thanks for letting me know."

He watched her walk away. Shaking his head, he returned to his office. Several minutes later he finally pulled his thoughts together enough to focus on the business in front of him. He'd have to talk to her soon. The Agreement would have to be dealt a deathblow one way or the other. Figuring out how to do it with the least amount of confusion needed some thought.

In the middle of the afternoon Selena drove to the road and quickly packed five energetic children into her van as the bus pulled away. Trina jumped into the front seat with a pronouncement of "Yuck! Boys!" Before they were halfway to the house, she asked when she could have her friends over. Selena laughed. She wondered how long she would have to wait for that question. "We'll talk about it when we get in the house."

Selena fixed hot chocolate and set out a plate of cookies for the boys. Putting her arm around Trevor's shoulder, she asked if he and his friends would please stay in the family room. And, yes they could go to the kitchen for more drinks. He pulled away from her and sullenly agreed.

Selena took Trina's hand and allowed the child to lead her to her room. "What would you like to do this afternoon?"

"Let's play a game on my computer."

Selena looked around while Trina turned on her computer. Trina had more things in her room than Selena and all of her sisters had owned collectively. Selena marveled at the children's unpretentiousness in the face of so much wealth.

Spying a picture propped on the bedside stand, Selena picked it up and studied it. She could see Trina in the face of the woman along with the same long blond hair, blue eyes, and doll-like features. *Kate.*

"Trina, where did you get this picture? I never saw it out before."

"That's my mom. Daddy gave it to me a long time ago. Sometimes I put it in the drawer." Trina's tone was nonchalant.

"Why do you put it in your drawer?"

"She's not real. I want a real mom. But, since I can't have a real mom I look at her sometimes. Is it a bad thing if I don't remember her?"

Speechless, Selena stared first at the picture and then at the child. Where had Trina gotten the idea she couldn't have a real mom?

Remembering that she waited for an answer, Selena said quickly, "No, honey, it's not a bad thing. You were so little when she went to Heaven that it would be hard for you to remember her. It's nice your daddy gave you this picture. She's really pretty, isn't she?"

Selena sat beside Trina and put her arm around her. "Why do you say you can't have a real mom?"

Trina hung her head. "I asked Daddy if you could be my mom and he said not now. I guess he doesn't want me to have a mom. Everybody in my class has a mom but me."

Selena felt the tears begin to form. Trina didn't understand Graham's answer to her question. *How can I explain that things could change, that the answer could be a temporary one?*

The Agreement had once again caused more problems than it solved. And the letters raised questions that begged for answers. But where would she find them?

Selena gave her a hug, kissed her on the cheek, and declared she would beat her at her game. It turned out to be an empty declaration. Trina won all the games they played and announced the fact the entire evening to anyone who would listen.

During dinner Trevor had little to say. He went upstairs to do his homework without being told. The food put away and the kitchen cleaned up, Selena knocked on his door and walked in at his acknowledgement.

"Did you have a good time this afternoon with your friends? I wanted to thank you for your good behavior." She began awkwardly, not knowing where to start to get him to talk about whatever bothered him.

"Why are you doing this? I wish you'd just leave me alone."

Stunned, Selena stared at him. "Have I said or done something I shouldn't have?"

"You're always touching me and you're not my mom and I don't like it."

"I'm sorry, Trevor. I didn't know. I won't do it again."

She went to the family room and picked up a book. She couldn't concentrate. She tried looking at a magazine, but only turned the pages without reading them.

First, Trina wanted a mom, then Trevor didn't. Trina's statement made more sense than Trevor's did. Why all of a sudden did Trevor not want to have anything to do with her?

She went to the kitchen to heat some water to make tea. Seeing Graham walk down the steps she waited for him to catch up with her.

"The children are ready for bed. You don't have to go back up," he said as he followed her to the kitchen.

Sitting at the table in the dining nook, Selena said, "I had a conversation with Trevor this evening after dinner. I noticed he'd developed an attitude about something. He said

181

I'm always touching him and he doesn't like it. I apologized and left, but I don't know what to make of it."

Graham smiled. "Oh, yes. The ten-year-touch-me-not stage. It's a guy thing. He'll eventually outgrow it. In the meantime don't worry too much about it. He wants to know you care about him, he just doesn't want you to show it.

"I thought he hated me." Should she tell him about Trina? For some reason she hesitated. That would open up other issues she didn't want to deal with yet.

She said good night and went to her room. Turning out the light she opened the drapes at the balcony door. The moon reflected a yellow glow on the landscape, magnifying the details of the fence around the corral and the branches of the trees. Shadows fell across the snow like sentinels standing at attention.

A movement in the moonlight caught her eye. She backed into the room, watching the base of the old oak tree. Two figures stepped out of the shadows, both looking towards the balcony, one pointing in her direction.

Her heart pounded. She knocked sharply on the adjoining door and yelled for Graham. *He has to be in there! If not, where did he go? Why's he never there when I need him?* She panicked. The figures hadn't moved.

She pulled her hand back to pound on the door again. It opened suddenly and Graham ran into the room. Not seeing her in the dark, he collided with her, her arms flailing, trying to find something to grab onto to stop the momentum. His body against hers, they stumbled across the room and fell onto her bed. He rolled over and landed on the floor with a thud, frantically asking, "What's the matter? Are you all right? Selena? What is it? What's the matter?"

"The oak tree by the corral. There's someone down there looking this way and pointing. I saw them." She struggled to remain calm and not let the hysteria take over.

He went quickly to the door and stared into the darkness. "Where? Come and show me. Where are they?"

Selena stood beside him. No one was there. "They stood right there on the left side. I saw them. Really. I did

Graham turned to walk out and Selena grabbed his arm. "You have to believe me. I'm not making this up. Please believe me!" Graham placed his hands on her shoulders. "I believe you. I'm going to go check it out."

"No! Don't go down there. Please don't go down there. You could get hurt. Graham, please don't go." She could hear the hysteria creeping into her voice as she clung to him.

He gently pried her fingers from his arms. "I'll take Jerome with me. I need to go down there tonight. Tomorrow may be too late. Pray, Selena." He rubbed her cheek with his finger.

She watched from the balcony door as Graham and Jerome walked to the oak tree. They shone flashlights several feet around the base of the tree. Remaining there for what seemed to her like hours, they finally returned to the house and she heard him open the door to his room. He tapped on the adjoining door and entered.

"We found one footprint. That was all. Could you tell from this distance if it was men or women?"

She shook her head. "It's too far away."

"It doesn't matter. I'll report it to the police. The footprint looked too large for a woman's shoe."

Selena sat on the sofa and shook. What did they want from her? She felt knots in her stomach as the fear returned. She didn't want to cry, not in front of Graham; she wanted to be strong. A sob escaped before she could stop it.

Graham moved to her side and took her hand. "We're going to make it, honey. I promise."

She took a couple ragged breaths. "I'm all right. You need to get some sleep. I'll see you in the morning."

He walked back to his room, torn between insisting on sleeping on her sofa, and honoring the terms of The Agreement. He didn't sleep much, expecting another knock on his door. He heard her moving around in her room most of the night. In the gray light of morning he fell asleep after wrestling all night with his emotions, his dreams, and reality.

They both arrived on time for breakfast. She'd covered up the dark circles with make up. They kept the conversation lively for Trevor and Trina. Selena took them to the bus stop and went into town to run errands.

She carried her packages into the kitchen and set them on the counter where Joyce would find them. Walking to Graham's office to pick up her mail, she found him staring despondently out of the window.

Instead of picking up her mail, she took his hand, pulled him out of his chair and led him down the hallway to the Closet. Locking the door she sat down on one of the chairs and waited for him to do the same. He slowly sat down, not looking at her.

Finally she broke the silence. "I can't go on like this, Graham. Every time I turn around someone scares me out of my wits. I find myself looking over my shoulder everywhere I go. I'm getting paranoid, thinking everyone is out to get me. I don't know who I can trust, and I find myself getting suspicious of everyone's actions and motives. I was upset the other day because I saw Babs coming out of my room, until I remembered it was cleaning day. It felt crazy being suspicious of Babs."

Graham reached over and took her hands in his. "I would never have brought you here if I'd known this was going to happen. The last thing I want is to hurt you. What I'm going to ask of you is really difficult for me. I want you to be here with us, but I know that I have selfish reasons. I can't watch you go through this again so I've decided to have you go to your mom's for a couple weeks. We'll see what's going on here by then and talk about whether or not you should come back

Selena listened with mixed emotions. *Go away from here? But, this is home. For a couple weeks? That's a long time. But, that would mean not having to worry about being watched and having my personal things rifled through. That would also mean not seeing Trevor and Trina. They wouldn't understand. And Graham. How can I leave him looking so depressed? And I haven't talked to him about The Agreement. How can I leave? But then maybe he's right. How can I stay and maintain my sanity?*

"Isn't there some other way we can deal with this? Running away never solves anything."

"I can't put you in any more danger." He placed his fingers on her lips as she started to protest. "I'll call you every day. I'll work on this end to try to get to the bottom of things. Do this for yourself, and do this for me."

Remembering the scripture she'd read the day before about submitting to your husband, she nodded. "Pray with me before I go."

Selena packed her suitcase and opened the gray box in the bottom of the closet to take some traveler's checks with her. Lying on top was the last letter that she'd found in the sofa. She opened it and reread the allegation that Graham had hit Kate. She remembered her promise to him that she would give him any letters she found. Replacing the ribbon, she went downstairs.

She found him in the breakfast nook, his hands in his pockets, staring out the window. She placed the letter behind her back, turned the light on and walked across the room.

He turned and gave her a tentative smile. She hesitated then began quickly before she lost her courage.

"Graham, I promised I would give you any letters I found. I found one more in the sofa, which doesn't make sense. That's my sofa, so there's no way that Kate could have left it there. I'll let you read it, then I have some questions

Graham's face blanched as he read the letter. He responded the same as before. He tore it until he could no longer find a piece large enough to tear.

"What are your questions?"

She cringed at the anger in his voice. "Is any of that true?"

He turned to her in disbelief. "How can you ask me that? What happened to the other letters you mentioned?"

"When I put everything away I couldn't find them. I looked everywhere. But, I don't understand if all of these things are lies why would anyone say those things about you? Especially since someone wrote them more than five years ago."

"What're you saying, Selena? You think those things are true? You think I'm capable of cheating on my wife and beating her? Is that what you're saying? Is that what you think?" His voice rose as his anger boiled over.

"I don't know, Graham. How am I supposed to know the truth from the lies? All I have to go on is what you tell me and I don't expect you to be up front with me if you have those kinds of problems."

"I don't believe I'm hearing this. I refuse to justify that question with an answer." His eyes pierced into hers. She'd never seen that look on his face before, a mixture of anger and pain.

"Graham, give me a chance. I didn't know you before I came here. You don't make it easy when you won't answer my questions."

She watched him leave the kitchen. Tears came to her eyes. Maybe he was right. Would she believe him if he denied the allegations? She wanted to, but would she?

After breakfast the next morning, Graham tersely told her that Jerome would take her to the airport. When Jerome carried her suitcase downstairs, Selena couldn't find Graham to say goodbye. She left a note on the table and walked out with Jerome.

Madelyn Cordell took one look at her daughter's face and remarked, "You look tired."

"Yeah. I guess I am. Thanks for agreeing to the visit on such short notice

"You're welcome here anytime. Is everything okay with Graham and the children?"

"Sure."

"Would you tell me if it isn't?"

Selena stared straight ahead, wondering how much to tell her mom. *As uncertain as things look right now they could change soon. I don't want to worry mom. Maybe I'll wait a few days to tell her.*

"I'll tell you sometime, Mom. Right now I don't even want to think about it."

Madelyn took Selena home. They ate dinner, watched TV for an hour then Selena went to bed long before her usual bedtime.

The next morning Madelyn waited for Selena to come to the kitchen for breakfast. She finally ate alone. Concerned, she opened the door a crack into Selena's room. Sound asleep. She ran errands and returned by noon.

"Good afternoon, sleepy head." Madelyn sat her packages on the table.

"I'm sorry, Mom. I can't believe I slept that much. I must have been more tired than I thought. 'Course I haven't been sleeping much lately."

By the end of the week, Selena had come no closer to the truth than when she arrived in Columbus. True to his word, Graham called her every day, his conversation short and impersonal. She always hung up close to tears, remembering the last conversation between them at the Estate.

One evening he put Trina on the phone. "Are you going to pick me up at school tomorrow, Selena? My dance lesson is tomorrow and I have to be there on time." "No, honey, I'm too far away. I'm at Grandma Madelyn's house. Maybe Jerome can take you if your dad is busy. I'll come home soon. I promise. I love you."

She talked to Trevor for a few minutes and he seemed to have forgotten his touch-me-not attitude. Now Graham didn't want to talk to her or have her touch him. She hung up, despondent.

"Is everything all right there?" Madelyn asked, noticing Selena's tears.

"Sure, Mom." Selena blew her nose and dried her eyes.

"Are you going to tell me what's going on before you go home?"

"I haven't been fair to you. I'm sorry. The problem is, I don't really know what's going on."

She started at the beginning with Howard harassing her. She told her about The Agreement, the terror, her changing feelings for Graham, her love for the children, the love and support of their staff, Graham's attentiveness, her involvement with the church, the footprints, the strangers on the property and the letters.

She ended by saying, "If I didn't care for Graham and the children so much, I wouldn't even consider staying. It seems like someone has something out for me. Now, Graham barely speaks to me because I questioned him about the allegations in the letters. How am I supposed to find out the answers?

"At first I thought Howard had followed me there, but Graham did some checking and said he's pretty sure it's not Howard that's causing the problems. Graham thinks someone is terrorizing me to get to him. He insisted I stay with you to get me out of danger. But, it's almost harder being away from them than being frightened and looking over my shoulder all the time. We really need your prayers, Mom."

Monday Selena took Madelyn's car and left early in the morning, hoping to find answers to her questions. She stopped at Clarinda's to pick up the mail that had accumulated. Still no divorce papers.

"Do you remember me telling you the name of Howard's attorney?" Selena asked her friend.

"Yes. Somebody Morefield."

Selena's eyes opened wide. "You're right! May I borrow your phone book? If I can find his name maybe I can make an appointment and talk to him." She ran her finger down the page until she came to Morefield, Scott, Attorney at Law. "Here it is."

Dialing the number, she made an appointment for three in the afternoon. "Thanks, Clarinda. You're a genius. Now maybe I'll get some answers. In the meantime, I'm going to look up an old friend of Howard's and see if I can get some more answers. See you Wednesday for lunch. Thanks." She gave her friend a hug.

Checking the address on her slip of paper, Selena drove to a unfamiliar section of the city. The narrow streets, the run down buildings, the ever-present graffiti, and the trash clinging to the half standing fences gave her an uneasy feeling.

Bobby had been a friend of Howard's for as long as she'd known the two of them. A burly person, too big for his frame, he looked like the kind of person she wouldn't want to meet in a dark alley if she didn't know him. *I'm glad he's my friend. He told me once that if I ever needed anything to let him know. I'm depending on his loyalty now.*

Catching sight of the building number, she locked the car, went into the building, found the apartment number and knocked on the door. She shivered as she felt the draft in the hallway. *Must be a broken window somewhere*, she thought, looking around. She took shallow breaths to keep from filling her lungs with the stench. She knocked again and heard movement inside the apartment. She waited as the door opened a crack. "Bobby, it's Selena."

The door opened wider, and he motioned her inside. His grin looked like a toothless smirk. "Hey, Selena, ain't seen much a ya lately

"That's right, Bobby. I moved. Have you seen Howard?"

"Yeah. Seen him last week. He been lookin' for ya. He real mad."

"Can you tell me if he's spent a lot of money lately? Like buying a new car or going on a nice vacation or maybe buying a house? I know he's your friend, Bobby, but it's real important that I know." Selena asked her questions slowly as if talking to a child.

"Nah. He ain't got no money. Ain't got no car. He livin' at Jana's house. She doesn't like me

Time stood still as Selena stared at him. "Jana? Jana Behnken? Is she his girlfriend?"

She watched in disbelief as Bobby nodded his head. She took a deep breath as the room started to spin. Her vision cleared as she heard herself say, "He's living with her? Jana? His step-sister?"

Bobby continued to nod his head and shifted his weight from one foot to the other, staring at a spot on the floor.

"How long has he been there?"

He shrugged. "Long time."

She felt nauseated as she remembered confronting Howard about him being too familiar with Jana. The implications of his actions could no longer be ignored.

So, Howard didn't have her money. *I wonder if Jana had anything to do with him not wanting to reconcile our marriage. I should have guessed. Why did it take me so long to catch on after the way he acted around other women? Adultery. At least now I can put the past behind me knowing I did everything I could to make the marriage work.*

"One more question, Bobby. Has Howard told you about any trips he's taken into the country?"

"Nope

"Thanks, Bobby. You've been a big help. Let's keep my visit here today just between you and me, okay? It would just upset Howard if he knew I talked to you and we don't want to do that, do we?" Selena patted him on the arm and left.

At ten minutes before three o'clock, Selena scanned the roster inside the door of the large office building and climbed the stairs to the second floor. She found the door with Scott Morefield, Attorney at Law, etched in the glass. The door opened easily and she stepped into the plush office. She wondered how Howard could afford an attorney on this side of town. *Maybe he does pro bono work.* Giving her name to the receptionist, she sat down.

What was it about that name, Scott Morefield? Why did she have a feeling it should mean something?

She walked into his office, even more impressive than his waiting area. The large oak desk, the ceiling to floor oak bookshelves on three sides of the room, the decorative plaques on the wall, the plush carpet, and his immaculate three piece suit all smacked of success.

"Mrs. Kensington, what can I do for you?"

Selena smiled, noticing that he seemed little older than Graham. His slightly graying, dark hair, and wire-rimmed

191

glasses gave him an air of sophistication. He had a ready smile; his gaze fixed on her face as if he had all the time in the world to solve her problem.

"First of all, I want you to know that I understand attorney/client privilege. I'm not asking you to tell me about your client, Howard Mulvaney, who is my ex-husband. I want to know why I haven't received the court documents. I understood that I didn't have to be at the hearing to receive them." She stopped at the look on his face. His mouth dropped open. He removed his glasses and leaned back in his chair.

"So, you're the elusive Selena. Isn't this a surprise? Well, yes. Uhhhh. There's a problem. Howard didn't show up at the hearing in August, so I had no recourse but to file a motion for dismissal. He came to my office the following day and demanded that the motion for divorce be filed a second time, which I did. However, that meant waiting until they could get it on the court docket again. That hearing is scheduled for February twenty-eighth. The divorce should be final on that date with you receiving the documents around the tenth of March."

Selena felt her heart race. The room spun and she felt cold.

"Are you all right?" She heard his voice, his face blurred.

She shook her head and willed her voice to be steady. "I thought the divorce would be final the first of September. No one told me any different. I remarried the middle of September. How could I get a marriage license if the divorce papers hadn't been filed with the court? Aren't they supposed to check those things out?"

"Yes, they are. It looks like yours slipped through the cracks. You say you married again? In the state of Ohio we call that bigamy."

"Oh, please. I have enough trouble as it is. Let's just forget we even had this conversation. You say the divorce will be final the end of February? Can you hold the document here for me to pick up? I prefer not to give out my address. Howard doesn't know where I moved and I'd like to keep it that way."

"I don't blame you for that. By the way, you said your last name is Kensington. You wouldn't know a Graham Kensington would you?"

"Yes. He's my husband. How do you know him?"

Scott righted his chair to an upright position and put his glasses back on. He stared at her for several moments before answering.

"Graham and I were college buddies. Too bad about Kate. I often wondered how that marriage worked considering how it started."

Scott Morefield. Of course the name sounded familiar! The letter.

"Mr. Morefield, I'd like to ask you a personal question. You said you and Graham were college buddies. What can you tell me about him as a person.

"Graham? He was one of my best friends. I could always depend on him to keep me on track. He's the only person I've ever known who told the truth one hundred percent of the time. Only once did I see him refuse to deal with an issue and I'm partly to blame for that. He's straight as an arrow. He had some kind of spiritual experience in our junior year in college and he tried to talk me into getting my life straightened out."

"Mr. Morefield, I found a letter with your signature on it telling Kate that Graham asked her to marry him on a dare from you. In another letter you advised her against divorcing Graham. Did you send those letters to her?"

"Letters? No. I figured Graham told her and they decided to go ahead and get married anyway. I didn't think he needed me to intervene in his business as level headed as he is.

"Thank you very much. Could you please call me when you get the papers in hand for me? I'll come and pick them up personally. If you can get them for me by the first of March, I would really appreciate it. Here's Graham's business card. I can be reached at that number."

He nodded and stared at the card. "What kind of business does he have?"

Selena smiled. "CPA. Call him and talk to him. Thanks again. Send me a bill if I've taken up too much of your time."

Chapter 14

Graham opened the door at the sound of the doorbell. "Dad! This is a nice surprise. Come on in."

"Hello, Graham. Are Selena and the children around? I'd like to take all of you out for lunch."

"The children are at a friend's house for the day and Selena is at her mother's."

"Well, come on then. It'll just be the two of us."

Graham wished his dad had picked another day to stop by the Estate. Since Selena left, he couldn't concentrate for more than a few minutes at a time. His mind jumped from one thing to another and always came back to her. In spite of the pain at her apparent refusal to believe him, he missed her.

How were they ever going to get things straightened out? Had Kate really said those things to her friends? If so, why? What would it prove? And if she hadn't, where did the letters come from? The personal information in them ruled out a lot of people. There weren't very many who knew the actual circumstances surrounding their lives together.

"Graham. Graham! Where are you, son? Your mind hasn't been with us all day."

"Sorry, Dad. What did you say?"

"How long is Selena going to be in Columbus.

"I don't know. Until we agree on a time for her to come back.

"What does that mean? She's the best thing that ever happened to you and the children. Why would she want to leave.

Graham hesitated. How much should he tell his dad? He'd always felt comfortable talking to him, unless the issues became too personal. However, he might have some insight into how to work things out with Selena.

"There've been some things going on at the Estate that have frightened her. She went to her mother's at my insistence to get away for awhile and get some rest."

"What's going on? Why don't you put a stop to it?"

"I would if I could. Neither of us knows who's responsible. I'm trying to find a detective now to stay at the Estate to flush them out. That's bad enough. But, before she left we had words and I don't know how to resolve it."

"You want to tell me what that was about?"

"Selena found some letters in her room, the same room Kate used before she died. Supposedly, Kate's friends sent them to her. They accused me of adultery and spousal abuse, blatant statements meant to assassinate my character. She questioned me about the truth of the statements and I refused to answer. She should know me well enough by now to know that none of it is true."

"How long did you know her before you married her?"

"I don't know exactly. We met about a year ago. I saw her off and on when I went to Columbus or Zanesville on business but didn't really spend much time with her. I may have known her six months. Why do you ask?"

"It doesn't sound like you saw enough of her before you married her for her to learn to know you very well. Why do you expect her to automatically take your word for it? Could you be letting your pride get in the way.

"Pride? I wouldn't call it that. And, yes. I do expect her to take my word for it that I could never do those things to Kate or to her. I've never lied to her before and I have no reason to start now.

"Son, think about your pride. You have a lot of it. Some of it's okay. You've done a lot of good things. But, when you let it get in the way of your relationship with Selena that's not good. Do whatever you have to do to keep her with you."

Graham spent an hour in the Closet that afternoon. *If it's my pride keeping me from having an open relationship with Selena then it has to go. But, does she have a right to question my character? Would I question hers if the tables were turned?*

Turning to the thirteenth chapter of First Corinthians he began to read at verse one. He stopped at the verse that said that love never demands its own way and hung his head. He fell on his knees and asked God to forgive him for his pride and his failure to show compassion to Selena when she questioned him about his character. How indeed was she to know if he just told her those things about himself to talk her into marrying him? How was she to know the difference between the truth and lies?

"Mom, do you have some writing paper? I just need one piece."

"It's in the desk drawer. Look in the middle drawer on the right."

Selena pulled the drawer open and gasped. The turquoise colored folder with her name printed on it lay on top. She slowly reached in and lifted it out.

"Mom, how did you get my portfolio?"

"You told me I could look at it and I guess I forgot to give it back to you. You can take it with you. It looks like you chose a good company to invest with."

"I've looked everywhere for this folder. I need to call them and have Howard's name taken off of the account. God really answers prayer. I just wish He would answer some more of them.

"He will, Selena. Just give it some time.

Selena picked up the phone when it rang. "Hi, Trina! Did you have a good time at your party this afternoon?"

"Yes. When are you coming home? Who's going to fix my hair tomorrow before we go to church? It never feels right when Daddy does it. Are you going to be here for my music recital next week? You're not going to leave us are you?"

Selena felt her throat constrict as she tried to keep up with the child's questions. "No, honey, I'm not going to leave you. I'll be home soon. I promise."

She talked to Trevor for a minute then heard Graham's voice on the line.

"Hi, Graham. Is there a time next week when you could come to Columbus? I need to talk to you as soon as possible. It's really important. Please don't tune me out again."

"I'm not going to tune you out, Selena. Would Tuesday be a good day for you?"

"Tuesday would be fine. Do you want me to pick you up at the airport?"

"That would be helpful. I'll see you Tuesday then."

She hung up the phone slowly. He had sounded different, more like the way he used to be. *Will he be ready to listen to me? What will I do if he isn't? I'll think about that when the time comes.*

"Mom went over to Peggy's for the day so I thought we could go back to her house to talk." Selena's heart pounded as she felt his presence close to her in the car. Graham's fingers had brushed against hers as he opened the car door for her, sending a feeling of warmth up her arm. His eyes, no longer angry, looked into hers. His lips had lost the hard line. The smile he gave her caused her to respond with a smile of her own.

Seated on the sofa facing him, she felt uncertain about where to begin. She felt his fingers rub the top of her hand and looked into his face. Seeing only love there, she took a deep breath.

"Graham, I talked to Howard's attorney last week, questioning him as to why I haven't received the court documents concerning the divorce. The attorney turned out to be an old college buddy of yours. Do you remember Scott Morefield?"

"Of course I remember him. He was one of the fearsome foursome as the others used to call us. Didn't you tell me he wrote one of those letters to Kate?"

"Yes, I told you that. But, when I questioned him about it he denied it. He said he figured it was your business and you could take care of it. Anyway, if he didn't write those, which were the first ones I found, I'm guessing it's safe to assume that the others weren't written by the people whose names were on them either. I don't understand why anyone would write those things about you. I'm really sorry that you had to read it and that I had nothing to base the accusations on. However, I'm convinced now that they're all lies and I'm sorry that my questions caused you so much pain."

"Honey, I wish I could take back what I said to you before you left. I talked to Dad last weekend. He's right. I have too much pride and it gets in the way of common sense sometimes. I'm sorry I didn't answer your questions and give you the chance you asked for to believe in me. That was the least I could do for you.

"There's something I've wanted to talk to you about for some time now. The Agreement. I know it says we're not to talk about renegotiation until March. But I think since we created it we can uncreate it if we want to."

Selena stared out the window. She hadn't planned on talking about The Agreement. With things even more complicated now than before, The Agreement would have to remain as written. She felt his hand touch her face and gently turn her head to look at him. "Talk to me, Selena. Don't tune me out."

"I'm not trying to tune you out. I just don't know how to tell you this. Scott Morefield told me that Howard didn't show up for the hearing in August. Therefore, the divorce is still pending. The hearing is scheduled for February twenty-eighth. Scott said he would call me when he gets the documents."

"The divorce is still pending? Why didn't he tell you that before?"

"Actually, he tried to reach me after Howard asked him to re-file the lawsuit, but I'd already moved to Serendipity Estates. All of my mail went to Clarinda, but other than that I left no forwarding address or phone number so Howard wouldn't be able to find me. I asked everyone not to tell anyone where I'd moved."

Selena watched his face, waiting for the question. When his eyes opened wide and his jaw dropped open she knew it was coming.

"How could we have received a marriage license if your divorce is still pending?"

"Good question. I don't know. I got the classic answer when I called the license bureau. 'Sorry, all we can do is chalk it up to human error.'"

"So, I guess your nuptial agreement turned out to be a prenuptial agreement. How do you feel about it now?"

Selena thought for a minute. "I think God inspired me to write it, but I wish now it didn't stand between us. The way things have turned out I'm glad it's there. At least now when I get the court documents, we can start over and do it right the next time. That is if you want to. Start over that is."

"I want to." His voice soft, she almost missed it. She didn't miss the meaning in the kiss, though, as he pulled her to him.

Seated on the plane on Saturday going back to Serendipity Estate, Selena smiled. They'd all be back together again and that's all that mattered for now.

Graham met her at the airport. "I have something I need to talk to you about."

Seated in the restaurant ten minutes later, Selena didn't have to wait long to find out. Close beside her, he took her hand and began. "I've added one more person to the staff. He should be there when we get back. The three of us will meet in my office. I'd like for you to hear everything. He needs to meet you, as he is to be your shadow at all times while you're home. He's an undercover detective and will be given access to every room, nook, and cranny at the Estate. I need to come up with a plausible title for him, so the rest of the staff won't suspect who he is or what he's really doing there."

Puzzled, Selena asked, "Why aren't you going to tell the rest of the staff who he is? If we can't trust them who *can* we trust?"

"That's a good question. There's been too much information leaving our house and I don't know how or when. I've been advised by the police not to tell anyone. I'm not even telling the children. I'm still trying to think of a good cover for him while he's there."

"What's the one thing about Jerome's job that he likes the least?"

Graham thought for a moment and shrugged. "He never complains, but I guess I would say household maintenance and the remodeling project I asked him to do last summer. It still isn't finished."

"What's this detective's name?"

"Cyrus Abbott."

"Put Cyrus to work inside then. With the remodeling, it'd give him an excuse to go out for tools if he needed to check something outside."

"Good idea. I knew there was a reason I wanted to bring you home." She warmed to his light teasing tone as he looked into her eyes.

As they ate, Graham spoke. "There's another thing I want you to know. Cyrus is going to install a security system.

Every time a door is opened a picture will be taken with the date and time recorded on it. We'll have a record then of everyone's comings and goings. If something happens, which I pray it won't, at least we'll know if someone in the house is involved or if someone from outside is coming in. I know this is going to really inconvenience you, but I've asked him to place a camera in your room. The only private place there will be the bathroom. You'll need to remember that in order not to embarrass yourself. The camera in your room will be running twenty-four hours a day, with the monitor being in Cyrus' room."

"Oh, thanks. Just what I need. I hope he catches the person soon. I feel a major invasion of privacy about to begin."

"I know it's not going to be easy for awhile. I hope and pray, too, that this will all be over quickly. I have something to confess. I don't want you to take this wrong. You know how much I missed you while you were at your mom's. But, there's another reason I wanted you to come home. Nothing happens when you aren't there. I've struggled with this for days. I know it looks like I'm deliberately bringing you back as bait. I don't want to do that to you. I've talked to Cyrus on the phone for several hours trying to find another way to flush these people out in the open without involving you. If you think of something, please let us know. Also, if you refuse to be part of this, I'll take you back to your mom's. I don't want you to think that we are using you and are knowingly putting you in danger."

Selena stared at her food. Her thoughts tumbled over each other. Was she going to walk back into something worse than when she left? Were all the security measures going to work? Some of the things that happened had been outside her room. So, how were they going to connect all the events on a property as large as Serendipity Estate? All the home security systems in the world wouldn't give anyone a clue as to who the footprints in the snow belonged to. Or who stood under the oak tree at night. Or who walked back from the stable in the middle of the day.

Graham took her hand and waited for her to answer. Finally she said, "I'll meet with you and Cyrus this evening. I have a lot of questions about my safety there. I'd turn around right now and go back to Columbus, except Serendipity Estate feels like home to me now. Being at Mom's seemed like being on vacation, and I feel like I need to get home and get back to work. Plus, I missed you and the kids a lot. I'll have to admit, though, I'm really scared. I don't understand why it takes me to get to the bottom of this. I don't want you to get hurt either, but if it's you they want, why me?"

"It's called psychological warfare. If they can force me to make a decision I don't want to make in order to protect my family, their theory is--they win. They don't care who gets hurt in the process."

"Just what is it they want you to do?"

"Six months ago I received a phone call from someone saying they wanted to buy my business. I told him it wasn't for sale. A few days later he called again and offered me a huge sum of money to sell out, about ten times what the business is worth. I asked him where all the money would come from and he wouldn't say. I suspected that the person I talked to was only a spokesperson. Anyway, a week later he called again and I again refused. There were veiled threats and I hung up. I didn't think too much about it, until I brought you to the Estate under the pretense that we had married. I'm pretty sure they want me to sell out so that the threats on you will stop. I may have to do that.

"If bringing Cyrus in doesn't get us the results we want I can't continue to live this way. Your safety is more important to me than the business, even though the business will have wide rippling effects if I quit. I need your cooperation to do this. If you don't want to, for whatever reason, just tell me. I know it's asking a lot."

Selena took a deep breath. "All right. I'll do it for you. No one should have to feel forced to make a decision that is contrary to God's purpose. You haven't done anything wrong, so it doesn't make sense for them to force you to sell. But, do me a favor, will you? Keep praying for that double protection for me."

Graham squeezed her hand. "Always, sweetheart."

When they arrived home, Trevor and Trina almost knocked Selena down. Trina jumped into her arms and wound her legs around her waist. "Thank you for coming home. I really, really, really, really missed you." She planted a long hard kiss on Selena's cheek.

Graham unwound her and placed her back on the floor. "Can we have hot chocolate and cookies with you before we go to bed?"

"Of course, honey."

Graham took her luggage upstairs with Trina following closely behind. Trevor looked at Selena self-consciously. Selena held out her hand to him. He walked over and put his arms around her waist.

"Are you going to go away again? I'm sorry if what I said made you go away."

Startled, Selena said, "Oh, Trev. That didn't have anything to do with it. I hope I don't have to go away again, but if I do it won't be because of anything you said. And I promise I'll always come back. Okay? Come on. Let's go fix the hot chocolate."

After the children went to bed, Graham and Selena walked to his office. Within minutes they heard a knock on the door and a man entered the room. "Hi. My name is Cyrus Abbott. Here's the application you asked me to fill out. Is there any other information you need on the form?" He placed his fingers on his lips, indicating they should not answer. As he talked he walked around the room picking up the phone, feeling under the computer, looking under the vases, and looking under the surface of the desk and the chairs. He took out his pocketknife and pried a round metal object from the phone and from under the desk. Sticking the knifepoint into the middle of each one, he twisted it until it came apart.

"Is there somewhere else we can meet?" he mouthed.

Graham led the way into the north wing opening the door to one of the unoccupied rooms. Its use as a conference room had never materialized. They chose a corner and sat on the floor. Graham sat next to Selena and put his arm around her, pulling her close.

"I couldn't take any chances that I might have missed one. I'll check it more thoroughly tomorrow."

Cyrus looked at Selena. "I'm sorry all this has happened to you, Ma'am. I understand you've been gone for a couple weeks. How much has he told you about our operation?"

"We talked about it this evening. Graham said he talked to you for several hours about how to handle the situation here. Does that mean, with the bugging devices you found in his office, that they know now who you are and what you're doing here?"

"I didn't call him from here," Graham explained. "The first call I made from the police station. I went over there one day to look at the file to see if I could make a connection between all the things that have happened. The police couldn't find one and I couldn't either. The only connection was you. The rest of the calls I made on my cell phone in a restaurant. I'm not sure about my car either or the van you drive. This probably seems like overkill, but we're just trying to be as cautious as we can."

"Once my purpose for being here has been established, I'll begin placing the monitoring devices. When will you be talking to your staff?"

"Without raising any questions, it'll have to wait until Monday morning. I'll bring the staff together and introduce you. Selena has come up with the best idea so far. I'm going to announce that you will be taking over the inside maintenance, which will include a remodeling project of one of the rooms. That will mean, of course, that noises will need to be made on a regular basis from that wing. However, that'll also mean that you will have lots of reasons to look for materials and tools in the garage, the barn, the stables, and anywhere else you want to go."

Selena looked at Cyrus as Graham spoke. He appeared to be forty-something in age. His thinning hair and receding hairline made him look ten years older. His eyes looked alert and penetrating behind his glasses. He and Graham stood shoulder to shoulder, but Cyrus' thin build gave him the appearance of being taller. *He could probably move pretty quickly if he needed to.*

Selena's eyes widened as she heard him say, "Are you still certain you don't want me to carry a gun?"

"Yes. At least for right now."

"Okay. I'll have a knife on me then. I never work without a concealed weapon. I prefer a gun, but I'll honor your wishes."

"Is the weapon thing necessary?" Selena asked Graham later. "I can't believe that it'll come to that."

"I hope it won't, but we don't know. At least he went along with the gun thing. Too many innocent people get hurt when there are guns around."

Graham went to his room and stood in the dark, looking out the balcony door. The weak moonlight barely illuminated the landscape. A cold wind blew the bare branches first one way then the other. He stuck his hands in his pants pockets and shivered in spite of the warmth of the room. With Cyrus here it looked as if things might finally come to an end.

Why did things have to get complicated now with her divorce? He sighed deeply. It sounded like a groan. He lay down on the bed fully clothed and stared at the ceiling, watching the shadows from the dim light of the lamp he had turned on. And he prayed.

Monday morning, Graham called the staff to the dining room for a meeting. The temperatures outside, barely in the twenties, had climbed only a few degrees in the past couple weeks. Selena returned from taking the children to meet the bus.

Laying her coat across a chair, she sat beside Graham at the head of the table. When Cyrus walked in she almost gave him away. She exercised every ounce of will power to remain expressionless. He wore a toupee so natural looking she wouldn't have known had she not seen his lack of hair Saturday night. He now wore glasses with very thick lenses which distorted his eyes and gave him a very different look. The lenses dulled the alertness in his eyes, and she wondered how he could even see anything. *This guy is good! He must think he's going to run into someone who might recognize him.*

Graham introduced the new maintenance man, Cyrus Abbott, explaining his duties, and the room he'd be occupying. He introduced the rest of the staff members by name then dismissed them to go to work.

During the introductions, Selena watched. Joyce smiled and waved her fingers at Cyrus, Jerome stood up and offered a hearty handshake and a verbal welcome, and Babs smiled. Cyrus acknowledged each one and made no comment.

Selena wondered. If Cyrus went to such lengths to hide his identity, was that his real name? Exactly who had he come here looking for?

When everyone had left, Selena squeezed Graham's hand, smiled, and went to her room. She felt stifled. Putting on another layer of clothing and her boots, she went to the stable. She cleaned Star's stall and picked up the blanket to place on the horse's back under the saddle, when she heard the door open and close. Expecting Jerome, she looked around the gate to say something and saw someone at the phone in the walkway. She quickly ducked back.

Slowly looking around the corner again, she heard, "Yes. Yes. Yes. No. Yes. Okay." She couldn't tell the gender of the person by the clothing or the voice. The clothing looked familiar, but she couldn't remember where she'd seen it before. Who was it? And why use the phone in the stable with the abundance of phones in the house? Or hadn't the person come from the house?

The horse saddled, Selena walked her around the corral. Jerome climbed the fence and shouted his usual greeting.

"Hey, Jerome." Selena waved. Walking Star over to the fence where he stood, she asked, "Have you ever seen anyone out here using the phone in the stable?"

"No, ma'am." He gave her a puzzled look. "No one as I know of uses the phone out here. I never could figure why they put one there in the first place."

"Thanks." She placed her foot in the stirrup, threw her leg over the saddle, and nudged Star to a cantor. It felt great to be back on horseback and feel the wind in her face, no matter how cold it blew. The sun brightened her spirits. Who could touch her out here?

The wind burned her cheeks, so she turned Star toward the stable. Walking back to the house, she wondered if she should report what she had seen and heard. How significant was it?

Selena changed her clothes and went to Graham's office. He'd stepped out. She looked in the kitchen. Not there either. She noticed his car parked in the driveway, but that didn't mean much. He could have taken one of the other vehicles.

Going to the north wing, she found Cyrus measuring two by fours in the room that Jerome had begun to remodel. "Hey, how's it going the first day on the job?" she asked loudly and pleasantly. With her back to the door she handed him a piece of paper with the information regarding the phone call in the stable. He stuck it in his pocket without pausing in his explanation of materials he would need to purchase to finish the work.

"Make a list and I'll pick up what you need when I go into town tomorrow."

Going back to Graham's office, she found him talking on the phone. He motioned for her to come in. She walked over to the window to admire the view, noticing the plaques hanging on the wall next to the window. They'd always been there but she never took time to read them.

Intrigued, she read the certificates for the degrees that he'd earned in college. One, a Bachelor of Arts degree from a university she'd never heard of in another state; the next one, a Masters of Business Administration from Ohio State University; and the last one a Doctorate of Ministry degree in theology from a seminary in Dayton. If he had a D. Min. degree why had he gone into the accounting business for himself?

He hung up the phone and said, "What can I do for you, my lady?" She turned around, smiling at the grin on his face.

"Are all the bugs gone," she whispered. He nodded, explaining that Cyrus had gone over his office yesterday and found one more, now convinced he'd destroyed them all.

She told him about the incident in the stable and that she gave the information to Cyrus. Turning to the wall, she pointed to the last certificate and said, "Explain this one to me."

"What do you want me to explain? I worked on that one and the MBA at the same time. I didn't know what to do with either one of them when I finished, but the Lord knew what he was doing when he prompted me to do both."

"I don't understand. How are you using the D. Min. now? Don't most people who have them use them in the ministry as a pastor or in a related position?" Graham smiled. "I guess you could say I'm in a related position. I work closely with pastors and teachers to help them keep their ministry operating."

"I came to ask you a question. Have you hired anyone else recently?"

"No. Why do you ask?"

"I went to the stable to take Star out and I heard someone using the phone. I looked around the corner but I didn't recognize the person. I couldn't tell by the voice or the clothes if it was a man or a woman. If no one else works here, then could someone just walk onto the property without being seen? And if they can, how did they know there's a phone in the stable?"

Graham stared at her. His brow furrowed and his eyes narrowed. "I don't have the answers to your questions, but we'll find out. It looks like we'll have to place a camera by the phone in the stable, too. Thanks for letting us know about this. And, please, Selena, promise me you'll be very careful. I don't want anything to happen to you."

In spite of his attempt to reassure her with a kiss Selena left the office feeling uneasy. She had the feeling that Graham and Cyrus knew more than they'd told her. How could she be very careful and take care of herself if she didn't know what to expect around the next corner?

Graham ran his fingers through his hair and stared at the ceiling after Selena left his office. How long could he continue to not answer her questions? He needed to talk to Cyrus about his suspicions. How indeed would anyone know the location of the phone in the stable unless he or she worked for him? Highly unlikely that someone walked onto the property to use the phone, that narrowed the suspects. He would have to remember to have Cyrus dust the phone for fingerprints even though there probably wouldn't be any, as usual. How much longer could he ask Selena to stay at Serendipity Estate? If anything happened to her he would never forgive himself for his selfishness in wanting her close by. His thoughts suddenly seemed disconnected, jumbled. She'd given her consent to return here knowing about the danger, but that still didn't resolve him of his responsibility to provide a safe place for those he loved. And her name held first place at the top of the list of his loved ones.

The two weeks she'd been gone had been difficult. Seeing her everyday had added a dimension to his life he'd never experienced prior to meeting her. He felt a longing to just be near her. Her pleasure at seeing him after they'd been apart and after they talked about their disagreement had given him hope that they could make a marriage work. Was this the over-the-edge kind of love he'd been searching for? He certainly felt on edge in her presence.

Selena went to the kitchen to make a sandwich for lunch. As she opened the refrigerator, everything suddenly blurred. Her heart raced and she gasped for breath. Closing the refrigerator door, she sat down on a chair and concentrated on taking deep breaths. As quickly as it started, it left. *What could that be? Oh, well, it's gone. No sense worrying about it.*

That evening, as she read from the scriptures and prayed, she thought about Graham's statement at her mother's house that he wanted to start over when she finally had the divorce papers in hand. Had she been premature in her desire to want the same thing? Even though she cared deeply for

Graham, that didn't mean she could be the wife he needed and deserved. Would he understand that she had given everything she had to Howard, but it wasn't enough?

Of course after her talk with Bobby she wondered if anything she did for Howard would've ever been enough. However, with no guarantees that she could give Graham what it took to make a marriage work, would he understand if she had second thoughts? But Graham was different.

Unconsciously, she began to compare the two men. Astounded at the comparison a peace washed over her. Howard stood for nothing and refused to participate in anything. Graham stood for everything right and good and embraced all that he stood for. Howard demanded he be given everything. Graham asked for nothing and gratefully accepted his gifts. Howard took everything he could get and destroyed it, giving nothing in return. Graham shared everything he had, and worked at restoring the damaged, whether in material items or emotional distress.

Being married to Graham would be much different than what she had experienced with Howard. Hadn't Graham said that marriage meant the same to him as it did to her? That he believed it to be a life time commitment? Maybe, just maybe, it could work.

Chapter 15

Selena looked at her watch. Not another one of those days! Too many errands and not enough time to do them in.

The weather had changed for the better. The temperatures daily climbed into the thirties with the sun shining most of the time. The snowstorms were farther apart and the snow lay on the ground for shorter periods. She longed for spring.

She placed a check mark beside each item on the list after she made the stop. She checked off lumberyard, halfway down the list, and started for home. She planned to make the rest of the stops after she gave Cyrus the things he requested.

A mile from home she slammed on the brakes and pulled over to the side of the road. At least she hoped it was the side of the road. Her blurred vision made it difficult to know exactly how far off the road she'd actually stopped. She gasped for breath as her heart raced and she felt a dull, squeezing pain in her chest. Leaning her head on the steering wheel she waited for it to ease up.

She jumped at the knock on her window. Her vision cleared enough for her to see Jerome.

"Are you all right, ma'am?" She saw his mouth move.

Selena rolled her window down and reassured him. "Just a little dizzy spell. I'm fine now. Thanks for stopping and checking.

When they arrived at Serendipity Estate, Selena put her hand on his arm and said, "Thanks again, Jerome, for stopping. Let's keep this between us. I'd prefer that Mr. Kensington not know. He'd just worry and there's nothing to worry about."

"Whatever you say, Ma'am." He frowned as he helped her carry several bags of items into the house.

Selena took the children to music lessons after school. She'd finally been able to change Trina's lesson to the same time as Trevor's, which got them home earlier in the evening. That had solved one problem and presented another one. That meant Graham usually ate dinner with them. So far, she'd been able to excuse herself early in the evening, and had thus avoided opportunities to spend a lot of time with him. She didn't know what to do with the feelings that developed after their discussion in Columbus. She realized with dismay that The Agreement, rarely mentioned, no longer held the same meaning.

At the end of the week, Graham asked Selena to come to his office before they had their weekly prayer time in the Closet. She couldn't think of a good reason to say no. Taking longer than usual to put the food away and place the dishes in the dishwasher, she finally walked to his office. He smiled and leaned forward on his desk as she walked in. She sat opposite him and waited for him to begin.

Graham watched her and couldn't understand why she seemed to be on edge. Recently things had gone smoothly as far as he knew. There had been no more threats or incidents. He hoped that was a good sign.

"This is my weekend to be out of town and I wanted you to know where you can reach me." Handing her a list of numbers, his fingers brushed hers. The warmth of her fingers reminded him he hadn't spent much time with her lately. He'd have to change that when he returned. Each time he left, it got harder to go. What if something happened while he was gone? At least this time Cyrus would be here.

"Do you know how to get in touch with Cyrus?"

He saw the barely perceptible nod. Why wouldn't she talk to him? Expressionless, she looked at him, her hands folded in her lap. He rubbed his eyes with his fingers. Something still needed to be resolved and he didn't know what

214

it could possibly be. He'd have to talk to her when he came back.

Graham stood up, walked around the desk, and held out his hand. Tentatively placing her hand in his, she walked with him to the Closet. She visibly relaxed as he chose a scripture to read then took her hands in his as he bowed his head and closed his eyes for prayer.

Since the first time she discovered this room it felt like a safe place. She felt a peace here that she hadn't found anywhere else in the house. An unspoken understanding had developed between them. They didn't talk about problems and issues here; they only brought them to God to work out.

Graham left early the next morning, barely having time to say goodbye to the children before breakfast. Trina, agitated that her dad would be away again began to cry.

"Why do you have to go away all the time? It's like we don't have a dad or a mom when you're gone. Can you stay home this time?"

Selena saw the pain on his face. She wished she could give the child some hope that things would be different soon. Not having that assurance herself yet, how could she give it to someone else?

Graham held Trina in a long embrace. "I'm sorry, honey, I have to go. Selena will be here. Doesn't she always take good care of you? I'll be back Sunday afternoon and we can all do something together in the evening. Think of something while I'm gone that would be fun." Giving Trevor a hug, he picked up his briefcase and his luggage and started for the door.

Stopping, he turned and looked at Selena. "You have my numbers if you need me?" Walking over to her, he looked into her eyes. "Be careful," he whispered, as he leaned down and kissed her on the cheek. She smiled tremulously and nodded her head.

She watched him go with mixed feelings. *When he's gone I don't have to wonder what to say if he wants to talk about the future.* But, she had to admit she missed him when he left. In spite of the tension, she liked the way he showed his appreciation for her and the way he put her at ease in every situation. She remembered the way he looked at her sometimes with a little smile on his face. It always made her heart pound.

"Selena, can you come to my gym program tomorrow after school?" Trina's voice brought her out of her reverie.

"Of course, honey. What time does it start? Find out today and let me know. I'll be there." She squeezed Trina's hand and smiled.

Graham called that evening and talked to the children. Trina handed the phone to Selena and said, "Dad wants to talk to you."

When she hung up the phone, she wished she hadn't talked to him. His tone caring and tender, he wanted to make sure she was safe. He said he missed her. Her heart constricted; she didn't know what to say.

The next day Cyrus approached her in the stable where she talked softly to Star and brushed her coat. "I know this is difficult for you, but I need to ask you to let me know when you're going to be away from the house while Graham is gone. I get a little paranoid after awhile if I haven't seen you around the property on the cameras. I don't want to be in your face all the time, so if you'll let me know it will be helpful. "

"I wish I knew why all this is necessary. But, if it will make things easier for you, I'll let you know what my schedule is until Graham gets back. The only time I plan to be gone today is this afternoon for a program for Trina at the school. We should be home all evening. I'll let you know tomorrow about the weekend."

Arriving at the school a few minutes before the program began, Selena found a seat in the bleachers with the other

216

parents. Finding an empty seat, she sat down and looked for Trina. She saw her halfway across the gym with a group of children beside the tumbling mats.

"May I sit here?" Selena looked up at a woman about her age.

"Sure."

"I'm Sharon Fleming. That's my son, Jeremy, over there by the trampoline."

Selena introduced herself and pointed Trina out to her.

"Is that your daughter?"

"Trina's my step-daughter. I married her dad, Graham Kensington." The explanation flowed automatically. She felt a pang of guilt as she heard herself tell the half-truth. She longed for the time when she could say it honestly.

"You're Graham Kensington's new wife? I'm really pleased to meet you. I dated Graham for awhile. He's a really nice guy. I wanted to have a relationship with him, but he didn't seem interested. You're a lucky woman."

Selena laughed with her. "Is there anyone around here that he hasn't dated?"

A whistle sounded and a man stepped up to the microphone, introducing himself as the physical education teacher. He explained that they traditionally had a gymnastics meet in February as a way of getting the kids physically fit for the sports programs in the Spring. He finally blew the whistle again, officially beginning the program.

The children lined up, snaking around the equipment and the mats. One by one they did tumbling exercises, cartwheels, and flips. A second line formed. The first line finished, the children in the second line did more advanced flips and twists. Applause filled the auditorium. Trina dropped behind, standing to the side with those not involved in the last part of the mat exercise.

The second segment of the program involved rope-climbing, exercises on the uneven bars and the pommel horse. Trina did well on the rope and the horse, but didn't attempt the uneven bars. A half dozen children attempted all three, one of them being Jeremy Fleming. His mother, beside Selena, screamed encouragement to him.

The children lined up for the third part of the program, the trampoline and floor exercises. Trina walked to the side, joining with those scheduled to jump on the trampoline. One adult stood on each side of the apparatus along with a couple children between each adult. Each child took a turn, doing the practiced level of flips, twists, and turns.

Selena watched with a smile as Trina climbed onto the trampoline. Trina often talked about the jumps she did in class. She began by doing small jumps and flips.

Selena held her breath as Trina increased her height and attempted a flip and a twist in the air. She landed on her back, bounced to her feet, and began to pump herself up to the same height again. Reaching the height, she completed the flip and started to twist.

From the bleachers, Selena saw her lean sideways, and her body bounced off center on the trampoline. The height and the speed from which she fell sent her back up into the air, still spiraling sideways. The adults ran to the side to catch her, but only one stood back far enough to cushion her landing.

Selena jumped out of the bleachers and ran halfway across the gym floor in seconds, dodging children and equipment, watching Trina and the adult land in a heap on the floor. Medical technicians appeared and the physical education teacher and his assistants steered the children to the other side of the room and moved the equipment.

Selena found Trina to be non-responsive, her face white, and her eyes closed. Her right foot lay at an odd angle and a pool of blood formed on the floor beneath it. "Trina.

Trina. Open your eyes. Talk to me. Come on. Talk to me." Selena patted her face. Trina moaned and rolled her head.

"I'm sorry, Ma'am, but you're going to have to leave the area."

"No. I'm her mother. Has anyone called the paramedics? She's unconscious and she has a broken ankle. I would appreciate it if someone would call them please. It's all right, Trina. I know your leg hurts. We're going to have the doctor look at it."

Selena prayed all the way to the hospital. Trina could have internal injuries. A thought almost stopped her in the middle of the road. *Graham. How am I going to reach him? What did I do with that paper that has the phone numbers on it? Think! Think! Think!*

She found a parking place next to the door, and ran into the Emergency Room as the paramedics wheeled Trina in on a stretcher. The child moaned. One of the paramedics talked softly to her. They directed Selena to the registration area and took Trina through the double doors to the treatment room.

Selena searched her purse for the numbers to call Graham. At the same time the clerk asked for information and tapped keys on the computer.

"Do you have an insurance card, Mrs. Kensington? I'd like to make a copy of it, please."

With a feeling of despair, Selena remembered that she'd forgotten to ask Graham for a copy of his insurance card. "I'm sorry. I'll have her dad bring it when he gets here. I'm not her legal parent; you'll have to get phone consent for treatment. As soon as I find a number where he can be reached, I'll let you know." She continued the search in her purse, which had now taken on a frenzy.

Think! What did I do with it when he gave it to me? We went to the Closet. Then I put it in my pocket. I went upstairs, opened my purse and. . . the side pocket! She pulled the paper out of the side pocket of her billfold and took it to the clerk who copied it onto the registration form.

"Could you let me see her as soon as possible? I need to talk to the doctor."

She found a pay phone in the waiting area and dialed the first number Graham had written on the paper. The phone rang, but he didn't answer. She tried the second number. Still no response. She dialed the third number, answered by a clerk in a motel. He offered to ring the room, then came back on the line. No answer. She left a message for Graham to call the hospital immediately.

She asked the registration clerk to please check again and see if she could go back to the treatment room. She paced the floor. *What will I do if something happens to Trina? Graham will never forgive me. Why didn't he answer at the numbers he gave me to call? Where is he anyway? Why do I have to be responsible for his children when he's out of town and out of reach?*

"Mrs. Kensington, you may come back now." A nurse stood at the door. Selena followed her to a large room with small curtained cubicles in a circle around the walls of the room. She saw Trina lying in the far corner and walked quickly to her. She put her arms around her and talked softly to her for several minutes.

Turning to the nurse she said, "Whatever permission you can accept from me, I'll give. If you can accept my permission for x-rays and blood work, you have it. I'd like to have the doctor do a thorough physical examination as she fell on a hard floor from about ten feet in the air."

"My leg hurts real bad, Selena. Don't let them move me. It hurts too bad. Is Daddy here?"

Selena shook her head.

"Oh, that's right, he's gone this weekend." She began to cry again.

"Honey, they have to take x-rays to see if you broke anything when you fell. You can cry if it hurts. Big girls cry sometimes. You can be brave and cry at the same time. I've called your daddy. I'm waiting for him to call back."

When Trina went to the x-ray department, Selena went back to the phone and started down the list of numbers. The clerk at the motel said he still hadn't returned. She looked at her watch. Probably at dinner.

She waited an hour and tried the numbers again. No answer to the first two numbers and he hadn't returned to the motel.

As she walked back to the treatment area to see Trina, the registration clerk stopped her. "We can't seem to reach your husband, ma'am. Are there any other numbers we can try?"

"No. I'm sorry, I don't know of any others. I've been trying also. Eventually one of us will catch up with him, I'm sure." Selena sounded more assured than she felt.

"Mrs. Kensington, we have the results of the x-rays." The doctor hung the film in a display unit and turned on a light behind them. "As you can see here, both bones are broken. This one is in two and this one is splintered and bulging. We need to do surgery to repair both bones. With your permission we would like to take Trina to surgery as soon as possible."

"My permission won't help you much. I'm trying to reach her father to get phone consent. He should be calling back any time now. I'll see if I can reach him again."

She retraced her steps to the phone and dialed the numbers from memory. The motel clerk put her on hold and she heard another phone ringing.

"Hello, Graham Kensington."

"Graham! Where have you been? I've been trying for hours to find you. You didn't answer at any of the numbers you gave me. We're having an emergency here

"Selena, calm down and tell me what's going on. What do you mean you're having an emergency? Are you all right? Has something happened again?"

"No, it's not me. It's Trina. She had an accident at school and she needs to have surgery. You need to call the nurse in the Emergency Room and give them permission to operate. I don't suppose you could come home, could you? There are too many papers to sign, I don't have an insurance card, and I can't give permission for treatment. Why did it have to happen this weekend? Do whatever you want to, but don't do this to me again."

"Selena, wait." Graham heard the click. He heard the hysteria in her voice. Dialing the number given to him by the motel clerk, he gave his consent for treatment and surgery. He hung up the phone, gathered up his personal items, checked out of the motel and drove to the airport.

He prayed all the way home. Selena had been more distraught than he had ever known her to be. Did that mean Trina was in serious condition? Or had he just put too much responsibility on Selena? She talked pretty fast and he hadn't understood everything she said. He prepared himself for an emotional storm when he got there. *I probably deserve it. Maybe it's time to make her their legal guardian. But, is she ready? Is that really the issue? Whenever Trina mentions it, Selena makes excuses. Why does life have to get so complicated?*

Selena suddenly thought of Trevor. She had given him permission to go to a friend's house for the afternoon. Making her way back to the phone, she dialed the number and apologized for the inconvenience. She explained the situation with Trina and was assured it would be no problem for Trevor to spend the night. Sighing with relief, she thanked the mother, and returned to Trina's bedside as the surgical assistant arrived to take her to surgery.

Placing the chart at the end of the cart, the nurse said, "Mrs. Kensington, your husband called and gave consent for surgery. Please remind him when you see him that we have other forms for him to sign also. Bye, Trina. You get better real fast, okay?"

Selena followed Trina to the surgical unit, kissed her, and promised to be there when she returned from surgery. Finding the waiting area, she sat down, and felt the ache in her chest. She leaned her head back against the wall and waited for the wave of dizziness, racing heart, blurred vision, and tightness in her chest to subside.

Cyrus. She jumped up and ran to the phone. It seemed all she'd done this evening was call people and apologize for something. She explained the situation and apologized for not calling sooner.

Two and half hours later Graham walked into the surgical waiting room looking haggard. He'd shed his coat and tie and his shirt looked rumpled. Selena took one look at him and felt the anger rise from the pit of her stomach. Afraid to say anything, knowing she would say things she would later regret, she clenched her teeth.

He walked over and sat down beside her, reaching for her hand. "Are you doing all right?" She snatched her hand away and tucked it under her arm.

She stared at him. Why did he ask a question that he already knew the answer to?

"Instead of asking me a bunch of dumb questions why don't you try explaining to me why it took me two and a half hours to find you when I had a list of numbers to reach you on a moment's notice. Or why don't you try explaining to me why I don't have an insurance card for emergencies for the children. It really stinks when you go out of town for days at a time and I don't know where you're going or who you're with. That leaves me totally responsible for your children. If anything ever happened to them...I just don't recall that this is part of my job description and it's definitely defined in The Agreement as your responsibility

Graham waited for her to finish. He ran his fingers through his already tousled hair. She was right. He'd given her too much responsibility. However, this was neither the time nor the place to change that. What could he say to appease her? Would she listen if he tried?

"You're right. I haven't been fair to you. I went to Atlanta to see a client. Evidently, you began calling as we went for dinner. I'm sorry you had such a hard time reaching me. The first number I gave you is my cell phone, but I forgot that Atlanta is out of the calling range. I need to get a new phone with an unlimited range so you can contact me no matter where I am. The second number is the client's number, which didn't help you since we went out together. I'm sorry, Selena, that you had to go through this. We need to talk about making some other changes, too. But, we'll do that some other time."

"I'm looking for the Kensington family," said a green garbed figure. Graham and Selena stood up while the doctor introduced himself and explained that the surgery had gone well with no complications. A pin had been placed in the ankle to hold the bones together while they healed. They could see Trina in about an hour when she awoke.

Tears of relief slid down Selena's cheeks. She took deep breaths to hold onto the small amount of control she had left. Graham held out his hand to her, but she refused to take it. She saw the pain in his eyes and looked away. Why give him hope when she felt none? No use to talk about a marriage now. After what she'd said to him on the phone, he certainly wouldn't be interested.

"I think I'll go home. There's nothing more I can do here." She picked up her purse and coat from the chair.

"Please stay, Selena. I want you to stay, and I know Trina will be asking for you when she wakes up. After we talk to her we can go home together and come back for the van tomorrow. You're too upset to be driving. Please." Refusing to look at him she wondered why he suddenly seemed to care so much, then realized the unreasonableness of the thought. He always seemed to care, sometimes too much. Nodding her head, she returned to her chair, leaned her head back against the wall and closed her eyes. She felt him sit down beside her, but he made no effort to touch her.

When Trina awoke from the anesthesia, she begged for someone to stay with her all night. Selena, afraid if she offered, that Graham would also stay, shook her head. Thinking of being near him all night overwhelmed her, knowing that she couldn't cope with it.

"I'll stay if you'll go home and get some rest." She looked directly at him for the first time that evening.

His expression inscrutable as his eyes pierced into hers, he said, "You need the rest more than I do. Why don't you go on home? I'll call Jerome to come and get you. I'll be home in the morning and we can both come back in the afternoon. Do this for yourself, Selena."

Her lip trembled as she nodded her head. How could he be so nice in a situation like this? How could she stay angry with him when he always seemed to be looking out for her? Too tired now to even think it through, she concentrated on walking to the front lobby to wait for Jerome. Maybe she'd think about it tomorrow.

Selena picked Trevor up from his friend's house the next morning. He had a hundred questions about Trina. When he asked if he could go to the hospital to see his sister, she replied, "You'll have to ask your dad."

As she pulled into the driveway at Serendipity Estate, she saw Graham's car in the driveway. Her heart sank. What would she say to him? She had to try to smooth things out from last night. They still had five weeks left on The Agreement and the pending divorce. Too long to have this much tension between them. Maybe she could buy some time by going to the stable.

She brushed Star's coat with slow, deliberate strokes and felt the tension easing from her neck and shoulders. Hearing the door open and close, she ducked behind a bale of straw. Her breaths came unevenly as the footsteps stopped at Star's stall. She let it out when she heard Graham talking to the horse. Standing up she said, "You scared me to death. Next time say something when you come in the door so I know who's there. How's Trina?"

"She's doing much better this morning. The doctor said there didn't appear to be any internal injuries. Just some bruises. She would only let me come home if I promised to bring you back with me when I returned. How're you doing this morning?" He leaned against the fence and searched her face for an answer.

"Better. Thanks for asking." She watched him, not knowing how to say what needed to be said. She raised her eyes to meet his and watched him hold out his hand to her as he'd done the night before. Slowly she placed her hand in his then allowed him to pull her into his arms.

Burying her face in his coat, she felt the strength of his embrace. She looked into his eyes. "Graham, I owe you an apology. I could have gotten my point across last night in a much nicer way. I was so upset about Trina, but that's no excuse to take it out on you. Please forgive me."

The corners of Graham's mouth curved slightly. "You told the truth last night. There's nothing to forgive. I want to thank you for being there for Trina and seeing that she received the proper care. I don't know what I would've done if you hadn't been there. You know I trust you completely with the children. You always have their best interest at heart and make good decisions for them. That's no excuse for me not to plan better for things like this. But, since this is the first major emergency, I was simply unprepared for it. I'm sorry it was difficult for you. I'll straighten it out. And I promise to be more specific about where I go the next time I go out of town." He caressed her face with his fingers. She laid her head on his shoulder, her arms behind his back, choosing to forget about The Agreement.

They walked to the house together. Remembering the camera in the corner of her room, she took her clothes out of the closet, went in the bathroom and closed the door. She stared in horror at the mirror as the light illuminated the message scrawled with her favorite lipstick in large letters across the glass. "Go back to Columbus before someone gets hurt."

She ran to the adjoining door and pounded as hard as she could. Getting no answer, she ran from her room, down the stairs, into Graham's office.

He looked up from opening his mail. "What's the matter?" he asked, alarmed, as she gasped for breath.

"Come." He followed her back to her room. Looking at the mirror, he clenched his teeth and took a deep breath. He pulled his phone from his pocket and dialed a number. "You need to come to Selena's room immediately."

In less than a minute, Cyrus appeared at the door. He went into the bathroom, took several photographs and started to leave. Graham stopped him. "Did you see anything on the screen?"

"Yes. Someone entered this room."

"Well? Did you recognize them?"

"Yes. I know who it was. But, the door to the bathroom was closed and I can't prove anything." Cyrus shrugged as he left.

Selena sat on the side of her bed and shook. What did it mean, 'before someone gets hurt'? Should she go back to Columbus? Someone could mean anyone here. If she didn't go back to Columbus, would it be her fault if he hurt the children--or Graham?

"What am I going to do? I can't bear the thought of someone getting hurt because of me." Graham sat down beside her and pulled her to him. "If you want to go, I won't stop you. I want you to know that whatever decision you make, I'll support you in it. If you go, I'll miss you terribly, but I won't ask you to stay if you don't want to."

He lifted her chin to look at him. "Just don't think if you leave that that's the last you've seen of me. I'll move to Columbus before that happens. I can operate my business from anywhere."

"Wouldn't that defeat the purpose of me leaving? If you're going to follow me, there's no sense in me going anywhere. If we're going to be together, we may as well be together here. He'll follow you wherever you go if it's your business he wants. I told you I'd stand with you to fight this thing and I will. Thanks for your support."

He pulled her into his arms and held her, speaking softly. "Do you have any idea how much you mean to me?"

She looked at him, tears welling in her eyes, and nodded.

Chapter 16

Trina arrived home from the hospital on Sunday. Despite the discomfort, she took advantage of the attention she received. All week the doorbell rang after school, with teachers and students alike stopping by for a few minutes with get well cards and gifts to cheer her up.

"If she gets any cheerier, she'll be bouncing off the walls," Selena remarked to Graham one evening.

True to his promise, Graham returned on Monday afternoon with a new phone. Sitting beside Selena on the sofa, he handed her a sack. Her mouth dropped open.

"What's this for?" She took the phone out of the bag.

"That's for you. Carry it with you wherever you go. I wrote the number down so I can call you directly. It'll probably be beneficial to you if you memorize the number of my phone. With this one you can reach me anywhere in the United States, so there won't be any more fiascoes like last Friday night."

The middle of the week the doorbell rang in the morning. Remembering that she still wasn't to answer the door, she watched as Joyce went to the front of the house. When no one arrived in the family room, where she'd propped Trina up on the sofa, she looked for Joyce. "Who rang the doorbell, Joyce?"

"It wasn't for you, ma'am. I took the package to Mr. Kensington," Joyce said haughtily. Selena sighed. She'd tried to win Joyce over, but to no avail. Joyce's actions indicated she had an attraction to Graham. No one had been told about The Agreement. Had she found out somehow and thought there might still be hope for her?

Knocking first, then walking in, Selena found Graham at the computer. He stopped typing and turned his chair to face her. "To what do I owe this pleasure?"

"Joyce said she brought you a package. I wondered if it's for me?" She returned his smile.

Graham rolled his eyes and shook his head. "It's supposed to be a surprise. But, since you insist, I'll give it to you now." He reached under his desk and handed it to her.

"You don't have to. I thought maybe it's something from the court. But, since you insist on giving it to me, I'll take it."

His heart skipped a beat at the smile that played across her face, lighting up her eyes, and softening the look around her mouth.

She tore the postal paper off, cut the tape on the box, and lifted the lid. Her eyes opened wide as she gasped. Inside lay a red dress of the softest material she'd ever seen. The material caught the light that caused shimmers of colors as it moved. A heart had been cut out near the high neckline and a diamond pendant hung from the point in the middle. As she carefully took the dress out of the box, she noticed the long, closely fitting sleeves, and the calf-length hem. A wide belt covered with the same material had a belt buckle in a scroll design.

"Am I to assume that there is a special occasion coming up?" Unable to hide her pleasure, she folded the dress carefully and placed it back in the box.

"Well, since Valentine's Day is this weekend, I thought I'd take my favorite lady out on the town. How does dinner and a concert sound to you?" Overwhelmed, she nodded her head. Valentine's Day had crept up on her. Not only had Graham remembered, he probably already had the reservations made. And he'd bought her a new dress, too.

She walked around behind him and put her arms around his neck. "What am I going to do with you?" she asked. "I'm not used to surprises like this. The dinner and concert sounds great. When are you planning on doing this?"

He reached up and caressed her arm. "How about Friday night? We'll need to leave here at five in order to have plenty of time to deal with the rush hour traffic. Will that work into your schedule?" He pulled her face gently down to his.

Just as their lips touched, the door opened. "Whoa! Bad timing, I guess." Selena stood up quickly, her face warming.

"Hi, Justin. Actually it's good timing. I'm leaving." She turned as she closed the door behind her and found Graham watching her.

Justin grinned. "I've never seen you so enraptured by a woman before. I'm really happy for you, Graham. How are things going with the business?"

"Not good. I mean business is great, but we're still being harassed. Last week he threatened Selena again. I have an undercover agent working with me so I hope to flush him out soon, whoever he is. Have you gotten any phone calls?"

"That's why I stopped by today. I received a phone call the first of the week asking me to sell my business. I refused. I'm wondering what's next. I haven't told Sherry yet that I got the call. How much does Selena know?"

"She knows most of it, that someone wants to buy my business bad enough to threaten my family. It's putting a strain on our relationship, and I need to make sure our relationship remains intact. She's the best thing that's ever happened to me." Friday afternoon Selena returned from her errands and went to her room to get ready for her evening with Graham.

The children had moaned at breakfast about spending the evening alone. "Someone will be here with you while we're gone. It's a surprise." Graham tried to appease them.

Selena's anticipation of the evening left her puzzled. Did she really want to spend the evening with him? Or did she just want to get out of the house? Since the lipstick-on-the-mirror incident, she looked over her shoulder at every turn.

Who had access to her room that could easily slip in and out without any questions being asked? With only three employees, and their loyalty beyond question, she knew they'd have reported anyone on the property that didn't belong there.

Despite all the questions, she promised herself to enjoy the evening with Graham. She pushed all her doubts below the surface of her consciousness and concentrated on looking nice and being amiable. Just for this evening. He'd planned a nice evening and she planned to show her appreciation.

She thanked God many times for Graham's integrity. He wouldn't mention The Agreement again until the first of March. She hoped and prayed that Cyrus had apprehended the person behind the incidents by then so they could go forward with their lives.

At five minutes until five, Selena emerged from her room with her coat over her arm. She hoped Graham liked the accessories she'd purchased on her shopping trip the day before to go with the dress. She felt nervous, as if going on a first date with him.

She took a deep breath and started down the stairway. As she reached the bottom step she heard his door open. Turning, she waited for him to descend. He reached the step she stood on and took her hands. "Beautiful." That one word and the look in his eyes told her what she needed to know.

The children, excited when their grandfather walked in to spend the evening with them, said good-byes hurriedly. Trevor pulled Sylvan into the family room where Trina anxiously waited to tell him all about the autographs on her cast and all the people who'd stopped to see her.

Selena, in awe of the posh restaurant where Graham had made reservations, looked around wide-eyed. To her surprise she realized that she no longer looked at prices.

"You spoil me, you know that?" She kept her tone light, teasing. Her breath caught in her throat as she saw the look that played across his face in the soft light.

"Good. That's what I want to do; spoil you so much you won't ever want to leave me."

She closed her eyes, too surprised to respond. Did he really think she wanted to leave him? *I'll be so glad to get The Agreement and the pending divorce out of the way so I can tell him how I really feel about him.*

When they pulled into the driveway after midnight, Selena wished the night would never end. She'd never felt so contented, peaceful, and loved as she did with Graham that evening. He'd been attentive to her needs and moods, and showed her in a hundred little ways that he loved her deeply. *I wonder when he's going to tell me?*

Selena kicked off her shoes as they walked into the family room. She didn't know how to say good night. She really didn't want to.

"I guess we should call it a night, huh? I want to thank you for a very special evening. I loved every minute of it." She spoke softly, watching the emotions play across his face.

"There's one more thing before the evening is over." Graham walked to the stereo. Turning the volume on low, he held out his hand to her. Delighted, she placed her hand in his and followed him to the middle of the floor.

A bright moon shone in the February sky, casting shadows on the freshly fallen snow. By the corral, partially hidden in the shadow of the old oak tree, a lone figure watched the scene unfold through the window of the family room.

Graham took Selena's left hand and placed his left one on her shoulder. They began to sway as one as he looked deeply into her eyes. The observer watched as Graham's right hand caressed Selena's face, and her arms crossed behind his neck.

He pulled her closer and placed his cheek against hers. They continued to move as one to the music.

Only one sound was heard in the cold night air. "Perfect." A slow crooked smile preceded a low harsh laugh. One of the horses whinnied. The light in the family room went out. The lone figure blended with the shadows in the woods.

Two weeks left in February. *If Scott Morefield hasn't called by the first day of March, I'm going to call him.*

Selena wanted to have papers in hand when she talked to Graham again. He'd promised that they'd talk about their marriage license when she received the divorce papers.

With all those thoughts going through her mind, she started for the stable. The sun shone from a blue sky, with the temperatures in the forties, warmer than normal. The soft breeze felt warm on her face. The ground remained frozen, but the snow and ice had melted.

Selena saddled Star, took her out for her warm up around the corral, then mounted and guided her to the trail through the woods. It seemed forever since they'd been on the trail. She breathed deep of the cool air, catching a whiff of the wet earth, and felt it clear her head. Riding in sync with the horse, she gave Star the lead and relaxed. Star knew this trail as well as she did.

She looked around for signs of spring, hearing the water in the stream before they rounded the bend. Run off from the melting snow had swollen the stream winding through the property, but the bridge was intact with the water several inches below it.

The trees remained bare with no signs of buds, as if daring spring to arrive. She looked closely for new growth under the trees, but the shade from the large branches blocked the sun and kept the ground temperature below freezing.

As they rounded the bend, Selena gasped. Across the trail stood a five-foot high section of fence. She pulled back on the reins, too late to alter the speed of the horse. The untrained animal and rider approached the fence in a panic. The trail sloped steeply on both sides, making it nearly impossible to go around the fence without causing serious injury to one or both of them. Selena prayed that Star would know to jump and clear the obstruction.

Star reared up, attempting to clear the fence at the last possible moment. Her front legs crashed down on the wooden structure. Selena held on as the horse reared. When Star's front legs splintered the fence, Selena felt herself, as if in slow motion, lose her grip on the saddle horn and sail through the air. She hit the ground with such force that she gasped over and over for breath. Sharp pains stabbed her in the side with each breath she took. Sliding down the slope toward the stream she stopped suddenly, feeling another shooting pain in her side.

She opened her eyes, not caring to guess how close she'd slid to the stream. It looked wider and deeper from this angle. She turned her head slightly at the sound of the water gurgling over the rocks. Inches lay between her and the water's edge. She moved her head and found herself curled around a small tree that had blocked her descent on the slope.

She waited several minutes for her head to clear. Trying to raise herself up on one elbow proved too painful. She dropped back to the frozen earth, unable to bear the stabbing pain. What now? No one would ever find her out here. The young horse wouldn't know to return to the stable without her.

She lifted her head and looked around. What had happened to Star? Was she lying somewhere hurt? *I hope they don't have to put her down. What about me? How am I going to get help? I can't even get up.*

She heard a buzzing sound. Disoriented, she looked around. The phone. She'd placed it in her pocket before going to the stable. Reaching slowly, her fingers closed around it. By the time her vision cleared enough to find the button to receive the call, it'd stopped ringing.

She tried to recall Graham's number. After a couple attempts, she lay the phone flat on the ground to place the call. The first two numbers she dialed she got a recording. The third time she almost cried when she heard his voice.

"Graham, I've been hurt. I need help. Please help me."

"Selena? What happened? Where are you? Talk to me. Say something. Okay. Keep talking. You're on the trail? I'm on my way out the door. Where did you say you are? By the bridge. Okay. Hang on. I'm on the trail. Keep talking to me. I need you to tell me where you are. What? Who put this fence up? Beside the trail. Under the bridge."

When he leaned over her, he froze. Her face, a mass of scratches, swollen tissue, and mud made her almost unrecognizable. She cried out when he tried to turn her over.

"I think my ribs are broken. I can't move, it hurts too bad." She gasped between each word as her voice became weaker.

She drifted in and out of consciousness, hearing Graham phone for medical assistance. Then he talked to someone else about the paramedics. He sat down next to her and placed her head on his leg.

"I'm s-s-so c-c-c-cold."

She felt him place something warm and heavy across her shoulders and around her neck. Graham, frantic that the ambulance wouldn't get there in time, stoked her hair. Who would have done this to her? Who knew she would be out riding?

"Keep talking to me, honey," he said aloud as he prayed silently. He prayed harder than he'd prayed for anything in his life. *Lord, please heal her. Don't take her away from me now. You know how much I love her. Please don't let her die. Just don't let her die!*

He talked to her and rubbed her forehead, the only place on her face free of injury. Occasionally she responded.

Graham heard the paramedics on the trail and yelled to get their attention. He heard Cyrus utter an exclamation at the fence across the trail.

"Under the bridge!" Graham shouted to get their attention.

Selena, only slightly aware of her surroundings, realized she drifted in and out of consciousness. She knew Graham would get help for her when she heard his voice and he sat beside her. Her face hurt where it lay against his leg, but she'd rather have it there than on the cold ground.

When the paramedics lifted her onto the cart to wheel her to the ambulance, she cried out from the pain and lost consciousness. Phrases drifted around her in a swirling fog, but none of it made sense. Someone else must be hurt. But, who? They couldn't be talking about her. "Blood pressure low. Start an IV. Probably shock. Check for internal injuries. Blankets. Keep an eye on her B/P."

When Selena roused again the bright lights hurt her eyes. She closed her eyes and moaned. She heard Graham talking softly, soothingly, and squeezed his hand. A few minutes later she felt the bed moving and heard him say she was being escorted to the X-ray Department.

Frowning, she tried to remember what had happened. Everything seemed to be moving in slow motion.

Graham heard her cry out when they changed her position to get the x-rays. Each time, he clenched his teeth and exercised more self-control than he thought he possessed to keep from demanding that they stop. Why did it have to be her? Why didn't they come after him if they wanted him? How much longer could he refuse to give them what they wanted? Angrily, he ran his fingers through his hair and paced the floor.

"Mr. Kensington, we have the results of the x-rays. Your wife has sustained fractures to four of her ribs. I don't detect any fractures in her face or head, but I suspect she has a concussion. I want to keep her in the hospital for a couple days to keep a close eye on the head injury. It's amazing to me that her injuries aren't more severe. Someone was watching over her."

When Selena awoke, the first thing she noticed was the soft bed and the warm blankets. It seemed like she had been cold for a very long time. Her vision blurred, but she could see someone sitting by the bed. "Graham?"

"I'm right here." She felt him take her hand and kiss her on the forehead.

"How are you feeling?" he asked, his voice gentle, almost a murmur.

"I don't know. My face feels funny and my vision's blurred. Could you help me turn on my side? Oh, never mind. It hurts too much. What happened to my side?"

"You were right. You have some broken ribs. Your face feels funny because it's all scratched and bruised. Your vision should clear up in a couple of days; you have a concussion from hitting your head on the ground."

She tried to process all the information, but it didn't make sense. She couldn't remember anything about the accident. Feeling again the wind in her face as she rode Star on the trail, she smiled. And that hurt. Lying perfectly still to keep from generating any more pain, she drifted off to sleep.

Graham watched her struggling with the memories and the pain. When she went to sleep, he dialed Cyrus' number. "Have you found out anything?" "I don't have any proof of anything yet. I'm going to set up a stake-out tonight."

"Good. I want these people stopped, and I want them stopped now. If you can't do it, than find someone who can.

No one will ever get a chance to do anything to my wife again. They almost killed her this time."

"I know. I'm really close to breaking this case."

"I don't care how close you are to breaking this case, if you don't do it in the next two days while she's in the hospital, don't bother. You're not getting another chance."

"I have to wait for them to make their next move, otherwise we'll blow the whole thing and won't be able to make the arrests."

"I don't want your excuses. Either do it or get out!"

Selena awoke to find that someone had turned her on her side. The darkened room, the drawn curtains across the window, and the closed door to her room made it difficult to determine the time of day, but it seemed she'd been asleep for only a few minutes.

Feeling Graham's hand over hers, she slowly moved her hand so as not to wake him. She touched her face and felt the tautness from the swollen tissue. What had happened? Who brought her to the hospital? She tried to turn over and moaned.

"What's the matter? What do you need?"

"I'm sorry. I didn't mean to wake you. I tried to turn over and it hurt. What time is it?"

"It's four in the morning."

"You can go home and sleep. You don't have to stay."

"I know I don't have to. This is a want to

She felt his fingers moving back and forth on her forehead and tried to smile. His hand felt good, and the messaging motion dulled the ache in her head.   The nurse opened the door and walked into the room. "I need to take your blood pressure, Mrs. Kensington."

"Can I get up to the bathroom for a minute when you're finished?"

"Sure. Let me get some help. I'll be right back."

Back in bed and lying on her back, Selena reached for Graham's hand and held it tight. She felt his breath on her cheek as his lips lightly touched her swollen ones. He placed his hands around one of hers as her other hand caressed his face.

"Did I hurt you?"

She brushed the tears from her eyes. "No. You've never hurt me. I don't know why you care so much for me, but I'm glad you do. I've been nothing but trouble for you ever since we met."

"Sh-h-h-h. You're not the trouble and you know it. I'd do it all over again. I can promise you one thing. No one will ever get a chance to hurt you again."

The memories seeped back into her mind.

"Graham? What about Star? Is she all right?" He didn't respond.

"Did they have to put her down?"

"Yes. She fell on her head and broke her neck. Jerome took care of her. I'm sorry. I know how much she meant to you." He massaged her forehead gently.

Selena drifted into a troubled sleep. The pitch-black night made it impossible to see anything. She felt the wind on her face and blowing through her hair. Something chased her; something nameless and faceless. She heard water running and the motion stopped. Feeling a hand on her face, she didn't know whether to be fearful or feel safe. Then the darkness enveloped her again and she heard voices laughing. A figure dressed in black emerged from the darkness.

She sat straight up in the bed. She moaned at the stabbing pain, unable to lay back down again.

Graham supported her back with a pillow as she eased herself down.

"What is it, honey

"The person making the phone call in the stable--it's the same one I saw on the balcony, the same one I saw under the old oak tree by the corral. Whoever did this to me is someone who's there a lot, or someone who lives there. I don't understand. There's only three besides the four of us there all the time."

Silent, not wanting to voice the thought that intruded into her mind she thought of each of the staff. Jerome would do anything for them. He couldn't be capable of doing something like this, could he?

Babs watched the children, went over and beyond the responsibilities required of her to keep the large house clean and functioning, and showed only love to everyone. Could she be. . .? No!

Joyce. Sometimes sullen, and often distant. But following through with a plan to cause serious injury? Could she really do it?

Graham watched her struggle with the thoughts and wanted to assure her that it wasn't any of them. But, he couldn't lie to her. He'd known before Cyrus joined the staff that one of the three, acting alone or most probably with someone else, had perpetrated the situations to frighten her. How else would the bugging devices have been placed without him knowing about it? The marriage had been so sudden that no one from the outside would have started the scare tactics so soon after Selena arrived. The Thanksgiving incident had to have been done by someone in the house, or someone who had been let in through the side door. The balcony door couldn't have been unlocked from the outside. Rifling through her boxes had to have been done during the day by a trusted person, as a stranger would not have been able to enter the property undetected, and he kept the garage locked at night. He suspected one of the women because most of the incidents had to do with a woman's personal things. Either that or a woman called the shots.

"Try to get some rest. You're safe here. I'm not going anywhere and I won't let anything happen to you." His voice, assuring and confident. She tried to smile again. Graham. Always confident.

Selena awoke late in the afternoon gasping for breath. She tried to cough, but the pain in her side stopped her. "Graham, could you help me sit up? I can't get my breath."

Sitting straight up helped for a short time. "I need to stand up. I feel like I don't have enough room to breathe."

She stood up and stretched to her fullest height, but it didn't help. Graham reached for her call bell and caught her as she collapsed.

Easing her back on the bed, he yelled that he needed help and then got out of the way as nurses and medical carts arrived from every direction. An x-ray machine arrived moments later as the nurses carried packaged trays into the room. When a doctor hurried in, they asked Graham to wait outside.

"Would someone care to tell me what's going on here?"

"The x-rays show that her lung collapsed and her chest is filling with fluid. We need to insert a chest tube. It'll involve making a small incision, then placing a tube in her chest to drain the fluid so the lung can inflate again. It'll only take a few minutes and then you can come back in. This is a relatively simple procedure. She evidently sustained a small tear in her lung from the accident."

Graham dialed Madelyn's number. The lack of sleep and the emotional distress had taken its toll on him. "Hi, Madelyn. This is Graham. Selena sustained some injuries in an accident yesterday and is in the hospital. I'm sure she's going to be all right. It's just that she has some broken ribs, and a concussion. Now one of her lungs has collapsed

"Is she going to be okay

"Yes, they're putting a chest tube in, and she'll be in the hospital for two or three more days. I wondered if you could come over for a few days. I don't want to leave her alone, but I need to check on the children. I'll get you a plane ticket if you want. How soon do you think you could come

Madelyn walked into the hospital room late in the evening. She stifled the sound that rose to her throat at the sight of Selena's swollen face and the machine hooked up to a tube in her side. Graham, unshaven and his clothes wrinkled, looked haggard. Struggling for control, she gave him a message from Jerome. "He said he'll wait to take you home. He's in the parking lot outside the front door."

By the next morning, Selena breathed normally and the pain in her side had decreased. It still hurt when she tried to take a deep breath. Medication to reduce the swelling had begun to be effective. Her face felt almost normal and the tissue felt softer to her touch. It didn't take as much effort to open her eyes or talk and her headache had decreased from a pounding pain to an ache.

"Thanks for coming, Mom. Graham didn't get much sleep last night. He looked almost as bad as me."

"I'm glad I could come, Selena. And I'm glad you're feeling better. Try to rest."

Graham called early in the morning, then showed up at noon. "Thanks for your help, Madelyn. Jerome is waiting outside to take you home. Get some rest. The children will probably overwhelm you when they get home. If you need anything, call me at this number. Joyce is staying the night to help with the children."

Puzzled, Selena frowned. Why did Joyce spend the night when Babs lived there? Maybe Babs took a day off.

The day of the accident, Cyrus returned to the bridge after the paramedics left. Looking for footprints turned out to be an exercise in futility with all the people tramping around getting Selena out from under the bridge. He looked at the fence across the trail and measured the distance the posts had been driven into the dirt. Less than six inches. Either the frozen ground made the digging difficult or the person doing it didn't have enough strength to do the job well. He carefully examined the ground around it, not sure what to look for. Anything to give him a clue.

Cyrus feared for Selena's life. The scare tactics were bad enough. But, this incident took on an ominous aspect not seen in the others. The serious injury that occurred had been well thought out. It had to be an act of desperation. He cringed to think of what could've happened--Selena's death--and really didn't understand why it hadn't. No matter what it took he planned to make sure that he apprehended the criminals and that they wouldn't be free to do anything to anyone else for a very long time.

The phone call from Graham made Cyrus more determined to get these people out of society. Positive that he knew their identity, he seethed that they'd been cunning enough to escape detection.

The day they found the message written on Selena's mirror, no one had entered or left the house. The day Selena heard the one-sided phone conversation in the stable, one staff person had left and re-entered. The same person entered Selena's room, although the appearance had been altered.

The past week he'd spent every night in the stable so he could watch the side of the house where the staff quarters were located.

Tonight he stood again by the window in the stable. The moon had moved to the western sky. Past midnight. About to give up and go inside, he saw a movement at one of the windows. Grabbing his binoculars, he watched as a rope ladder eased over the side of the window. A figure crawled over the sill and down the ladder, closed the window, then disengaged the ladder and dropped it behind the bushes. He dialed a number, asked for re-enforcement, and followed the figure from a distance.

He walked softly on the frozen ground, keeping track of the location of the lone figure by the crunching of the footsteps. Then silence. He reached for his weapon, having gotten permission from Graham to carry it after the accident. He crept closer in the darkness. Thud. Thud. Thud. He rounded the bend in the trail and watched the fence being dismantled. As the last piece lay on the ground, he emerged from the darkness, shone a spotlight into the eyes, and ordered, "Freeze!"

Two hands twitched as if to reach for a weapon. "I wouldn't do that if I were you. Get your hands up, now!"

He handcuffed his prisoner, pulled the hood off the face, and grinned coldly. "Well, well. So, we meet again, Melinda Brown. Did you think you could go underground forever? I knew we'd have this little talk eventually. So, who are you working for this time? Cat got your tongue? How about if we sit down over here for a few minutes and rest from our little ordeal?" He dragged her to a tree several yards away from the trail and confiscated a gun in her waistband and a knife in her sock. Placing chains on her legs, and a gag across her mouth, he waited. He surmised someone would be coming from the other direction before the darkness dissipated, assuming that she didn't work alone. He shivered and pulled his coat around his neck.

He didn't wait long. He heard the footsteps before he saw the figure. Activating his two-way radio, he said softly, "Move in." Black clad police officers emerged from behind several trees as he barked an order. "Halt! Drop the weapon!"

Shining the light, Cyrus raised his eyebrows in surprise. "Tommy Stanger. Why am I not surprised? Cuff him." Picking Melinda up by her arm, he shoved her towards the officers as he said, "Take this one with you, too." He removed the gag and ducked as she spit at him. He had one thought as he walked back to the house. *She's good. Real good. I hope I don't see her again.*

Graham walked into the house and poured a glass of orange juice. Cyrus met him in the hallway.

"I made the arrests last night."

"Thanks. I'll talk to you later. I need to get some sleep."

Going to his room, Graham fell across his bed in sheer exhaustion. The story could wait. He didn't want his worst suspicions confirmed until he'd slept and could ask the right questions.

The next morning, after Graham called the hospital to check on Selena, he and Cyrus went to a local restaurant. Graham listened to the whole story, shaking his head in disbelief.

"Don't be too hard on yourself, Graham. These people are professionals. I'm hoping this will put them away for a long time. I've asked that they be booked for attempted murder. They knew when they put the fence up that the horse had received no training in jumping. If they'd just wanted to scare Selena, they'd have built the fence lower."

"I guess I got a little rough on you the other day. I apologize. It was tough seeing Selena suffer, but that's no excuse for jumping on you. I really appreciate all your hard work. Send me a bill."

Chapter 17

Selena smiled when Graham walked into her hospital room. He handed her a bouquet of roses and kissed her on the cheek.

Turning to Madelyn, he gave her the usual message, "Jerome is waiting in the front parking lot. Thanks for being here for us."

"Mom, don't forget the envelope. See you tomorrow."

After Madelyn left, Graham sat facing Selena. "What's that about an envelope?"

"Just something I need from my room. Don't worry about it."

"Speaking of worrying, the doctor told me about the panic attacks you talked to him about. Why didn't you tell me?"

"They came and went quickly and I didn't want to worry you. There was nothing you could do and there were so many things going on . . ."

"When are you going to realize how much I care about you? I hate hearing from someone else what's going on with you." He stared at her with a frown across his forehead.

"I'm sorry, Graham. If we ever get all this other stuff behind us and I can concentrate on us, I'll try to remember to tell you things like that. No one ever cared that much about me before."

"Well, now someone does, and don't forget it! There's something I need to tell you. I guess I'll start at the beginning. If you get tired, let me know. We'll have the rest of our lives to put all the pieces together.

"I want to tell you about my business. In my accounting service I work for non-profit organizations. At the present time, I have fifteen clients and have been contacted by three others for appointments to discuss providing services for them.

"Several of my clients are part of a loosely run organization that owns Serendipity Estate. They asked me to live there to keep up the property and the buildings, eventually turning it into a retreat/resort facility where conferences and seminars can be held. The only thing holding them back is the construction of a lodge where those who attend the meetings can spend the night. The last I heard, they're having problems finding a contractor to do the work."

"There's a man I know who goes to my church in Columbus who's a contractor. He builds motels in the tri-state area. Maybe you could contact him and have him give you a bid. He has several crews that work for him and he's done very well, so his bids have to be competitive."

Graham smiled and took her hand. "I knew there was a reason I was supposed to talk to you about this.

"Continuing my story, in August I received a phone call from a man who identified himself as Joe Samuels. Some of this I know I've already told you, but I need to repeat it to tie the loose ends together. Anyway, he said he wanted to buy my business and he'd consider any amount of money I'd ask to sell out. I told him my business wasn't for sale--end of discussion. He called me again in September. I got suspicious and asked him who he worked for. He wouldn't tell me. I told him not to waste his time calling back again, that my answer would always be the same. His reply? 'We'll see about that!' I had the phone company trace the second call and was told it had been placed from somewhere outside of the United States. I'd heard of a group headed by an anti-Christian oil magnate who spends most of his time trying to discredit the work of well known Christians around the world. I never thought they'd hear about me. I'm just a small fish in a big pond. But, evidently someone thought I was worth going after.

"I didn't think any more about it until you told me that you'd seen someone on the balcony and then other things started happening to you. I began to suspect that it revolved around my business.

"The longer it went on, with all the things that happened to you, the more I began to suspect that someone inside the house, one of my staff members, was involved. An outsider would not have known your schedule and entered your room when you were gone."

Graham stood up and went to the window. How to tell her about the arrests?

Selena reached out and touched his arm. "What's the matter, Graham? Did something happen since my accident?"

He sat down, holding her hands tightly. "Yes. Cyrus, whose real name is Dennis Jones, made the arrests last night."

"Arrests? More than one? Who are they?"

"Melinda Brown and Tommy Stanger." He glanced at her then looked away.

"Are those real names or are they also aliases?"

"I assume they're real names."

Selena thought for a few moments and asked, "Then is it safe to assume that the staff members had aliases also?"

"One staff member. I'd say that's a safe assumption. Barbara Smith is an alias."

"Babs? It can't be. Dear, old, sweet, Babs? She wouldn't hurt a flea. Would she? Babs! Please tell me this is a sick joke."

"To begin with, Babs is neither old nor sweet. She just wanted to win us over. Hers was the figure you saw on the balcony, going to and from the stable, in the stable, under the oak tree. She altered her appearance and voice when she worked for us. Your room, the mirror, the balcony door, your boxes, and the letters were all her doings. She also placed the fence on the trail. Cyrus caught her taking it down after midnight.

"Her accomplice from the outside showed up on the scene after her arrest. Cyrus had called for police assistance, so several officers emerged from the woods when Tommy Stanger showed up. Cyrus recognized them both. They've been working for terrorist organizations for years, but always disappeared just before the authorities caught up with them.

"He thought the day I introduced him to Babs that he knew her as Melinda Brown. They're still trying to find out exactly who they worked for. They may never know. They haven't found a way yet to get them to talk. The FBI is going to continue to work on the case, but as far as we--you and I--are concerned it's over. They won't be bothering us anymore." The sense of relief sounded in his voice.

"I wouldn't have been surprised if you'd told me it was Joyce. She doesn't like me very much."

"What do you mean? Is she bothering you? If she is we'll let her go and hire someone else."

"Let's wait and see what happens. She's been really resentful since I took over the scheduling and the meal planning.

"Graham, how did Babs get the information in those letters?"

"Babs cleaned out the room after Kate died. I went in and took a few things for the children and asked her to dispose of the rest. She evidently found a diary or some letters and used the information to make the letters look authentic."

Selena leaned her head back and took a deep breath to keep the tears of relief from spilling over onto her cheeks. Opening her eyes, she asked softly, "How can I ever thank you for all you've done for me?"

"We'll talk about it when we get home." Graham looked into her eyes and leaned forward to kiss her.

"Is this all you guys ever do? Or do I just have perfect timing?

"Justin! It has to be the timing. Hello, Sherry. This is real nice of both of you to stop by." Graham stood up, laughing.

"Selena, do you remember my wife, Sherry?"

"Of course. It's real nice to see you again, Sherry. Sorry you have to see me like this. Thanks for the flowers. They're beautiful."

After they left, Selena asked Graham to help her back to bed, then said, "You owe me one. You promised me the world one day if I would get you dismissed from the hospital. I can't give you the world, but please get me out of here. I know I'll get well faster at home. Please?"

"Honey, I can't get you out of here with that tube in your side. Believe me, I remember how frustrating it is. Try to be patient. I'll talk to the doctor and see how long he thinks it'll be. When the tube comes out I'll see if I can take you home and get a nurse to come out and stay with you. It's too dangerous for you to leave with it in there."

They heard a knock on the door as the doctor walked in. "The x-rays are amazing. The ones taken this morning show a marked improvement over the ones from last night. What I would like to do is clamp the tube for the rest of today and see how you do. If everything continues to progress, we can take it out tomorrow."

"Is there a possibility that I could take her home tomorrow? I would be willing to pay for a nurse to stay with her if you think it's necessary."

"Let's see how things look tomorrow. I may want her to stay another day. We'll talk about the nurse when I see you again. You probably won't need one."

Graham took several calls and explained he wouldn't be working until Selena returned home.

Overwhelmed by his attentions she said, "You can work if you want to. I'll be all right now; you and Mom don't have to be here around the clock. I'm not used to being waited on

"You better get used to it. I plan to be around for a very long time, and I'm not letting you out of my sight. I want to spend this time with you. The work will still be there when I get back."

He took her hand and held it to his lips. Swallowing several times, he said with a catch in his voice, "I love you, Selena."

"I know. You've shown me in so many ways." She placed her hand on his face and gently pulled him to her until their lips met. This time there were no interruptions.

"Graham, you've been so patient with me and I couldn't have made it the last five months without your love and encouragement. You've shown me what real love is. I don't know how things are going to work out for us but I want you to know that whatever happens, I love you. I remember thinking once that you aren't the type of person I'd want to spend my life with. I was wrong. You're exactly the person I want and need."

Graham reached in his jacket pocket and pulled out a small box. "Honey, I didn't do this right the first time. I didn't give you much of a choice. This time I want to get it right. Will you marry me? I love you more than words can say and I want you beside me forever."

She looked at the love shining from his eyes and nodded. "Yes, I'll marry you. I know now what a marriage should be and together we can make it happen."

Opening the box that he placed in her hand, she gasped. "You still have this?"

"Of course. I bought it for you and you didn't go anywhere. I've been hoping all this time that someday I could talk you into wearing it for me."

She held out her finger as he slipped the diamond ring on beside the matching wedding band. "You don't have to talk me into it this time

The door opened and Selena saw two little heads peek around the curtain. "Trevor! Trina! Come here you guys. How did you get here

"Jerome brought us. He said he'd wait in the car. Daddy said we could come." Trina leaned her crutches against the wall as Graham sat her on the side of the bed.

Trevor looked at the equipment beside the bed, then looked at Selena. "That looks yucky. Are you going to come home soon?"

Selena rubbed his arm. "Of course I'm coming home soon. I feel lots better."

"If you're coming home soon, then does that mean you're not going to leave us? I don't want you to leave. I want you to stay and be my mom."

Selena looked at Trina and pulled her into her arms. "I'm not leaving, honey. I plan to stay for a very long time. You know what? If it's okay with Trevor, I'd love to be your mom."

Graham placed his hands on Trevor's shoulders. "What do you think, Trev?"

Trevor shifted from one foot to the other, looking first at Graham and then at Selena. "It's okay with me," he finally choked out.

Selena hugged and kissed them as they prepared to leave. Graham went with them to the car and Selena said a prayer of heartfelt thanks for everything God had given her in the past year.

The next day Madelyn came and Graham went home. As soon as he'd left the room, Selena turned to her mother. "Did you find the envelope?"

"It's right here. I almost didn't find it since there's nothing written on the outside."

"Thanks, Mom. I'll be so glad to get this taken care of."

The doctor took the tube out of her side and the nurse bandaged the incision. "It looks a little red where I made the incision so I'd like for you to stay another day. I don't see any reason why you can't go home tomorrow, but I want to look at that incision before you go

When Graham walked in that evening, she smiled at the look of pleasure on his face. "Wow! You look great. Did your mom help you with your hair?"

She nodded as she reached for his hand. "The doctor unhooked me from all the tubes today. He said I can go home tomorrow if the incision looks okay."

"That's great, honey. It'll sure be good having you home again. I've missed you."

Selena reached for the envelope on the bedside stand and handed it to him. "Before I go home there's something I want to talk to you about."

He took the paper out of the envelope and looked at her copy of The Agreement. She watched his face as he read the words written in her handwriting across the paper. "Paid in full. Thanks for being so patient with me. All my love forever. Selena."

He knelt beside her chair, gathered her into his arms, and buried his face in her neck. "I love you, Graham. I don't ever want anything keeping us apart again. No more agreements."

"How about a marriage license that actually means something?"

"That I can handle. That'll bind us together."

"I guess we must've been on the same wave length. I brought something for you." He took an envelope out of his pocket and handed it to her.

Her eyes widened as she took his copy of The Agreement and read, "My dearest Selena, Watching God heal you and seeing you fall in love with me right before my eyes has made the wait bearable. You will always be my one true love. Forever yours, Graham."

"Thanks. I can't tell you how much this means to me." She reached for a tissue and took a couple deep breaths.

"Graham, I have one more request. Do you think that after we get the marriage license we could go to the pastor and say our vows again? I don't remember much about the first time in September. I promise this time I'll really mean it."

"With a promise like that, how can I say no?" Graham spoke softly as he looked past the bruises, deep into her eyes, and felt the love well up inside him.

For the first time, he thanked God for The Agreement. *Without it I would not have given her the time she needed to come to me willingly.*

"You know, we still have the certificate from your dad from Christmas. Where would you like to take me for our honeymoon?"

"Oh, I don't know. A cruise on the Mediterranean might be nice. What do you think?"

"I think as long as I'm with you, any place would be nice."

Selena took a deep breath of the cold, crisp air as the attendant wheeled her out to Graham's car the next morning. She felt a twinge of pain in her chest and reminded herself to breathe easy.

"I guess we're even now. I got you out and you got me out. Except, I have a confession to make." She smiled as they pulled onto the highway.

"The doctor planned to send you home that day anyway, so I really took credit for something I didn't do."

"I guess we're even then. I really didn't do anything either." Graham laughed as he reached for her hand. "Let's keep it even. No more hospitals.

"Oh, by the way, I took a message from Scott Morefield this morning. It seems a cancellation on the court docket yesterday moved Howard's hearing up. He said he'll have your papers in his office by the end of the week. When I explained that you're in the hospital he said he'd deliver them to you personally if you want him to. You can call him when you feel up to it

"How about today? How about seeing the pastor over the weekend? And how about. . .?"

"Slow down, honey. We've got plenty of time to do all the things we want to do."

"You're right, but we've waited too long to begin." She leaned her head back against the headrest, a soft smile creasing her face.

It's time to begin.

THE END

Selena Mulvaney is about to change her life from a quiet and fulfilling atmosphere in a large city, to a suspense-filled rural mansion. After losing everything she ever wanted, Selena is forced to make some difficult decisions. Calling on her faith in God to help her through, He leads her to Graham Kensington. When Graham offers her a job and a marriage proposal, she agrees only after he signs a nuptial agreement putting constraints on their relationship. Slowly, she reaches out to him-the one person who truly cares about her, but who also places her in a situation where strange happenings and threats shatter the illusion of peace. So strange, in fact, that the two of them must work together to discover who wants them apart and why.

Evelyn Longenecker grew up in a Christian home near Dayton, Ohio, graduating from high school and nurses' training in that area. For the next twenty-three years, she worked in various aspects of health care. She has moved all over the United States, and now lives in Southern California with her husband, Neal. They have one daughter and two granddaughters.

US$21.95

ISBN 1-58851-451-X

90000

9 781588 514516

AmErica House